AMY'S KOURT

A Young Girl's Effort to Help Her Community

JAMES A. GAUTHIER, J.D.

Cover illustrated by: Lauren Bouldin

Library of Congress Control Number:	9781951306496
Paperback:	978-1-951306-49-6
Hardcover:	978-1-951306-50-2
eBook:	978-1-951306-51-9

BOOK
ART
PRESS
SOLUTIONS

30 Wall Street, 8th Floor
New York City, NY 10005
www.bookartpress.us
+1-800-351-3529

Contents

CHAPTER ONE

....

Here Ye, Here Ye

"**A**my! Your brothers are fighting again. Please tell them to stop fighting or else they will be punished."

I replied, "Mom, what is the punishment. You can't threaten Tom and Gary without specifying the punishment if they don't stop." Mom replied, "Amy, you decide their punishment. You always seem to know what is best to get their attention."

I told my brothers that they would be grounded from swimming if they didn't stop fighting. I knew that removing swimming was a good form of punishment since the temperature was going to hit 95 degrees today.

Tom first, then Gary yelled back at me, "Make us."

I replied, "That's fine. Your punishment is that you are grounded from swimming today as I stated."

Gary replied, "You can't stop us. We are going swimming. Just try and stop us!"

I wasn't sure how to stop them. I am seven years old. I weigh 53 pounds wet and I am nearly a head shorter than either of my brothers. My brother Tom is nine years old and my brother Gary is eleven years old. I know that either could pound my face and I wouldn't be able to stop him. The only advantage I held was that I was a girl and their little sister. My brothers loved me except when my mother made me do her job of disciplining my brothers.

I turned to Gary and said, "I am sorry, but the punishment stands. You and Tom shall forfeit swimming today for refusing to listen to me.

You understood the consequences of your continued fighting and now you are being properly punished."

Gary asked me, "Will an apology remove the punishment?"

I went to reply to Gary when Tom said, "Do what you want. I am not apologizing to the little dweeb. She has no right to punish us anyway. We are older and bigger than her. I am going swimming with or without you Gary."

Gary looked at me and said, "Well? Will you accept my sincere apology? I should not have treated you like I did. I have too much respect and love for you as my little sister."

I told Gary, "I will accept a hug and apology this time." Gary gave me a big hug and said, "Amy, please forgive me for the disrespect I have shown to you. I promise to treat you better next time."

Tom looked at me and said, "Gary, you are a fool. She can't make us do anything that we don't want to do."

Gary replied to Tom, "You apologize to Amy or you are not swimming today."

Tom replied, "Shove it!"

The temperature was 89 degrees when the community pool opened. I was getting ready to go swimming and take Gary with me. The pool was two blocks away from our house and was safe to walk to. We were dressed and had our towels and some money for a snack. As Gary and I began to leave our house, I yelled back to Mom, "Gary and I are going swimming, but Tom is grounded from swimming today."

Mom replied, "OK, but where is Tom right now?"

I looked in his bedroom, but Tom wasn't there. He snuck out the back window and rode his bike to the swimming pool. I was angry with Tom.

Gary said, "Don't worry Amy; I will enforce the punishment for you."

I watched Gary walk up to Tom and take him by his arm and escort him out of the pool area. Gary made Tom ride his bike back home and then locked Tom in their bedroom. Mom promised to keep Tom in the room. Gary returned to the pool and we had fun swimming for the afternoon. I made sure to thank Gary for helping me enforce the punishment against Tom.

I explained to Gary, "All Tom had to do was apologize. Mom doesn't like fighting and both of you know it; so please stop. Mom is seven months pregnant and doesn't need more stress in this heat."

When Gary and I returned home, Tom apologized to me and said that he wouldn't disrespect me again.

I thanked Tom and said, "I hope not."

Mom had a baby girl whom she named "Cynthia". Cynthia looked exactly like me when I was a baby. I asked my mother if she thought Cynthia would grow up to look like me.

Mom replied, "Cynthia looks just like you as a baby. I wouldn't be surprised if she looks a lot like you when she is older."

I had a strong attachment to my little sister. I loved playing with her and just being her big sister. I commented, "One day little sister, you and I are going to change the world together."

Word spread through our neighborhood. It didn't take too long before Alice and Rebecca asked me to settle a dispute they were having. Alice lived across the street from me and Rebecca lived two houses away from my own. We were all headed to third grade in the fall. I asked Alice what the dispute was all about.

Alice replied, "I had Rebecca over at my house. We were playing with my dolls and doll house when Rebecca got mad at me because I chose a dress that she wanted for her doll. Before I could offer the dress to Rebecca, she grabbed my doll and tore off the dress. The dress tore and is ruined. Now my mom is angry because she paid $16.99 for the dress."

I told Alice that I was sorry that happened. I looked at the torn doll dress and I believed it was ruined as well. I figured the dispute was easy and I asked Rebecca what happened. My thought was that Rebecca needs to buy Alice a new doll dress.

Rebecca replied, "Alice and I were playing dolls. I wanted the dress that was on her doll because she was changing the doll into a different dress. I took Alice's doll and she grabbed it back out of my hands and that is how the dress got torn. Alice tore it; not me!"

I sat back and realized that the dispute was more complicated than I originally thought. Alice and Rebecca were both my friends and I didn't want to hurt either one.

Alice yelled, "Amy, are you going to help us or not?"

I replied, "Both of you are my friends. If I make a decision, one of you will be mad at me and I don't want to lose either of your friendships. Why don't you let your parents work it out?"

Rebecca replied, "No, I trust your decision and I will live with it." Alice replied, "I will accept your decision as well."

I listened to the facts once again and decided that both were the cause of the dress getting damaged. I decided that Rebecca should reimburse Alice for one-half of the cost of the dress. I wrote out, "Judgment for Alice in the amount of $8.50."

Rebecca said, "That's fine with me. I will get my mother to give you a check for the amount and then Alice; I don't want to play with you anymore. We are no longer friends." Rebecca left for home.

Alice looked at me and asked, "Amy, you are still my friend, aren't you?"

I replied, "Of course I am. By tomorrow, Rebecca will also be your friend again."

I didn't like being put into the position of having to decide, but my friends pleaded with me to decide their dispute and I did what I was asked.

The next day Alice and I were playing on the playground when Rebecca asked to join us. We were all friends again as I expected.

One of our neighbors on the next block had an aggressive dog that they kept in a fenced yard. The dog belonged to David, a sixth grader at my school. Kelly, a fourth grader was walking past the fenced yard with her frozen fruit drink when the dog jumped at the fence scaring Kelly and causing her to drop her drink. Kelly's friend suggested that she tell me about it and see if I could get her another drink.

Once again, it sounded so simple to solve. Why do they need me? I asked David if he would agree to participate in a decision on the lost drink and his dog.

David replied, "My dog, Daisy did nothing wrong. I will listen to what Kelly says, but she will be lying if she says my dog did something to her."

I arranged for David and Kelly to tell me their story. I heard both sides and thought that David should replace Kelly's drink. I was ready to make my decision when Joseph asked if he could talk. Joseph was nine and saw everything that happened. I asked Joseph to tell what he saw.

Joseph replied, "I saw Kelly walking past the fence. She had a stick in her hand and she was hitting the fence. The dog got mad and started barking and then jumped at the fence. That is when Kelly dropped her drink. I think that she caused the problem because she was tormenting Daisy who is usually a good dog."

I asked Kelly if she hit Daisy's fence with a stick. She admitted doing so and I ruled that she was the cause of losing her drink.

I thought about the cases that I had heard and realized that you need to listen to both sides carefully before jumping to any conclusions and making any decisions. My dad had previously told me that there are usually two stories of what happened and often one story is usually not the full truth. I thought of it differently. One side may not be telling me everything. Word of my little court spread through the neighborhood. I was surprised to receive a request from two of my neighbors. The claim was that one neighbor was spraying some kind of weed killer in his planter when he over sprayed and killed plants in the other neighbor's planter.

Their kids suggested that their parents let me decide the case.

Mr. Johnson asked me if I would decide their case. I said I could if Mr. Newell would agree as well. Mr. Newell thought the idea was ridiculous, but finally agreed to me making a neighborhood decision. This time I was being very careful to listen to the facts before coming to a conclusion.

Mr. Johnson said, "I just planted four azalea plants. The plants came direct from the nursery and were filled with purple flowers. Mr. Newell sprayed his planter last week with a weed killer and now my plants no longer have flowers; just leaves. The weed killer killed off my azalea plants."

Mr. Newell showed me the container he used. Very clearly on the container it was stated, "This product is safe around azalea plants." Mr. Newell said, "My product couldn't have killed his azalea plants."

I thought about the facts and remembered that my house had azalea plants with bright colors. We went out back to look at our plants and all the flowers were gone as well. My mother saw all the commotion and asked what was wrong.

I explained that we are in court and there is a question of killing off azalea plants because the flowers are all gone.

Mom replied, "Azalea plants only keep their flowers for a couple of weeks and then drop the flowers. If you check with the nursery, you will learn that by this time of year, the plants no longer have flowers and it would have nothing to do with the weed killer you mentioned. I use it in my flower beds all the time."

Mr. Johnson checked with the nursery and learned that the flowers should have dropped by now. Case closed.

CHAPTER TWO

....

Open Kourt House

At age seven, I began my career as a judge. My neighborhood knew me and understood that I could be fair and impartial in making decisions. I had learned about fairness, called equity in the law. I believed that when I made a decision to punish behavior that I did so impartially and without regard to the parties involved. I had proven my ability to resolve disputes early on and wanted to pursue my life as a neighborhood judge.

It was my eighth birthday and my brothers Tom and Gary asked me what I would like as a present from them.

I replied, "I like being a judge for the neighborhood. I would like to use our back porch, if it is all right with mom and dad, to set up a courtroom to hear cases arising from our neighborhood."

I called in some favors from my brothers Tom and Gary. Our back porch was fairly large and covered making it useable in the hot sun or rain. We had a desk in the garage and several tables and chairs that we used when entertaining guests at Thanksgiving and Christmas. I asked to use the desk and tables to set up my courthouse. My parents agreed.

Gary and Tom were wonderful. They packed the heavy desk and placed it on the porch along with two rectangular tables and four chairs. My desk had the old office chair that was a little dusty, but it still worked fine. The desk and chair were part of my dad's home office until the room was needed for Cynthia. When we set up the desk and tables, I noticed that I couldn't see over the desk very well.

Gary said, "Judge Amy, I will build a platform for your chair and your desk. That will raise you up like a real judge.

I was so excited and thanked Gary and Tom for their help.

Gary built a wooden box that raised my chair up by one foot and then built a narrow table on top of the desk for my writing area. The porch was beginning to look like a courtroom, but our tables and chairs were old and dirty looking from being in the garage for so long. Mom and dad gave us permission to paint the desk black and we used table cloths to cover the tables. I decided that I couldn't do anything about the chairs except wash them off.

We finished the initial courtroom set up and painted the outside of the desk. I liked my desk; at least until I opened the top drawer and a large brown spider was living in the drawer. I screamed and slammed the desk drawer shut. Gary came to my aid and cleaned out the desk so I wouldn't find any more unwelcomed visitors.

Mom informed us that we were going out for pizza for my birthday. After dinner, Mom handed me my first present. I opened it and it was a black robe like the judges wear on television. It was just my size too.

Mom said, "If you are going to be a judge, then you should look like one too."

I looked around and asked mom where dad and boys went.

Mom replied, "To get the rest of your birthday present. You will see it when you get home."

Mom and I pulled into the driveway and Gary yelled out, "Amy, we are in the courtroom. Come and see."

I walked around the house and when I stepped onto the porch, I couldn't believe my eyes. My family bought black table covers for the tables and bought me twelve black folding chairs for the tables and guests. I was so very happy that I hugged mom, dad, Gary and Tom.

Tom said, "Amy, there is one more present for you. I made this in shop class for you."

I opened the gift and it was my own gavel with my name engraved on the side of the hammerhead. Gary handed me a knock block that he made. Gary explained that that I am to hit the gavel on the block when needed. Gary burned into the wood, "Judge Amy".

Dad and mom let me put up a sign in the front yard which read, "AMY'S NEIGHBORHOOD KOURTHOUSE". So, what if Tom didn't spell 'court' correctly, I liked the way it was spelled.

I would come home after school anticipating receiving my first case in the new courtroom. Two full weeks went by without any cases. I became disappointed and believed that my idea was more a waste of time than a community service.

I asked Tom and Gary to spread the word that the neighborhood court was in session, but by appointment only. Still nothing! I became so discouraged that I was ready to quit.

I was taking off my black robe when Jamison stopped by the Kourt and asked me if I would hear his dispute with Roger.

I replied, "I will, but I can't discuss your case unless Roger is before me at the same time. I can't talk with just one side. That is the rule of my court. I believe in fairness."

Jamison left, but returned twenty minutes later with Roger and a witness to their dispute. I was getting so excited. I directed Jamison and Roger to the courtroom and I took the bench and called docket number one. I asked Jamison and Roger to swear that they would tell me the truth. They agreed and also agreed to my judgment, whatever it turned out to be.

I told Jamison to go first and tellme what happened.

Jamison said, "I rode my new bicycle to school. When I left school, I saw Roger riding my bike away from the school. I walked to Roger's house and retrieved my bike. He scratched up the side when he let it hit the ground and slide. Roger owes me a new bike or I am going to break his face."

I asked Roger to tell me what happened.

Roger explained, "My mother is pregnant and called me at school because her water broke and she slipped and fell. She called an ambulance, but I felt the need to get help to my mother right away. I saw Jamison's bike and I took it and rode it to my house. I was careless in how I set down the bike, but my mother was my concern at that time; not Jamison's bike. I'm sorry for taking the bike. My parents don't have the money to buy me a bike and I know that they won't be able to buy Jamison a new bike either. All I can say is that I am sorry."

Jamison then turned to me and said, "Well, Judge. What is your decision?"

I thought to myself…being a judge is hard work. I asked Jamison what he thought his damage was. I explained that the bike was scratched, but was still in good working condition.

Jamison replied, "I don't know for sure. My mom paid $127 for the bike at Christmas. It was almost new when Roger took it."

I decided that a direct decision may not work and I asked to take their matter under consideration. I would give them my decision tomorrow. In the meantime, I looked closely at Jamison's bike and only the metallic red paint was scratched. I contacted the bike dealer and learned that you can buy a bottle of touch up paint for $3.49. The next day, I entered judgment against Roger for $3.49 and he had to do the touch up painting if agreed to by Jamison.

Jamison rode his bike by my house and showed me that it looked as good as new and thanked me for my good job. He said that he and Roger did the touch-up work together.

I looked around and no one was present. I took my gavel and said, "Case closed."

It didn't take too long waiting for my next case. Jennifer called me on the phone to see if I was still handling disputes.

I replied, "Yes I am. Get the other party together and then arrange for a time for me to hear the dispute. Right now, I am available every day after 3:00 pm and all-day Saturday."

Jennifer said that she would try to talk Keri into participating in the problem solving.

I replied, "This isn't math. This is Amy's Kourt and I am the judge." Jennifer replied, "Ya Ya, I know already. That is why I am here."

Keri called me and agreed to have me hear their dispute. I was curious because I was close friends with Keri and Jennifer. We had been in school together since kindergarten. I felt good that they trusted me to hear their dispute and enter judgment.

I brought Keri and Jennifer into the courtroom. Each of them brought a witness and another friend. Everyone said they would tell me the truth.

I asked Jennifer to tell her story.

Jennifer said, "I had a sleepover and my mom would only allow me to have two friends. Sorry Amy. I invited Keri and Cynthia. My mom had already bought nonrefundable ice show tickets for me and two guests. At the sleepover, Keri told me for the first time that she couldn't spend the night because her family was going out of town in the morning. I asked about the ice show and Keri said, 'Sorry, I can't go.' It was too late to find someone else. My mom spent $32.50 on a ticket for Keri and she couldn't get her money back."

I asked Keri to tell her story.

Keri said, "I told Jenny that I might not be able to go to the ice show because my family was planning a vacation at the same time. I suggested that Jenny invite someone else, like you Amy, but Jenny said that she would take a chance. When my parents told me that we were leaving early that night, I couldn't go and Jenny knew that it was a possibility that I couldn't go. I am truly sorry that her mother bought the expensive ticket, but I had no choice."

I explained, "I had heard the facts and my decision is that Jennifer accepted the risk of Keri not going when Keri suggested someone else be invited instead of her. Jennifer knew that something might cause Keri to not go to the ice show and I find that it wasn't her fault. No judgment for Jennifer."

I then asked Jennifer, "Why didn't you call me? I would have loved to go."

Jennifer said, "I was going to call you, but I thought Keri would make it so I took a chance. Now I need to explain your decision to my mother and hopefully she will understand."

Jennifer's mother didn't understand. She came to my house and asked, "What authority do you have to make up judgments and decisions. You are an eight-year-old girl like my daughter and she definitely lacks the capacity to decide for others."

I replied to Jennifer's mother, "Jennifer and Keri chose to have me hear their dispute. I heard it and gave my judgment. Jennifer knew that Keri might not be able to go to the ice show, but she took the risk of not inviting someone else. Keri is not responsible for your ticket cost."

Jennifer's mother walked away saying, "You make sense."

My cases seemed to stop. I decided to hold an open kourthouse for the neighborhood. I prepared a flier that I hand delivered to every porch in the neighborhood. My flier read,

"AMY'S KOURT- COME AND MEET JUDGE AMY AND LEARN ABOUT RESOLVING DISPUTES BEFORETHE DISPUTE GROWS TOO LARGE TO FIX IN OUR NEIGHBORHOOD KOURT. CASES ARE FREE AND I AM FAIR AND IMPARTIAL. CASES FOR KIDS AND ADULTS ALIKE. PLEASE STOP BY AND SEE ME." OPEN KOURTHOUSE THIS SATURDAY 9AM TO 5PM.

In anticipation of a large gathering, I made lemonade and cookies and put a sign up saying "KOURTHOUSE IN THE REAR". I sat at my desk from 9 am to 11:15 am before someone stopped by. It was Billy and he saw the sign that I had lemonade and cookies so he stopped. I was really disappointed. I was also hot. It was 85 degrees and I was wearing my judge's robe.

I walked out front of my house and my friends Jennifer, Keri, Alice and Rebecca each carried signs directing people to stop by my Kourthouse and say hello. My friends were on each corner signaling people to stop. By noon, we had fourteen adults and twelve kids visiting my little Kourthouse. I explained how the kourt worked and why it was a community service I chose to do.

From the open house, I received seven new cases to be scheduled and heard before me. I was so excited. My hands shook as I wrote down information on the parties and their phone numbers and a brief description of the dispute. I began feeling like a real judge in our neighborhood.

On Saturday, I began court at 9:00 am with neighborhood Kourt Docket No. 2. The dispute was a noise complaint. Amanda was taking drum lessons and practiced in her family's garage until 8:00 pm daily. Kiefer lived next door and his bedroom window was next to the garage window. When Amanda played the drums, Kiefer was unable to hear his television. Many of Kiefer's favorite shows were on from 6-8:00 pm.

I asked Kiefer about his complaint against Amanda.

Kiefer explained, "I go to school and have sports after school. I don't get home until 6:00 pm every school day. I like to watch television in my bedroom, but I can't hear my shows with Amanda banging on her drums. I close my bedroom window, but then it gets hot in my room. I shouldn't have to shut myself in just to hear the television. I want Amanda to stop playing the drums after 6:00 pm."

I asked Amanda her story.

Amanda said, "Like Kiefer, I have after school activities and I don't get home until 5:30 pm. I am trying to learn the drums for school orchestra. I must practice daily and the garage is where my parents put me. I don't mean to interfere with Kiefer's shows, but I need to practice. I don't have a choice. I can't play in my bedroom because I would wake up my baby brother."

Both sides looked to me for a decision. As I was thinking of what to say, Monica asked, "Amanda, don't you still have that empty bedroom in your basement that isn't being used for anything?"

Amanda replied, "It is being used by spiders and other bugs. That room creeps me out and I don't want to go in there. It is also dark and depressing."

Monica suggested that a group of kids get together and clean out the room, paint it and turn it into a music room. It would be in the basement and wouldn't bother Kiefer and shouldn't bother your parents. I ruled that the decision will be put off until they see if the basement can be used. I learned the next day that the room was unfinished and Amanda's father would put acoustical sound insulation in the walls and finish off the room so Amanda would have a good place to play.

I ruled that Amanda can practice from 6-7pm nightly until her room is finished. Aftermy ruling, Kiefer apologized and allowed Amanda to practice until 8 pm until her new music room was finished.

I had two more cases scheduled for Amy's Kourt. I called docket No. 3. Mr. Perkins claimed that Robbie picked his prize roses that he was growing for his wife. The value of the roses was $19.50 I asked Robbie for his story.

Robbie explained, "I picked the roses to give to my girlfriend. I wanted to make Ginger happy by giving her the flowers. When Ginger learned that I stole the flowers, she threw them at me and we are no longer friends. How much more can I be punished. I told Mr. Perkins that I was sorry."

Mr. Perkins replied, "Robbie, do you know how hard I work keeping the rose beds free of weeds so my wife can appreciate the beautiful roses that we grow in our flower beds?"

Robbie said, "No, and again, I am sorry."

I said, "I am ready to make a decision. I am entering judgment directing Robbie to weed Mr. Perkin's flower beds for one month. Robbie will earn $2.00 per hour as credit against the judgment of $19.50 that I entered against him."

This was getting easier. I called my next case. I looked around and there were no more kids. Instead I had two men sitting in my courtroom. I asked if they needed help.

Mr. Wilson said that his case was next with Mr. Sarls. I called their case. Mr. Wilson said, "I put my garbage can on the corner of my driveway for pickup. It was the same place that I have put the can for the past ten years. A week ago, Mr. Sarls backed over the garbage can; got out of his car and kicked the garbage can causing garbage to spill out everywhere. I want a new garbage can at least."

I asked for Mr. Sarls' story.

Mr. Sarls explained, "My brother-in-law is visiting and took up my driveway causing me to park in a different part of the driveway. I backed out, but forgot where I was and cut the turn too short. I was mad. The garbage can shouldn't have been there since it was Thursday morning and garbage collection didn't come until Friday morning."

Mr. Wilson replied, "We were leaving town and had to put the garbage can out early."

I said that I was ready to enter judgment. I explained that Mr. Sarls was responsible for seeing what was behind his car. Mr. Wilson's garbage can was on his property and he did nothing wrong. I enter judgment against Mr. Sarls for a new garbage can and as further punishment he must put Mr. Wilson's garbage can at the curb for one month. Both men were laughing and shaking hands as they left my little Kourthouse.

My simple decisions caught on with the neighborhood. I learned that people were saying, "Don't argue. Settle or let Judge Amy decide your case in the neighborhood Amy's Kourt. I began hearing my name as 'Judge Amy' and I became so excited.

My next case was the following Saturday between a fourteen-year-old boy named Gerald and his seventeen-year-old neighbor Bullet. I learned that Bullet was the quarterback on the high school football team. I called the docket and both boys appeared with two witnesses. They accepted my authority as their judge which was my standing instruction before proceeding. They agreed to be truthful.

I asked Gerald to tell his story.

Gerald said, "I received a new football for my birthday. I was showing it to Bullet when Bullet threw my football as hard as he could to his friend, John. John didn't catch the football and it bounced and was run over by an oncoming car and ruined."

I asked Bullet for his story.

Bullet said, "What the dweeb said was basically true. I threw his football and I expected my receiver to catch it. John missed and the ball got run over just like he said. It wasn't my fault that the ball got run over."

I asked Gerald how much the football cost.

Gerald replied, "It is a professional leather model and it cost $48.99 before tax. I have the receipt from my dad.

I asked Bullet if he had Gerald's permission to throw his football. Bullet said, "I don't need permission. When I get a football in my hands, it is natural to throw it."

I thanked both parties and then I entered judgment in favor of Gerald for $55.00 to cover cost and tax to replace his football.

Bullet jumped up on one of my tables and threatened to hurt me. My brothers grabbed him and threw him off the porch. I banged my gavel and gave Bullet 48 hours to replace the football or provide the cash to Gerald.

Bullet yelled, "Up yours" as he walked away.

My brothers were going to go after him, but I explained that I had it covered. If he didn't pay, then he wouldn't play either. Two days passed and Gerald didn't receive payment.

I wrote up an order on judgment which said:

"To Coach Riley:

Amy's Kourt had jurisdiction over Bullet. He failed to honor a judgment. I am now ordering him to be grounded from playing football until he satisfies my $55 judgment entered against him plus a court fee of $10. I signed it, Judge Amy."

My brothers laughed at me and said, "Coach Riley would never honor your Amy's Kourt judgment. Bullet is the star player on the team and the coach likes to win games."

I said, "We will see who plays and who pays. I am the lawful judge and he agreed to participate in my kourt."

I received a telephone call from Coach Riley asking me to join him at the high school. He put me on notice that Bullet's dad was there and he is mad.

I asked Gary and Tom to go with me to the high school. The Coach told me that Bullet would not be playing until he resolved the judgment. When I arrived, Bullet told his dad, "That's the little creep that thinks she can order me around and prevent me from playing football."

Bullet's father asked me what my court was all about. I explained about the claim and my judgment and the reason for the judgment and the second order preventing Bullet from playing football until he took care of the judgment. I said that Bullet must learn that he is accountable for his conduct.

He said, "That's all fine, but what gives you the right to enter a judgment against my son?"

I replied, "Your son did. He consented to my kourt and my decision. He didn't like my decision and now he is trying to avoid taking responsibility."

He asked Bullet "Is that true son? Did you consent to Judge Amy's Kourt?"

Bullet answered, "Yes, but she can't stop me from playing football." His dad replied, "Maybe she can't, but I can and so can Coach Riley.

Now, how do you want to handle this?"

Bullet replied, "Fine, I will pay the judgment and the extra $10 to the court."

Bullet's dad wrote out a check to Gerald for $55 and a check to me for $10. He told Bullet that it would come out of his allowance. He said, "Next time you act like a man and be accountable for your conduct."

I was nervous, but Coach Riley said, "You are a tough kid. He didn't scare you?"

I said, "I have been shaking like a wet puppy on the inside, but I had to do what was right. I thank you for backing me up."

Coach Riley said, "I did what I thought was right and hopefully Bullet learns from this ordeal."

My tenacity spread quickly through the neighborhood and even into the schools. Many kids began calling me Judge Amy and I smiled at my accomplishments.

CHAPTER THREE

Amy's School Kourt Is Now In Session

I was called into the principal's office and asked questions about my neighborhood kourt program. Apparently, my principal learned about how tenacious I could be when he heard about Bullet and the Football Coach. Mr. Peters asked me if I thought I could create an Amy's Kourt for the school. It would be a dispute resolution system alternative to expulsion or suspension.

I replied, "I would be honored to give it a try." I would like a room that can be used as a courtroom. I have found that I receive more respect when the surroundings resemble a courtroom."

The principal explained that there was an extra classroom that could be used. He would have the janitor set it up to look like a courtroom. You can make any changes that you deem necessary.

I asked if I could wear my judge's robe and use my gavel. He replied, "You can use any of your props."

I replied, "Sir, they are not props. I treat my job as a judge seriously and I demand fairness and being impartial. If I am to do this job, then I need the authority to enforce my judgments or it isn't worth doing the job."

He gave me full authority to act as the school judge on a trial basis. Our school ran from kindergarten through eighth grade giving me a wide range of situations that could arise.

The principal called an assembly in the gymnasium and introduced me to the student body. I smiled when he referred to me as Judge Amy.

He told a little bit about my background and then let me talk to the students.

I explained that Amy's Kourt is a voluntary court to hear small disputes between students, or about students. In order to participate, you will need to agree to the kourt having the authority over your case. You will also have to tell the truth to me or I can't be fair. When I was done, many students clapped and my friends said, "I hope I never have to appear before you."

I created a complaint form for students to use at school and I could use it at home too. The form looked like this:

COMPLAINT FOR AMY'S KOURT

What is your complaint? _____

_____

Who is your complaint against? _____

_____

What are your damages or requested relief? _____

_____

Hearing date and time: _____

Response: _____

_____

By signing this form, you agree to be bound by the decision of Amy's Kourt and Judge Amy.

My school principal let me put my complaint forms in the office. I was excited to hear complaints, but no one asked for help. It was March and school was almost over. I just kept hoping to get a case at school.

At home, I had four cases for hearing the following Saturday. My first case involved Andrew stealing Mark's laptop computer. Both boys were in seventh grade. I swore Andrew and Mark and then asked Mark to tell his story.

Mark replied, "I was working with my laptop on the front porch when Andrew stopped by my house. We talked briefly and I excused myself to go to the bathroom. When I returned to the porch, Andrew and my laptop were both missing. I went to Andrew's house, but he denied taking my laptop. I haven't told my mother yet because I know she will be mad at me for not protecting my computer better. She told me that my laptop cost a lot of money."

I asked Andrew to tell me his story.

Andrew explained, "I stopped by Mark's house and visited. I saw his computer, but I didn't take it. I left while Mark was in the bathroom because I had a dental appointment that I forgot about."

I asked Mark how he could prove that Andrew took his laptop versus someone else.

Mark replied, "Andrew was there and so was my laptop. When I got back from the bathroom, both were gone. I think the answer is obvious. Andrew stole my laptop."

I ruled in favor of Andrew and denied judgment for Mark. Mark was angry at me.

Mark said, "I am going to tell my mother about what Andrew did. She will get my computer back." I called, "Next case please."

John appeared with a black eye. John was a sixth grader and said that he was hit by Dennis who was a seventh grader. I swore them in and asked for John's story.

John explained, "I was goofing off in the front yard with a ball. Dennis stopped by and asked me to throw him my ball. I tossed it to him and he hurt his thumb catching the softball. He got mad at me and threw the ball at me. It hit me on my right eye and it hurt badly. I still have the black eye and this happened two weeks ago."

I asked for Dennis' story.

Dennis said, "John threw the ball as hard as he could at me. I reached out to grab the softball and it bent my thumb back. I got mad and threw the ball back to John. He missed the ball and it bounced off his hand and hit him in the eye. It was just an accident on both injuries. My thumb still hurts.

After hearing their facts, I ruled that the injuries were both unintended accidents and no judgment would be entered. I dismissed their case.

My last case of the day was another theft case. Before I could call my next case, Mark returned to my courtroom and excused himself.

He said, "Judge Amy. Your decision was correct. When I went to the bathroom, my mother saw my laptop sitting on the table. She picked it up and took it inside. She didn't know that I was looking for it and I hadn't told her that it was missing. Andrew did nothing wrong."

I asked Mark to apologize to Andrew for falsely accusing him of stealing the laptop.

Jessica (9 years old) was next and she explained, "I had $5 on my night stand from my birthday. Rene (also 9 years old) was visiting and when she left, I couldn't find my $5. I think Rene took it."

I asked Rene to tell me her side of the story.

Rene said, "I was visiting and I didn't mean to take Jessica's $5, but it was just sitting there. I felt bad about taking it. I spent it on treats for my friends at school, including Jessica."

I granted judgment in favor of Jessica for $5 and gave Rene two days to pay the judgment or face community service.

Rene replied, "I don't have the money to pay the judgment and I am not about to tell my mother that I stole money from Jessica or I will be grounded for life."

I asked Jessica what chores she hated to do.

Jessica said, "I hate taking out the garbage, including putting the can on the curb for Friday morning pick up. I also hate weeding the planters. I have to weed one planter each week."

I asked what value Jessica would put on both chores.

Jessica replied, "I think that weeding the planter four times and taking out the garbage four times would be fair."

I entered judgment against Rene ordering her to do Jessica's weeding and garbage can removal. The next day I saw Jessica and Rene weeding the planter together as friends.

My final case dealt with gas from a lawnmower that was borrowed. I swore the adult men as I called the case.

Mr. Johnson said, "I lent Mr. Sims my lawnmower. At the time, the lawnmower was clean and full of gas. When Mr. Sims returned the lawnmower it was dirty and empty when I went to use it. I think Mr. Sims needs to clean my mower and fill the tank with gas. He refused."

Mr. Sims was asked to go next.

Mr. Sims replied, "I did borrow the mower because my mower was being serviced. I returned the mower in the same condition that Mr. Johnson returned my mower when he borrowed it. My mower was also dirty and empty."

I asked Mr. Johnson if that was what happened.

He replied, "I didn't have time to clean the mower or fill it up. Bob didn't say anything to me or I would have gladly filled his mower and cleaned it."

I entered judgment in favor of Mr. Johnson for a full tank of lawnmower fuel and to wash the mower the next time it was dirty. The men walked out of my court shaking hands and laughing. I heard Mr. Sims say, "She's good for an eight-year-old."

I was done with my home cases and I hoped that I would get some cases at school. It had been a month since Amy's Kourt was set up at school and no cases yet. I carried my judge's robe and gavel around with me just in case I was needed.

The principal stopped me in the hallway and said that he had a case for my court. It would be a trial case to see if it would work out or not. The boy was facing suspension for three days if needed. I learned that Elliott, an eighth grader was bullying James, a sixth grader by making him do things for Elliott like James was his servant.

I scheduled the hearing for the next day. Elliott and James appeared in Amy's School Kourt. I received their agreement to be bound by the kourt's decision and to tell me the truth.

I asked James for his side of the story.

James said, "I was minding my own business over lunch and Elliott made me give him my lunch. When he was done eating my lunch, he made me clean up the mess he made. He demanded that I carry his books to his next class and ordered me to be waiting for him so I could carry his books to the next class."

I asked Elliott for his story.

Elliott said, "James is a little dweeb that wasn't worth my time. I am bigger than James and stronger than James. I had a right to take his lunch and make him my servant. Someday he may grow up and get his own dweeb for a servant. I was teaching him how to be a man."

I asked James if how he was treated was humiliating.

He replied, "Yes. When Elliott sat at his desk, he made me kneel down on the floor and act like a foot stool in front of his classmates. When the teacher entered the room, Elliott took his shoe and shoved me over. I got up to leave and the teacher asked me what happened. I told her the truth and said that Elliott was bullying me."

I said that I was ready to enter judgment. I ordered Elliott to clean the playground lunch area every day for one week and to apologize to James.

Elliott replied, "No way!"

I explained that the alternative would be a suspension from school. Elliott replied, "You can't suspend me. You are nothing more than a little girl dweeb who plays at being a judge. Why don't you go and play with your dolls and get out of my face?"

I reminded Elliott that he consented to the control of my kourt. I do have the authority and the backing of the principal.

Elliott said, "Just try to suspend me. You are a stupid joke." I asked if Elliott had anything else to say.

Elliott replied, "Nothing you would want to hear."

I replied, "Thank you. I am entering judgment suspending you from school for three days and you are hereby ordered to clean up the outside lunch area for one full week."

Elliott replied, "That's not going to happen. Take off your little judge pajamas and I will kick your butt. I don't care that you are only eight years old and a little girl. You mean nothing to me."

Sitting in the back of the courtroom was Elliott's mother and Principal Peters. Elliott's mother stood up and said, "Elliott, get your things. We are going home for a week. The judge suspended you and I agree with her decision. You are also grounded for the next month. Do you want to challenge my authority too?

Elliott replied, "No mom."

Word spread through the school. The worst bully was taken down in my Kourtroom and my judgment was supported by Principal Peters. Within the week, bullies began acting nicer and bullying seemed to stop. I received a school complaint form from Susan claiming that Jessica stole her writing assignment and claimed it to be her own work. The teacher heard both students claim the report was theirs and suggested that Susan proceed with the complaint and see how it worked out in student court.

Susan and Jessica were scheduled for right after school at 3:00 pm. I swore them in and had them sign the agreement for accepting my judgment. I then asked Susan to tell her side of the story.

Susan said, "I worked on my report for two days. I printed it out and put a cover page on the front. My report is still on my computer. When the teacher was checking the assignments, she called me up to her desk to ask about my report. I said that I turned one in and I described the report. The teacher looked through the stack of reports and found mine with Jessica's name on the report. The cover page was missing.

I then asked Jessica for her side.

Jessica said, "I wrote this report for my class. I worked on it for three days." Jessica described the report and showed me that she had the report on her computer too. Jessica said, "One of us is lying and it isn't me."

Ms. Gamble, the teacher whispered in my ear, "See what I mean. Which girl is telling the truth?"

I replied, "I think I know how to determine that. I asked for both laptop computers to be put on my desk with the report on the screen. I confirmed that both computers had the identical report. I then told Jessica and Susan that when documents are created on a computer, the information about the document is registered under the document properties. My dad is a lawyer and taught me that. All I have to do is click on properties and I will know which one of you copied the other. Either admit your wrongdoing and receive a lesser judgment, or get the full judgment if I have to show that you kept lying after promising to tell me the truth in court.

Jessica began to cry and said that she copied Susan's report onto her computer. She apologized to Susan and Ms. Gamble and asked me to forgive her for lying in my court.

I thanked Jessica for telling the truth. I entered judgment requiring Jessica to apologize to Susan at the next school assembly. Principal Peters and Ms. Gamble agreed to the punishment. Ms. Gamble gave Jessica one day to turn in her own report or fail the assignment.

I thought I was done, but learned that I had one more case on the school docket. It involved two brothers fighting on school property. Principal Peters explained that the brothers would be suspended for one week for fighting unless I determined a different punishment was needed. I thought, two brothers fighting. That sounds like my brothers, but they wouldn't dare fight at school. Principal Peters walked in my brothers, Gary and Tom and said that they were fighting on school property.

I was angry and embarrassed to have my brothers before me. I kept reminding myself, be fair and impartial. Right now, Gary and Tom are just two students in a lot of trouble.

I looked at Gary and Tom and said, "Do you accept the judgment of this court regardless of the outcome?"

Both of my brothers answered, "Yes."

I asked Gary to tell me what happened.

Gary said, "Tom and I were playing catch. Tom missed my throw and I told him to go get the baseball since he missed the catch. Tom refused. I tried to make Tom get the ball and he hit me on the side of my head. I got mad and hit Tom in the mouth. We were wrestling on the ground when Principal Peters caught us fighting."

I asked Tom for his side of the story.

Tom said, "It is pretty much what Gary said. I missed the catch because Gary threw the ball completely over my head. I told him to get his own ball. He refused. Gary grabbed my arm and tried to make me get the ball. I got mad and hit him like he said. He then hit me and we went onto the ground fighting until we were caught."

I asked Gary and Tom if they knew that the school rules prohibited fighting on school property.

Both replied, "Yes."

I said, "You are my brothers, but I must apply justice equally. It is my judgment that both of you will perform crosswalk duty every morning and afternoon for one month in front of the school. You will wear the proper crossing guard uniforms and be timely for your job. If you don't do this job, then I will seek suspension under the school rules. Do I make myself clear? No fighting at home or at school."

Gary asked me if a hug and kiss would get him out of this judgment.

I gave him a hug and said, "No way. You and Tom need to learn."

My next home court was on Saturday. I called my first case which involved a baseball going through the side window of a neighbor's car. I swore in the parties when I heard swearing in my house. I heard my mother scream, "Amy, I need your help now!" I ran inside my house and saw that my mother's water broke and my dad was at work. I called an ambulance, but was told that it would take approximately 30 minutes to get an ambulance at our home. I began to panic and called several neighbors, but no one was home. I then looked at Gary and asked, "Can you drive Mom's car?"

Gary said, "Of course. I have driven with Dad several times."

I said, "Good. We need to get Mom to the hospital. She is having the baby and it will be too long for an ambulance." Tom helped me get Mom into the car. Gary carried Mom's suitcase and baby car seat while I grabbed Cynthia. We were off to the hospital. Gary did a good job driving, but when we pulled into the hospital, a policeman asked to see Gary's driver's license.

Gary replied, "My Mom is having a baby. I need to be with her right now."

The officer said, "Driver's license please."

Gary said, "I don't have a driver's license. This was an emergency and I had no choice."

The officer replied, "Tell it to the judge."

I watched the officer hand Gary a ticket. I told Gary that I was sorry about the ticket.

Gary replied, "I would do it again. Mom is my first priority."

Mom had a baby boy whom she named Steven. It was nice to have a brother smaller than me and Cynthia. I was ready to turn nine when he was born. Mom promised that five children were enough.

Gary received a trial date from the court. As part of the pre-trial preparation, Gary was asked if he agreed that the charge of driving a car without a valid driver's license was true. Gary admitted to the fact. At trial, Gary could argue against the penalty.

I was called to testify. I looked at the judge square in his eyes and said, "My brother drove a car without a valid driver's license because of an emergency. My mother's water broke and the nearest ambulance would be longer than thirty minutes. My brother Gary was legally justified in breaking the license law because of the medical emergency he was facing."

The judge asked, "Why didn't you explore any alternatives?"

I explained, "I called our neighbors, but no one was home, or at least didn't answer their phones. We couldn't get a timely ambulance and I gave Gary permission to drive mom's car. If someone is guilty, it should be me. My brother was acting as I directed."

The judge asked me if I was Judge Amy from Amy's Kourt. I replied, "Yes I am."

The judge askedme what punishment should be given in this case.

I looked at the judge and said "None. An emergency can serve as a justification when other reasonable options are not available."

The judge asked, "Where did you learn that?"

I replied, "I read about defenses to tickets and justified behavior. I think Gary qualifies. At least that is the judgment that I would give this case. Gary was acting as a Good Samaritan and shouldn't be punished for doing a good deed."

The judge said, "I agree. Case dismissed." The judge then invited me to sit in his chair and go into his chambers. I told the judge, "I would love to have a nice courtroom someday."

The judge replied, "I suspect you will have your own courtroom. In the meantime, I have an extra set of judicial scales and a new gavel that I never use. I would like to give them to you. The judge then asked why I carried a bag around with me."

I explained that it held my judicial robe and gavel. I never know when I will need to act as judge at school or at home.

The judge said, "Wait right here. I will be right back."

When the judge returned, he handed me a briefcase that said "JUDGE" on the side. He said, "It's yours. Good luck in your career Judge Amy."

I was about to say thank you when Judge Rodgers asked me what my plans were for the summer.

I replied, "I will be holding Amy's Kourt Monday, Wednesday and Saturday."

Judge Rodgers asked, "Amy would you be interested in sitting in my courtroom on Tuesdays and observing my courtroom in action?"

I was so excited. I turned to my mother. Before I could ask, she said, "Of course you can. I will drive you here on Tuesdays."

Judge Rodgers offered to pick me up and drop me off since he passed our house on his way to the courthouse.

Mom replied, "That will be fine ifAmy is comfortable."

CHAPTER FOUR

Training To Be A Judge

arrived in court with my mother for the first day. When I walked in, the lady sitting next to the judge said, "All rise for Judge Amy." I was in shock as she directed me up to where she sat and showed me my chair next to the judge.

Judge Rogers said, "If you are going to learn to be a judge, then you need to sit up here with me. We will talk about the cases when we take a recess."

I began to laugh and asked, "Do judges really have recess too?"

He replied, "Absolutely. At recess, you and I can talk about the cases and procedure and have something to drink."

Judge Rodgers made me feel so special. He even allowed me to wear my judicial robe in his courtroom. I received a lot of real funny looks from the people called defendants, but it was still a lot of fun for me.

I kept notes of courtroom procedure. I wrote down how to swear in a witness and learned who the bailiff was and which parties were called plaintiffs and defendants. I noticed that the cases weren't that much different from my cases.

Our first case dealt with lumber that the plaintiff's attorney said was non-conforming goods. The lumber would not be acceptable in a home construction and his builder client rejected the lumber. The defendant I learned was the lumber company who claimed that the lumber was conforming and was not timely rejected by the builder in any event. When showed a piece of the lumber. I didn't think it looked very good, but what did I know. The defendant was the lumber company. The plaintiff wanted credit for the bad lumber even though it was used in building the house. After the attorneys did their speeches, called 'closing arguments', Judge Rodgers said that he would take a ten-minute recess and then give his decision. He looked at me and signaled me to follow him to his chambers.

Judge Rodgers asked me, "Amy, what do you think? Do you have an opinion on who is right and who is wrong?"

I replied, "I heard what both sides said. On the one hand, the man building the house got some very bad wood. I understood what it should have looked like. Because he didn't get what he expected, he should, possibly, maybe, might, I don't know, get a refund? On the other hand, the builder used the lumber and then asked for a refund. It seems like the lumber was either good enough for the job or it wasn't. Since the builder used the wood, he seemed to have accepted it in the condition it was in. I guess my opinion is that he didn't timely reject the bad wood so judgment for the lumber company."

Judge Rodgers praised my rationale and said that I had a good grasp of common-sense law. He explained that under the Uniform Commercial Code, the builder had a limited period of time to reject the lumber as being a non-conforming good. That means that what he received wasn't what he ordered. However, once he used the wood in framing the house, he accepted the wood as conforming and he recovers nothing. Your decision is correct. Good job.

I listened to how Judge Rodgers reviewed the facts as he applied the facts to his decision. I could see that the builder man was mad, but I think Judge Rodgers was correct in his decision.

The bailiff lit up our light telling us that the next case was ready to be heard. Judge Rodgers introduced me as Judge Amy of Amy's Kourt and asked if anyone objected to my presence. He then called for opening statements. When we were in his office, he explained that at the beginning of the trial, the attorneys talk about the facts and what they intend to prove in their case. That is called the 'opening statement'. When the trial testimony is over, then the lawyers make closing arguments applying the facts to the law.

This case was a car accident case. The plaintiff was rear ended at a stop light. The plaintiff said that he hit his brakes when the light changed from yellow to red. When he was stopped, the defendant ran into the back of his car causing injuries to his neck and back. The defendant said that the plaintiff slammed on his brakes causing the defendant to smash into the plaintiff's car.

After arguments, Judge Rodgers asked me my opinion.

I said, "If the first car could stop at the red light, then the second car should have been able to stop if they left enough room between their cars to stop. Sometimes my dad follows too closely and I yell at him to back off a little. I think the rule is one car length for each ten miles per hour." Judge Rodgers told me that I had a good head for judging cases.

The defendant was following too closely and failed to maintain a safe following distance. I will rule for the plaintiff and award damages.

I asked, "How much in damages?"

Judge Rodgers said, "Once liability is established, then damages represents what is needed to put the person back into the same condition they were in before the accident. In this case, the plaintiff has $580 in chiropractor bills. I will award the medical bills and $1400 in pain and suffering damages."

I said, "I agree."

Judge Rodgers replied, "Good."

Our last case of the day was different than the others. Our light turned on indicating that the courtroom was ready. We walked in as two policemen were taking handcuffs off a man. Everyone remained standing as the bailiff said, "All rise for the prospective jurors." Our courtroom had thirty people who were called 'potential jurors'. Judge Rodgers whispered to me that this process of selecting the jury was called 'voir dire'. The attorneys could ask the jurors questions in deciding on whom to use for the jury. I quickly learned that the man had been charged with selling drugs at a school. He was called a 'criminal defendant'. It took almost two hours to choose the jury and then the trial started. The actual trial only took one hour. There was a video of the man selling drugs to children and undercover cops.

We broke from the room and Judge Rodgers asked my opinion again. I said it was pretty clear that he was selling drugs. I think he is guilty. The Judge and I discussed the day while the jurors decided the case. I also learned that the proper word for what the jury was doing is 'deliberation'. I learned so much with Judge Rodgers. The jurors came back in twenty minutes and found the defendant guilty as charged. Judge Rodgers said, "So say you one; so say you all." The jurors all answered "Yes" and they were excused, which meant that they could go home.

I was so excited and I couldn't thank Judge Rodgers enough. I had my notes and I intended to clear up my Kourt with the use of proper titles and phrases. I wondered if I could hold a jury trial in my court. It is all so exciting.

On Wednesday, I had my next neighborhood case. This time I had table notes that said, "Plaintiff" and "Defendant".

The case was between Philip and Sheryl. Both were going into 9th grade, but decided to let me hear their dispute. Philip was the plaintiff making Sheryl the defendant. I swore in both parties asking, "Do you promise to tell the truth and only the truth, so help you God." Both said, yes and agreed to my Kourt's jurisdiction for their dispute and that my decision would be final and binding on everyone.

I turned to Philip and said, "Please present your case."

Philip testified, "I loved Sheryl. I got a job during the school year and bought her a very nice opal ring which was her birthstone. She had been asking me for the ring for nearly six months when I decided to use all of my savings to buy her the ring. Sheryl was very happy to have the ring and every time she saw me; she would smile and show me the ring. I tried to go out with Sheryl, but she said that she babysat on Fridays and Saturdays. I went to the pizza shop and found Sheryl and Mike making out. When I said something, Sheryl told me that I could drown in a lake. She never liked me, but she did like the opal ring that I bought her."

I called for the defendant's case. I then said, "Sheryl – that's you. What is your side of the story?"

Sheryl replied, "Philip was like a puppy dog. He would follow me around like I would somehow like him as a boyfriend. Philip asked me what he could do to make me happy. I said he could buy me the opal ring at the jewelry store. He bought me the ring and thought that he purchased me for the value of the ring. I told him to leave me alone. He asked me for the ring back and I said no."

I asked Philip how much the ring cost.

He replied, "I paid $338 on sale. It took my entire savings."

I asked, "Did Sheryl treat you differently before and after you bought her the ring?"

He replied, "Before I bought the ring, Sheryl was very loving. She would hold my hand and give me little kisses while asking me about the ring and when I would get it for her. I thought we were very close. After she got the ring, she wanted nothing more to do with me."

I called for any closing arguments. Both parties said, "Huh?"

I then said I was ready to enter my decision. I summarized, "Philip and Sheryl had a relationship that encouraged Philip to purchase an expensive ring for Sheryl. At the time of the ring purchase, there was no relationship, but Sheryl deceived Philip into buying her the ring. Once she had the ring, she dumped all over Philip. I find that Sheryl acted badly and should have refused the ring if she had no continuing relationship with Philip. My judgment is for Philip for $338 or return of the ring in 48 hours." Sheryl took off the ring and threw it at Philip. I learned the following week that Sheryl's parents filed suit in small claims court seeking recovery of the ring from Philip. Judge Rodgers was the judge in the small claims court and it just happened to be a Tuesday. Sheryl walked into the courtroom with her father. She saw Philip and his mother and sat across from each other. Sheryl yelled over at Philip, "Get my ring out of your pocket.

I am getting it back today. I don't give a care about what Judge Amy said. The bailiff announced, "All rise for the Honorable Judge Rodgers and visiting Judge Amy."

Sheryl looked at her mother and said, "What is she doing here? She is the one that made me give the ring back to Philip." Sheryl's mother asked the bailiff why I was sitting in the courtroom in a black gown.

The bailiff answered, "Today is Tuesday. Judge Amy sits in this court on Tuesdays. Before she could say anything else, Judge Rodgers called the case.

Sheryl explained the facts and finished with, "Judge Amy ruled in Amy's Kourt that I had to give the ring back to Philip. I gave it to him, but Judge Amy is a joke. She had no authority over me or my ring. That is why I am here."

Judge Rodgers said that he had a few questions. His first question was, "Did you agree to the jurisdiction of Amy's Kourt?" She said that she did. Then he asked, "Did you have a trial in Amy's Kourt?" She said that she did. His final question was, "Did Judge Amy enter a verdict or decision in your case?" She replied, "Yes." Judge Rodgers then said, "This matter has already been fully adjudicated in a court of law and I have no authority to hear the case unless you reserved an appeal option." Sheryl didn't think so.

Sheryl's mother said, "Amy's Kourt is a joke. A nine-year-old is the judge. She is nothing."

Judge Rodgers said, "Not so. Parties to a dispute may elect to resolve the dispute through private decision making, such as Amy's Kourt. The decision is final and binding unless an appeal right is reserved. The decision of the sitting judge is the final decision under our state code

S.C. §18.358.3033. The fact that Judge Amy is only nine years old is irrelevant.

On recess, Judge Rodgers said that my decision was correct in his opinion. He then said, "Congratulations. Your decision survived your first appeal."

Our next case dealt with another traffic accident. This time the parties wanted a jury so the case took up the rest of the day. The plaintiff said the defendant failed to yield, whatever that meant. I wrote the word 'yield' in my notes and thought I would ask Judge Rodgers later.

Plaintiff said that he was turning left off the roadway into a restaurant. The defendant turned right onto the same street and hit plaintiff's car as it crossed in front of the defendant's car. I tried to draw a picture, but one of the first pieces of evidence was a police report drawing showing the intersection. I could see visually what the attorneys were talking about. The accident happened in the defendant's lane of travel which meant that the plaintiff was in his way. I wondered if the defendant could have avoided hitting the other driver.

When the case was given to the jury, Judge Rodgers and I went to his office, which I now understand to be his 'chambers'. We talked about the case and like usual Judge Rodgers asked me what my thoughts were. I replied, "It seems like the plaintiff turned in front of the defendant causing the accident. The plaintiff's car was hit on the passenger side by the front end of the defendant's car. The collision happened in the defendant's lane on the road. I think the accident was caused by the plaintiff, but I have a question. What if the defendant could have avoided hitting the plaintiff and he didn't. Is that wrong too?"

Judge Rodgers said, "Amy, you are smarter than you give yourself credit. Your analysis is correct. The jury will have to decide if the defendant could have avoided the accident. The rule is called the "Last clear chance doctrine" and it applies if the defendant didn't take any steps to avoid the accident."

I was so proud. The jury came back in forty minutes and said that the plaintiff was at fault. When I got home that night, I couldn't wait to share my cases with my family.

My mom congratulated me as she handed me a summons and complaint for superior court. My parents and I were being sued by Bullet because my brothers threw him off the porch and out of my Kourthouse. Bullet claims that he has lost every football game since then and I ruined his future as a professional football player.

I asked Judge Rodgers about the complaint and if he had any recommendations for a defense lawyer.

Judge Rodgers said that his former law firm will handle the case 'pro bono', which meant without charge to me and my family. My parents were very appreciative of the free representation, but still didn't like being sued. My Dad suggested that I shut down my Amy's Kourt.

I replied, "No way. It is my community service and I refuse to give in to a bully."

CHAPTER FIVE

....

Learning The Law The Hard Way

M y dad and I met with the lawyer from Judge's Rodger's former law firm. The people were nice and talked about my Amy's Kourt and my relationship with Judge Rodgers. Mr. Harper told me that he had heard nothing but praise from Judge Rodgers about my ability to make correct decisions using common sense. We talked about our case. He said that if Bullet had received a physical injury from being thrown off the porch, then we would 'tender', which means give the case to our insurance company. However, since the only injury claimed is mental, we will need to defend it ourselves.

My dad asked, "What chance is there for Bullet winning in court?" Mr. Harper replied, "There is always a chance the other side could win, but I am fairly confident that you will do fine. There is no clear 'nexus', which means connection, between being thrown off the porch and loosing football games."

Mr. Harper allowed me to help draft an 'answer', which is a written response to the complaint filed by Bullet's parents. I insisted the facts be accurate and rewrote the answer four times. We argued 'contributory fault', which meant that what Bullet did is what caused his damages. We also argued that he threatened me, as the sitting judge of Amy's Kourt, and that is why he was physically removed from the Kourthouse. The legal theory is called 'justification'.

Mr. Harper notified me and my parents that Bullet's family was asking for a twelve-person jury to hear the case. Served with the jury demand was a notice that Bullet's attorneys wanted to take my 'deposition', which is my sworn statement before we get to court. I was less worried than my parents and our lawyers. It was the aggression by the other attorneys that was making everyone nervous. That is, everyone but me. I knew that I did nothing wrong and getting thrown out of my court was justified and could not be tied to Bullet's ability to play football.

I arrived with my dad for my deposition. I turned ten years old three days before the deposition. I was asked my name and I told them. They asked me if I had a play courthouse. I said, "No, I have a real Kourthouse called "Amy's Kourt."

The attorney said, "But it is just a game you play, isn't that correct?" I replied, "No. It is my community service. I am licensed to provide

Amy's Kourt"

He asked, "And who licenses Amy's Kourt?"

I replied, "The city and state licensed me. I have a valid city and county business license and I have authority to hold Amy's Kourt under S.C. §18.358.3033.

He asked for my licenses and I handed him a copy. He seemed really surprised that I was licensed. He turned to Bullet's parents and said, "Judge Amy is legitimate."

He asked me about the incident when Bullet was thrown off of our porch. I replied, "Bullet was never thrown off of our porch."

He said, "Then you tell me what happened that day."

I explained that I held Amy's Kourt and Bullet consented to the jurisdiction of my Kourt. I entered judgment against him requiring him to replace an expensive football he ruined or pay for the football. He jumped onto one of the tables in my Kourtroom and threatened me. My brothers grabbed him and removed him from my Kourthouse. If you check my business license, you will see that the rear porch is the designated Amy's Kourt. My brothers were justified in removing Bullet. He threatened an officer of the court and rightfully, he should have been put in jail for what he did.

The attorney asked me about my involvement as an Amy's Kourt Judge.

I explained that during the summer, I sit in on cases with Judge Rodgers every Tuesday. I am learning the law first hand through this experience. I hold Amy's Kourt for my neighborhood on Monday, Wednesday and Saturday. I will be holding Amy's Kourt at the public school on Tuesdays and Thursdays when school starts up again.

He asked, "You even judge at the public school?"

I replied, "Yes. Ask your client what happened when he refused to pay my judgment."

He asked, "Please tell me."

I said, "I warned bullet that he needed to pay the judgment or he wouldn't play football. Coach Peters backed me up as did Bullet's father. Bullet agreed to pay and his father wrote out a check to the other party and a $10 check to my Kourt for sanctions.

The attorney said, "You seem so smart. Should my client receive damages out of this lawsuit?"

I replied, "I am not doing your job too. However, I would like to know what nexus can be shown from being properly ejected from a Kourthouse and the loss of ability to play football. Bullet was never injured and the only psychological injury would have been brought on by Bullet."

I saw Judge Rodgers the following Tuesday. He shook my hand and said, "I heard wonderful reports about your deposition. My former partners said that you are as tenacious as anyone in our office. You will make a good attorney someday."

I replied, "I plan to be a full-time judge one day with nice courtroom and court personnel like a bailiff."

Judge Rodgers replied, "I think you will get it too."

Trial was only two months away and school was starting up again. I refused to let my personal trial interfere with my duties as an Amy's Kourt judge. I heard cases at school on Tuesdays and eventually on Thursdays as well. In no time, our trial date arrived. I was the only one in our family that wasn't worried. Gary and Tom were pulled from school so they could testify about removing Bullet. I still didn't know what my parents had to contribute.

I sat with our attorneys during the voir dire process. I watched the juror's eyes as they were asked questions. We had the right to kick off three jurors for no reason, called 'preemptory challenges', and we could kick anyone off for 'just cause', meaning their minds were made up or they were influenced and couldn't be fair. We got to the last couple of jurors and I wanted this man and my attorney wanted a softer woman who might find favor in the fact that I was a little girl on trial. My argument was that I was a judge and the man might respect authority more. I won the argument and the man remained on the jury. We had three days of trial before the case went to the jury. The jury verdict or decision sheet asked some questions. The first was, "Did the defendants, or any of them, physically remove the plaintiff Bullet from the defendant's residence in such a manner that he was forcefully thrown off the porch. The jurors needed to mark yes or no. The second question was whether the removal of Bullet from the porch was justified under the circumstances. "Yes or No." The third question, "Is there a clear nexus between being removed from the defendant's porch and Bullet's inability to win football games? "Yes or No". The fourth question, "If a nexus exists, then what are Bullet's damages."

The jury took twenty minutes and returned a verdict in favor of the defendants. I told my parents, "I told you so." I realized that I didn't like sitting on the other side of the courtroom. Being a named defendant gave me respect for the parties that appear before me in my kourtroom. Judge Rodgers indicated that the fall judicial conference was being held in September. It would be highly unusual, but he would like to invite me to be his guest at the conference this year. I checked with my parents and they were not thrilled since it was being held on the other side of the state. I had been offered to stay with Judge Rodgers and his family. He had a twelve-year-old daughter that was also going to be attending. My family finally gave in and let me go.

Judge Rodger's daughter was named Patty. She and I attended numerous workshops while receiving many strange stares from other judges. Patty said, "Amy, at least you are a judge of sorts. I am nothing except my father's daughter."

One of the older judges stopped me and asked what Patty and I were doing at the judicial conference. I introduced myself as Judge Amy. He looked at his list of judges and said, "I don't see your name on my list." As we talked, a woman handed him an updated list and my name was on it thanks to Judge Rodgers. I received a name tag with my name and the word Judge underneath. I was just like all of the other judges, which I later learned included our Supreme Court justices. I was in heaven for a new judge trying to learn my way in life. I may have been an Amy's Kourt Judge, but I was accepted as a judge and I was quite proud of it.

The judicial conference lasted five days and there were seminars held daily for torts, contracts, criminal, civil, real estate, probate and guardianship, land use and ethics. In each course, the latest decisions were reviewed by the attorneys and judges that decided the cases. I decided to sit up front, but the table was too high for me. Judge Arnold, the Chief Justice of our State Supreme Court, carried in a large phone book for me and Patty so we could see better over our tables. It was wonderful to be respected at our age. I learned so much about the law that week that I couldn't wait to get back to Judge Rodger's court and apply what I learned. I repeatedly thanked Judge Rodgers for the opportunity to attend the judicial conference.

He replied, "I have you penciled in for next year too if that is all right with you."

My smile said it all. I was so happy and it showed.

CHAPTER SIX

School Kourt is Changing

started school late due to the judicial conference. It was an excused absence so I wasn't worried. I was also a straight 'A' student. I started up School Kourt with my first case of the year.

The school had a fall fair that included bringing in the largest pumpkin for the fall carnival. The grand prize was $200 and four tickets to a theme park. Elise's grandfather brought in a 768-pound pumpkin and Kennedy's uncle brought in an 810-pound squash. Elise told Kennedy that the squash didn't qualify because it wasn't a pumpkin. The rules said, "Pumpkins only." Kennedy got mad and destroyed Elise's pumpkin before the judging began. He contended that he should be the winner because he had the largest squash. Brady intervened and said that he had a 230-pound pumpkin which would be the winning pumpkin.

The first prize went to Brady. Elise filed a complaint against Kennedy for the loss of the prize money and tickets.

I accepted the complaint, but I was concerned that my decision may not be honored by the parents if they weren't also part of the Amy's Kourt jurisdiction. I insisted that Elise's parents and grandfather be joined as plaintiffs and Kennedy and his parents be joined as defendants. I got to thinking about the case and decided that if Elise prevailed, then Brady would need to return the money and tickets so I made Brady and his parents' parties as well. It took two weeks to get everyone signed up and then I held the trial on a Saturday at my Amy's Kourt.

Brady's parents asked why they were consenting to Amy's Kourt. Kennedy's parents wondered the same, but didn't complain. I handed out an agreement for the court which confirmed that my decision was final and binding under S.C. §18.358.3033. Everyone signed off.

I asked for an opening statement from Elise or her grandfather. Elise chose to speak.

She testified, "My grandfather delivered to the school a 768-pound pumpkin for the fall harvest contest. It was the largest pumpkin and I should have won the $200 and the four tickets to the theme park."

Elise then called her grandfather and he testified that he did deliver the 768-pound pumpkin. He had a weigh scale measurement and a picture of the pumpkin that he delivered.

I called on Kennedy to testify. He admitted that he delivered an 810-pound squash and that Elise told him that his squash didn't qualify for the contest. The rules called for a pumpkin. I got mad and broke up the pumpkin and hauled it away over the weekend.

I then called Brady and he testified that he presented a 230-pound pumpkin that was there for the judging. He admitted receiving the $200 and the four theme park tickets.

I asked Brady if he saw Elise's pumpkin before it was destroyed. He said, "No. He just heard about it, but never saw it."

I asked Brady if he had any reason to dispute the size of the pumpkin produced by Elise's family.

He said, "Yes. I won, she lost."

I was considering the case when Abagail walked into the Kourthouse. She asked to testify.

I asked, "Who are you testifying for?" She said, "Me. I am the rightful winner."

I asked why she wasn't part of the complaint process.

Abagail answered, "We went on vacation and when we returned, I learned what happened."

I said, "You may testify."

Abagail said, "I saw the two squash plants produced by Elise and Kennedy. Neither were pumpkins. I told Kennedy that neither were pumpkins and would not qualify. In the meantime, I put my grandma's 230-pound pumpkin into the contest just before leaving on vacation. The pumpkin had my name, address and telephone number written on the bottom of the pumpkin. When we got back from vacation, my pumpkin was gone and Brady had entered a 230-pound pumpkin. My dad rolled Brady's pumpkin over last night and my name was on the bottom. As such, I believe I won. I also have a picture of me and the pumpkin when we delivered it."

I asked all the parties and parents if they had anything more to add to the case. No one answered. I said that I would take the case under advisement and issue my ruling in two days.

I called Judge Rodgers to ask his opinion on how he would decide the case.

Judge Rodgers said, "Amy. You are the decision maker. You heard the testimony. Now enter your decision. You don't need me. Just use your brilliant mind. You will make the right decision. I promise you."

The next day I entered judgment in favor of Abagail. I ordered Brady to deliver the $200 and the four tickets to the court within 24 hours for distribution to Abagail.

Brady's parents refused to return the money and tickets to the court or deliver it to Abagail. They denied that I had any authority over them even though they signed accepting my jurisdiction and authority.

Abagail's parents sued Brady's parents in small claims court seeking enforcement of the Judgment I entered in favor of Abagail. I also 'sanctioned', which meant that I gave a penalty to Elise, Kennedy and Brady for 'perjury', which meant lying to the court. I charged each of them with a $25 fine. Kennedy and Elise joined in Brady's response on the court judgment.

I knew this could happen. The case went to the local court and Judge Rodgers received the case. When he learned that the case was an appeal from Amy's Kourt, he denied the appeal of the decision, but granted jurisdiction on the sanctions. Judge Rodgers decided that Amy's Kourt didn't have statutory authority to assess sanctions and he dismissed my perjury sanctions. The case was appealed in its entirety to the superior court. The superior court judge upheld Judge Rodger's decision and the case was further appealed to the state Court of Appeals. Two of the three judges upheld Judge Rodger's and the superior court's decision and Brady's parents took the case to the state supreme court. I appealed my right to apply sanctions out of Amy's Kourt since the parties granted me jurisdiction. Given my authority as a private court to issue sanctions, the Supreme Court granted 'certiorari' which means that it would agree to hear the case. I learned that the court decides what cases it will hear or reject.

Our little case tied up the state Supreme Court for ten days. When the decision came out, the Supreme Court upheld my authority as a private judge under S.C. §18.358.3033. The court sustained my decision as to the prize award and denied my authority to assess sanctions without legislative authority. I won part and lost part. The exciting thing was that I was part of the court system up to the Supreme Court.

Things returned to normal at school until my state representative asked to talk with me after school. He said that he followed my Amy's Kourt case to the Supreme Court. He was a news reporter before joining the legislature. He asked me if I was interested in pursuing the ability to make penalties and sanctions out of my kourt system. I smiled and said, "Of course. If I can't enforce what I say, then what good is my role as the judge?"

He replied, "Well, the state Supreme Court has upheld your right to decide cases as a final determination. That's pretty good for a ten-year-old."

I replied, "I turn eleven next week thank you."

Representative Brunt authored legislation granting private courts the right to sanction parties that willfully violate the court rules, including perjury and intentional delays. The penalties could not exceed $50 per incident. Over the next year, the legislature messed around with the legislation and it was finally adopted near my twelfth birthday. I now had a hammer if needed. Part of the legislation required more formality in how I handle my cases.

Representative Brunt then put my name in as a community leader and highlighted my Amy's Kourt for the news article that aired on television and in the newspaper. Amy's Kourt became the alternative court for the neighborhood and schools. I wasn't aware of it, but my name was put in for kid of the year for our county. When I received notice that I won, I couldn't believe I had even been nominated.

A television reporter interviewed me and took pictures of my Amy's Kourthouse on my back porch. I talked about going to judicial conferences and my desire to become a future judge with a nice courtroom like the regular judges had. I smiled and said, "Until then, I love my Amy's Kourt on the back porch."

Mr. Burns was a wealthy builder that graduated from my school and lived in our community. He had seen the television report and also read about my little Kourt in the local newspaper. Mr. Burns stopped by and asked me if I would consider hearing business cases affecting his company. I was thrilled, but said, "I have to treat everyone the same. No one gets special treatment from me."

Mr. Burns replied, "I would never ask for special treatment. I am just impressed with your tenacity and I don't like the public courts that much."

I agreed to give it a try. I asked, "How many cases do you have over one year?"

Mr. Burns replied, "Less than five."

Mr. Burns stopped by my Amy's Kourt and showed me how he changed his business contracts to include a venue provision for Amy's Kourt. Anyone signing a contract with his business must consent to hearing disputes exclusively in Amy's Kourt. He cited S.C. §18.358.3033 as the authority for using Amy's Kourt.

I asked Mr. Burns what his business was about.

He explained, "I have a lumber store and a plumbing store and a large construction company. Sometimes a case will be brought to collect money. Other times a case may deal with defects in construction, etc. Your job will be to hear both sides and make the best decision you can make. I don't expect you to have the full knowledge of a lawyer. I want you to use your God given common sense that I have heard so much about."

I thanked Mr. Burns and then reminded myself that I had school Kourt today and I had to get going or I would be late. When I arrived, I was handed three complaint forms and told that the parties were all present.

I quickly put on my black robe and carried my gavel and block to my table. I banged the gavel and asked everyone to sit down and be quiet while court was in session.

I called my first case. The complaint said that Steven (6th grader) took an apple out of the lunch of Shelly (2nd grader). Shelly wanted another apple or $0.50 to buy another apple in the school dispenser.

I swore my parties and asked Shelly to make her opening statement. Shelly replied, "My what?"

I explained, "Please tell me what you intend to prove as the plaintiff." Shelly replied, "The what?"

I said, "You are making a complaint. You are called the 'plaintiff'. Steven is the person you are complaining about and he is called the 'defendant'."

Shelly replied, "Oh."

I asked Shelly to proceed and tell me what happened.

Shelly said, "My mom gave me $0.50 to buy an apple from the apple machine at lunch time. I bought the apple and put it on my desk. I bought a carton of milk and when I returned to my desk, my apple was missing and some of the kids in my class were laughing at me. I thought they were joking. I asked that they please return my apple, but no one returned it."

I asked, "You are claiming that Steven took your apple. What proof do you have that it was Steven?"

Shelly replied, "I have a witness." I replied, "Who is your witness? Shelly replied, "My friend Amanda. She is in my class and sits next to me."

I called Amanda to step forward and I swore her in. I asked Amanda to tell me what she saw.

Amanda testified, "I saw Steven walk by our room at lunch time. Shelly's desk is near the door. Steven stopped and grabbed her apple and left our room."

I thanked the plaintiff and then called upon Steven to testify. Steven said, "I forgot my lunch at home. I saw the apple and I grabbed it. I would have bought an apple, but I didn't have any money. I knew it was wrong, but I did it because I was hungry."

I said, "I am granting judgment for Shelly in the amount of two fresh red applies, or $1.00. The judgment is to be satisfied within two days. If you don't take care of this, then you will be in contempt of this court and further judgment can be entered against you. Do you understand?

Steven said, "Yes. I will bring Shelly a dollar tomorrow."

My second case dealt with a student lying to her teacher. The teacher filed the complaint claiming that Sylvia copied her work off the Internet.

I called the parties. Ms. Prosser taught fifth grade. Sylvia was in her class.

I asked Ms. Prosser if she had an opening statement. She did. I said, "You may proceed with your opening."

Ms. Prosser said, "I will prove that I gave a writing assignment that required original thought. I received a paper from Sylvia on the Great Wall in China that was written beyond what I believed to be Sylvia's ability. I checked the Internet and found the same paper written by someone else. I asked Sylvia after class if she copied the report. She denied having done so. I failed Sylvia on the assignment. I will prove that Sylvia copied the work. I am handing you the Internet version and Sylvia's report. You will see that both reports are identical."

I called Sylvia and asked her if she had a response to what Ms. Prosser said.

Sylvia replied, "I didn't know the work was from the Internet. My older sister helped me with my report. When I went to bed, she typed up my report for me and I handed it in. I didn't read it before I handed it in. When Ms. Prosser accused me of copying, I cried and said that I didn't copy. She refused to listen to me. I have my hand written report in my jacket pocket. May I give it to you?"

I said, "Please get your hand-written report and give it to me." Sylvia handed me a two-page report and I looked it over and handed it to Ms. Prosser.

Ms. Prosser apologized to Sylvia for not listening to her before accusing her of wrongdoing.

I banged my gavel and said, "Call the next case."

My next case dealt with something much more serious than usual. It was a school truancy case. The principal was going to suspend Alfred (8th grader) for two weeks because he skipped school again to ride his skate board at the local park.

I swore in the principal and Alfred and asked the Principal to make his opening statement or his proof.

Mr. Thomlinson testified, "This is the fifth time this year that I have personally caught Alfred riding his skateboard instead of being at school. He is now subject to a two-week suspension. I decided to bring this complaint against Alfred and hear your decision.

I called on Alfred to give his side of the story.

Alfred replied, "The principal is right. I skipped school again. This is actually eight times this year. School is boring and I need time to get away from the boredom. I don't mean to cause trouble. I'm just bored."

I asked Alfred what his grades were like.

He replied, "I get straight 'A' grades. I usually get 100% on all my tests and I know this stuff forwards and backwards. That is why I am so bored."

I asked if anyone had tested Alfred for his IQ. Alfred said, "No."

I asked Principal Thomlinson, "Does the school district have any provisions for getting students tested for IQ. I suspect that Alfred's boredom is due to his academic ability. I don't want to punish Alfred with suspension because he is smart."

The principal said that he would look into it.

I talked with the principal and Alfred and asked if there was a way for Alfred to act as a tutor to slower students in any of the grades at the school. That was something both were interested in. I entered Judgment against Alfred requiring him to work as a teaching aide at least five hours a week for the rest of the school year. The teachers could determine where he would be the best help. Alfred thanked me and said, "It is nice being needed and having something to do."

I talked with Principal Thomlinson after court. I wondered how I was hearing a case from a different school than my own.

He replied, "Didn't you receive the notice. You are going to be the Amy's Kourt Judge for all K-8 schools in our district. The schools have agreed to hold cases at this school.

All I could think of is WOW! I worked my way through school and heard thirty-one school cases before the end of the year. I must have been doing a good job because the teachers decided to keep Amy's Kourt working.

Over the summer, I heard neighborhood cases more regularly. I had started carrying around a calendar and I started requiring cases to be scheduled in advance of the hearing. I was only one person and I was spread quite thin. I loved being a judge. The paperwork ... not so much!

CHAPTER SEVEN

Moving Up

I received my first case from Mr. Burns. I laughed because the case was covering plumbing supplies that the other side said was non-conforming goods. Mr. Burns said the supplies met the job specifications. This was similar to my case with Judge Rodgers and the lumber yard.

I scheduled the hearing and Mr. Burn's store manager was there to represent the company. Mr. Lee was the plumber that ordered the plumbing parts. There were no other witnesses. I swore everyone in and asked Mr. Lee to please make his opening statement or offer his proof that...; what did your complaint say? Oh, here it is. The plumbing goods were non-conforming. Please explain to me why the parts were not meeting job specifications.

Mr. Lee asked, "How old are you?" I replied, "Twelve."

He said, "This is ridiculous. I am not putting up with this insanity. I want a real judge."

I looked at Mr. Lee and said, "For this case, I am a real judge. I am licensed and my authority comes from S.C. §18.358.3033. The contract you signed with Burn's plumbing set venue in my private Amy's Kourt. Now you can tell me about your complaint, or I will dismiss your case for refusing to present it in a timely manner."

Mr. Lee walked out of my Kourthouse and I entered judgment dismissing his complaint 'with prejudice', which means he can't ask for another case on the same subject matter.

I learned from Mr. Burns that Mr. Lee filed a lawsuit in the superior court of our county asking for the same relief as he asked for in my Kourt. Mr. Burns said that his lawyers needed a declaration from me about what happened. He said the lawyers would prepare what I needed to say.

I replied, "No thank you. I will prepare my own declaration so no one puts words in my mouth that don't belong there."

I wrote:

"Amy Lynn Jefferies, Judge of Amy's Kourt, makes this declaration of facts under penalty of perjury under the laws of our state. On Saturday, June 10, I had Kourt scheduled to hear the matter of Mr. Lee, plumber vs. Mr. Burn's plumbing store. Mr. Lee objected to me being the judge because I am only twelve years old. I cited S.C. §18.358.3033 as my authority and the venue clause of Mr. Burn's contract as my right to sit as the judge. I told Mr. Lee that if he failed to proceed with his case that I would dismiss it with prejudice. Mr. Lee walked out of my Kourthouse and I entered judgment dismissing his case with prejudice. Signed: Judge Amy."

In response to my declaration, Mr. Lee provided pictures of my back porch Kourtroom in partial support of his claim that my Kourt was nothing more than 'Amy's playground'. He called me a pretentious and excitable little girl that was too big for my britches.

The case was to be heard by Judge Patricia Stewart. I was sitting with Mr. Burns at his table when the bailiff said, "All rise. The superior court is now in session. The honorable Patricia Stewart presiding."

The judge asked for identification of who was sitting at counsel tables. Mr. Burns' attorney introduced himself and Mr. Burns. He then explained that I was Mr. Burn's guest. The judge asked for my name.

I replied, "Your honor, my name is Amy Lynn Jefferies." The judge asked if I was a defendant in this matter.

I said, "No."

Are you an attorney, or are you assisting the attorney?

I said, "No. I am the Amy's Kourt judge that first heard this case." The Judge said, "I wondered. Please sit out there. Only parties and their attorneys are to be seated at counsel tables. I suspect that you will be a key witness at this hearing."

Judge Stewart then turned to Mr. Lee's attorney and said, "As I understand your petition, you are seeking to void a judgment from a private court which dismissed your client's case with prejudice."

He replied, "That's right your honor. The little girl that you had removed from counsel tables is the pretend judge that made the order. It is ridiculous that we even need to be here arguing this matter."

Judge Stewart said, "We'll see." She called me to the witness stand and said, "Judge Amy. I read your declaration. I have a few questions and then I will let the attorneys ask you any questions."

"Are you licensed to have a private court in this county?"

I replied, "Yes. I am licensed by the city and the county for Amy's Kourt which is a private kourt hearing neighborhood disputes and school disputes. I can hear other matters as well if the parties agree to my kourt's jurisdiction."

Did you have on your docket the matter of Lee Plumbing vs. Burn's Plumbing Store?"

I replied, "Yes. I did."

Judge Stewart then said, "Tell me what happened in your court."

I explained, "Mr. Lee saw me and refused to let me hear the case. I pointed out the venue clause in the contract that he agreed to as well as his agreement to accept jurisdiction of my court. I also pointed out S.C. §18.358.3033 as my statutory authority to act as a private court. When he refused to let me hear the case, he started leaving. I told him that if he left my Kourtroom that I would enter judgment dismissing his case with prejudice which is what I did."

Judge Stewart said, "Thank you. I will now open you up for questions from the attorneys."

Mr. Lee's attorney asked me how many cases I had 'adjudicated'. I looked confused and looked to Judge Stewart.

She said, "How many cases have you heard and given judgment."

I said, "Oh. I'm sorry, but I had never heard that word before. I have now heard 385 cases and this is the only one that I have had a lot of trouble with."

He asked me about my training. I replied, "I am learning as I go. I work with Judge Rodgers on Tuesdays and I study what I can find. I attend the annual judicial conferences."

He said, "Please describe your courtroom to the judge."

I replied, "It is on my back porch. I have an old office desk that sits on a wooden box built by my brothers and another box where my chair sits so I can see over the desk. In front of my desk are two tables with chairs for the parties."

He then asked me, "You don't actually have a courtroom. What you have is a porch to play court in. Isn't that true?"

I replied, "My Kourt is on my back porch. It has a roof so court can be heard on sunny and rainy days. It is all I have. Someday, I will have a beautiful courtroom like Judge Stewart. Until then, what you saw is my Kourtroom. What is important is my decision and thought process; not my Kourthouse."

He said, "Nothing further. When are you going to dump this children's theater and get on with the real practice of law?"

Judge Stewart asked Mr. Burn's attorney if he had any questions. He replied, "One your honor." Judge Amy, would your decision making be different in a nice courtroom?"

I replied, "My job as judge is to hear cases and be fair and impartial in my thoughts and decision making. It makes no difference where I may hear a case. I must do my best to make the best decision on the facts and not on anything else. I would love a fancy courtroom, but I love being a judge and my little Kourthouse is fine for now."

Judge Stewart thanked everyone and then said, "The petition in this matter to set aside the decision of a private court is denied. The simple fact that Judge Amy's Kourt is on her back porch instead of in this courthouse makes no difference. Contracts providing for an agreement as to venue may be enforced. In this situation, the contract specified Amy's Kourt as the venue for any disputes. Our Supreme Court has already ruled that private courts are permissible and the decisions of the private judges are enforceable as if made by an elected judge. Judge Amy warned Mr. Lee that if he left her courtroom, she would dismiss his case with prejudice and she did. Like Judge Amy, I am likewise dismissing this case with prejudice."

I was so excited to have the judge agree with my decision. Mr. Burns shook my hand and then gave me a hug. He said, "See, I put no pressure on you. I will accept your decision making if you will agree to be the venue for my business hearings.

I agreed. I noticed that across from the school the formerly vacant lot had a new building going up. It was brick and really nice. I walked past the new building every day on my way to school. I was talking with Sheryl and I said that I would love a building like that for Amy's Kourt.

Sheryl replied, "You wish. That building is a lot of money."

One day I stopped to look inside the window. The building was mostly one big room. On my way home, I stopped by to see if I could look inside the building. I walked around when this man said, "Get out unless you are wearing a hard hat."

I replied, "I'm sorry, but I don't have one."

He picked up a hard hat and said, "Wear this if you are going to be walking around in here."

I asked the man what the building was going to be.

He replied, "I don't know. It is supposed to be done by Christmas. It is a Christmas present as I understand it."

I thought someone is going to be lucky this Christmas.

I carried on my court cases through the summer and fall. I noticed that I was receiving at minimum ten cases per month from the school. All student discipline was funneled through my court. The principals said that I had a good grasp on punishment that worked better than expulsion or suspension.

The time came and Christmas was here. I was on school break waiting for Christmas day along with millions of other kids. I was now thirteen and I was growing up quickly. Christmas day arrived and we opened our presents and had a really nice Christmas. Mr. Burns stopped by to invite my family out for coffee and treats as part of his appreciation. He said, "I have something to show Judge Amy too."

My family followed Mr. Burns and I was surprised to see him pull into the new building's parking lot. He handed me the key to the door and said, "Amy, will you please open the door and I will show your family around."

I walked into this beautiful building. The side room was an actual courtroom with a judge's bench, a jury sitting area, counsel tables and pews for people to sit on. I had a bailiff's station and a clerk's station. On the front of my bench was the name, AMY'S KOURT.

I asked Mr. Burns if the courtroom was really for me.

He replied, "It is yours for as long as you, or your successors want it. I have a lease that requires your signature."

I asked, "How much is the lease per month?"

He replied, "It is a little pricy, but isn't a beautiful new courtroom worth the expense."

I replied, "I suppose so, but I don't have any money to pay the lease." Mr. Burns replied, "Please look at the lease."

I looked and it read, "Terms. $1 per year. Received on account. $100."

I said, "It looks like the lease is paid for the next 100 years."

Mr. Burns smiled and thanked me for my services to my community. What was even more exciting was the sign in the front of the building and that I received the keys for my new Amy's Kourt. When I arrived at my new courthouse the next day, Mr. Burns had added under the courthouse sign, "Judge Amy Presiding." I was so happy that I sat down on the steps of the building and cried for a few minutes.

A policeman stopped and asked me if I was all right. I assured him that I was fine.

He replied, "I'm sure the court will be open soon. Which are you, plaintiff or defendant?"

I replied, "I am the Judge. I am Judge Amy."

The officer said, "I am pleased to meet your honor."

I had the first real opportunity to walk through my new courthouse. I had a room with a door sign that read "Judge's Chambers" and underneath that was "Hon. Amy L. Jefferies" I had my own bathroom and a small kitchen and refrigerator. I had a male and female public bathroom and a records room just in case I wanted to keep records. The most special part of my entire office tour was the note card from Judge Rodgers inviting me to be his guest at the judicial conference.

I joined Judge Rodgers for my usual Tuesday learning day. Judge Rodgers complimented me on my terminology and said that I was starting to sound like a judge with considerable experience.

I invited Judge Rodgers to stop by and see my new Kourthouse. He smiled an approving smile.

Judge Rodgers said, "I knew you would have a beautiful courthouse of your own one day. I already stopped by. It is beautiful. In fact, I think it is nicer than this one."

I blushed and said, "Thank you." I hope I can live up to being a judge. There is so much to know."

He replied, "That is why I want you to attend the judicial conference with me again this year.

CHAPTER EIGHT

....

I Am A Judge

I explained to my mother that the judicial conference was here once again. Judge Rodgers invited me to go with him to the conference. I am so excited about this opportunity because I learned so much last year. I can go, right?

My mother replied, "Who else is going with you?"

I replied, "Patricia can't go this year because she has cheerleader camp that she is going to."

Mom replied, "I didn't ask who isn't going. I want to know who is going."

I replied, "I think it would be just me and Judge Rodgers. He said that he could get two rooms and hopefully you or one of my brothers could go with me."

Mom replied, "Amy. You are 13 years old. You are no longer a little girl. You can't stay with a married man in a hotel room and I don't care if he is a judge. You are my daughter and you are not going under those circumstances."

I asked if Mom could go with me. I said, "You can bring Cynthia and Steven with you and get away from home for a week."

Mom replied, "No. It is too difficult having little children away from home for that long. It will be unfair to Judge Rodgers."

I became angry and said, "Mom, I am a Judge and I am going to the judicial conference with or without your blessing. I want to learn the law and the conference is a good way to learn."

Mom replied, "I said No! Amy, that's final. You are too young to be going to a judicial conference with a married man. Why isn't his wife going?" I replied, "Jenny is a school teacher and can't get the time off of work to go with Jerry."

Mom said, "Now, it's Jerry and not Judge Rodgers."

I explained, "He asked me to call him Jerry when we are away from the court. He treats me like a professional and he cares about me learning the law and furthering my education. I wish you would understand."

Mom said, "I do understand and I already said no."

I asked, "Can Gary or Tom go with me or are you afraid that they will rape me too?"

My mother said, "No!!!!!"

I was sitting on my bed crying when my Dad came home. He came in and asked, "What's wrong Amy? How can I help?"

I explained what Mom said about the judicial conference.

Dad replied, "I agree with your mother. It is not a question of you doing something wrong, or even Judge Rodgers doing something to you. I trust your judgment. However, it is the appearance that may give rise to questions. What do you think the other judges would think knowing that Judge Rodgers has a young girl sharing a room with him?"

I said, "We wouldn't be sharing the same room. He was getting me my own room next to him."

Dad asked, "Exactly when is the judicial conference?"

I said it is from September 2 to September 6. It starts Wednesday and goes to Sunday at 4:00 pm.

Dad said, "You are lucky. My trial scheduled for October 31 settled today. I will go with you to the judicial conference."

I replied, "Don't tell mom. She will tell me that I can't go with a married man, including my father."

Dad replied, "Amy stop with the sarcasm or you won't go at all."

I thanked my father and he squared things with my mother so I could go.

Dad, Judge Rodgers and I arrived at the conference. Dad walked me to the convention center and into the initial greeting room where we would have breakfast and listen to speakers on the current law changes. We checked in at the registration table and Judge Rodgers found his name badge but I couldn't find one for me.

I turned to Judge Rodgers and asked, "Jerry, did you register me for the conference?"

My Dad apologized and said, "Please refer to him as Judge Rodgers." I said, "I am a judge too."

My Dad patted my head and said, "Not the same thing Amy. These judges are elected. Your position is created for Amy's Kourt. There is a big difference."

Judge Rodgers replied to my Dad, "No, Judge Amy was registered as a Judge and she should have a name tag here. I will look into this."

I heard Judge Rodgers ask the woman where Judge Amy Jefferies' name tag was.

She replied, "We found out that we misspelled her name and we are making her a new name tag."

Judge Rodgers smiled and said, "There you go."

Another woman arrived and handed me my name tag. It said,

AMY L. JEFFERIES, JUDGE
AMY'S KOURT

My Dad asked if he could sit in on the conference. The woman asked if my dad was a judge.

He said, "No."

She replied, "Sorry, but I can't let you in. Is Judge Amy your daughter?"

Dad answered, "Yes."

She handed my dad a copy of the conference agenda and said that I would be through at 4:30 pm tonight.

Judge Rodgers said, "I will bring Amy back with me and we can have dinner together."

Dad said, "What about me?"

Judge Rodgers apologized and explained that when he said he would bring me back with him that it was implicit that he meant delivering me to my dad so we could all go to dinner.

Dad said, "Have fun and I will find something to do all day."

At the breakfast, different speakers talked about the law and recent changes. The man in charge then said, "Today, we have a very special judge with us. Many of you have seen her and asked me about her. Her name is Judge Amy and she created a private court over which she is the judge. I would like to welcome Judge Amy up to the speaker's platform to talk with you about her court. This is unplanned, but I think she will answer many of the questions I am receiving about this spectacular young woman. Please welcome Judge Amy.

I was excited and shaking all at the same time. I explained about how I first got involved and how Amy's Kourt grew from a neighborhood court to a school court and now a community court. I am currently hearing cases between Kids and adults alike. Just recently I decided a uniform commercial code case dealing with nonconforming goods. I have heard personal injury cases from trip and falls to car accidents. I deal with bullies and theft of property. My judgments are unique at times as I try to match my judgment to fit the wrong. I have much more flexibility than the rest of you. I have had two challenges to my authority to hear cases and I prevailed in the Supreme Court and in the legislature. My court is authorized under statutory law and I treat my duty to be fair and impartial as my highest duty to those who enter my courtroom. Just recently I received a 100-year lease on my own courthouse. I was surprised when the conference had a series of pictures of my early court house on my porch and in the school to my current court. I heard many judges comment that my court and chambers was nicer than theirs.

There were pictures of me sitting on the bench with parties at tables. I heard one-woman judge say, "She sure looks like the judge."

I am excited about my future. I am a judge and I will remain a judge for many years to come. I believe in the law and applying the law fairly and without delay. I give people two days to pay off judgments under most circumstances. I am tough, but fair. If I am taking work from any of you, then I am sorry, but I love being a judge and I hope I will be viewed as a good judge when my time ends. Thank you.

One-woman judge asked me if there were any negatives in being the sole judge in my courthouse.

I replied, "Yes there is. When everyone else goes home, I am left to clean the courtroom and bathrooms so we are ready to go for the next court day. I wish I had a cleaning service, but I can't afford one because I am not paid for my community services.

One of the judges asked, "Why not get paid? Have you looked into your right to charge fees and get paid?"

I replied, "No. I have tried to be a no cost court to help people." He suggested that I obtain authority to charge a little for my cases. I could use the money to hire a maintenance service to clean up every day. I replied, "Thank you again."

When the conference ended, I was so excited to apply what I learned, including seeking fee authority. I contacted the Supreme Court and was told that I was a private judicial court. I didn't need permission to charge fees. It is a matter of private contract guaranteed under the Constitution. I decided to better organize my Kourt. On Mondays I heard neighborhood disputes. I charged a $0.10 filing fee to make the complaint. If the defendant wanted to dispute the claim, then he or she had to pay $0.10 as well. If the plaintiff won, I awarded the defendant's $0.10 fee to the plaintiff as cost recovery.

Tuesdays were kept for working with Judge Rodgers, and when he was doing criminal court, I worked with Judge Samuels on the civil calendar. She was always very helpful and willing to take the time to teach me how to be a good judge.

I used Wednesday for school court and charged students like I charged kids from the neighborhood.

I used Thursday for more adult type cases like personal injuries and business disputes with Friday being my everything day, including organizing. Saturday was reserved for cases that would take longer than one hour. My fee was $50 to file a case in my court. If there was a counterclaim then I charged them $50 as well. It seemed only fair.

The simple fact that I had the right to charge fees worked well. In my first month, I made enough money to hire a service to clean the courthouse for me. That extra help got me home a little sooner and relieved some pressure that I was receiving from my parents. They claimed I was spending too much time playing judge.

I replied, "I am not playing. I am the judge regardless of what you might otherwise think." My saving grace was that I maintained a 4.0 GPA while doing my judging work.

My reputation for being fair and quick seemed to bring in more adult type disputes. What changed was that I had real attorneys presenting cases before me at age 13. I seemed to have the knack to hear and decide personal injury cases. People read or heard others talking about my Kourt and the general reason for appearing in my Kourt was timing. If an adult filed in the superior court it took one year to get to trial. Our district court was six months. In my Kourt, you could be heard in six weeks or less.

I arrived at my Kourthouse one afternoon and there was a sticker over the door that said, "This business is temporarily locked down. The reason given was tax registration. I called my dad because he was a tax attorney. He laughed at my Kourt being shut down.

I asked dad why he thought it was a laughable matter. I was confused and angry. I had cases that day.

Dad explained, "I always thought you were doing a community service. It now appears that you are a recognized private business. I will get your Kourt registered with the various taxing authorities and have the sticker off your door within the hour. We can't have the judge locked out of her own courtroom.

Mr. Burns heard about my need for a cleaning service and my tax burden and need for operational funds. He put a bow on a thank you card and provided me with his cleaning service and $5,000 to help me get going in my private court system.

CHAPTER NINE

Amy's Kourt is Growing Up

My dad registered me with the taxing offices and the places were quick to send me a tax return to complete quarterly. One tax was called "Business & Occupation's Tax" and the other was "Income Taxes." I couldn't believe that the government takes what little money I make for taxes. I was doing all the work.

I decided to raise the adult cases to a $100 filing fee. That was because I had to hire a clerk to keep records of payments. I found a really nice high school girl that would work mostly for the work experience. I paid her $2 per hour. I received a visit from two Department of Labor agents that threatened to shut down my Kourt unless I paid them the estimated taxes due on Susan's wages.

I asked, "What wages? I give her $2 to help me as a volunteer. She is getting job skills and I get some paperwork help. I learned that I had to withhold taxes, whatever that meant. I sat down with dad and he explained it all to me. When I began taking taxes from Susan's pay, she quit and complained to the labor department that I wasn't paying her enough.

I received an audit notice by the labor office. They decided that I wasn't meeting minimum wage standards and they ordered me to pay anybody at $7.50 per hour that works for my Kourt. When the department determined that I was thirteen years old, they couldn't sue me and let Susan's case drop. I thought, good! They explained that they were shutting down Amy's Kourt. I agreed to fix Susan's pay and pay everyone at a minimum of $7.50 per hour.

My brother, Tom asked if he could volunteer at my Kourthouse. He learned that to get consideration as a fire fighter, he had to have some community service history. He thought being my clerk would be an easy way to get the hours clocked for when he applied on turning eighteen. I was excited because Tom had two years to go before he could apply.

I trained Tom daily and arranged for him to watch the clerk in Judge Rodger's court. Tom's first day was on Saturday. He stepped into the courtroom and said, "Amy's Kourt is now in session. The honorable Amy Lynn Jefferies presiding."

I entered the courtroom from my chambers. I carried my Bible and asked the Lord daily to help me make the right decisions and bring justice where due. As I sat down, I said, "You may be seated." My court room was full. I had a personal injury case; a breach of contract case and two theft cases between kids.

I called the first case. When the attorneys and parties were seated in the courtroom, I asked them to identify the people at their tables. I then welcomed them to my Kourt and confirmed that all parties accepted my jurisdiction and decision would be final and binding. There were no appeals from my Kourt. Everyone agreed.

I asked the plaintiff's attorney if he wanted to make an opening statement.

He said, "Yes your honor."

Just then I saw my Dad and Mom walk into my Kourt and sit down. I looked at the attorney and said, "You may proceed with your opening statement."

He replied, "I will make this very short because I can see that you are getting quite busy. This is a simple personal injury case. My client was stopped at a stop sign and the defendant rear ended his car. My client was injured. We will prove liability, injuries and damages to the court's satisfaction.

I thanked him and asked if the defendant wanted to do an opening statement. He said he did. I said, "You may proceed."

The defense attorney explained, "My client's brakes failed and he couldn't stop his car in time to avoid the accident. Had the plaintiff not been stopped at the stop sign, this accident wouldn't have happened? We believe the plaintiff is also at fault."

I asked the plaintiff's attorney to call his first witness. It was his client. Mr. Brown testified, "I was sitting at the stop sign waiting for the other car to complete their turn then I was going to turn. I looked back and saw the defendant coming fast. He smashed into the rear end of my car." I heard about his whiplash damages and his requested relief of $7,600.

The defendant testified that he had his brakes worked on at his local dealership. He produced a receipt showing that new brakes were put on his car. He didn't know that there was a problem until he couldn't stop at the intersection.

The plaintiff's attorney cross-examined the defendant and asked him, "How long ago was it that you had your brakes done.'

He replied, "Six months ago."

"And you have been driving your car to and from work since then, isn't that correct?"

He answered "Yes".

"Were you in a hurry that morning?"

He answered, "Yes, I was going to be late for work." I asked for closing arguments.

The plaintiff's attorney said that the defendant had been driving on the new brakes for six months. He lived 14 miles from his job and over six months he drove approximately 3,528 miles on the new brakes. He was also late for work and distracted by the time. This isn't an unavoidable accident. We ask for judgment of $7,500.

The defense attorney explained that the plaintiff could have turned, but he waited for another car that was not the favored car in the intersection. Had the plaintiff made his turn when he could have, then he wouldn't have been stopped at the stop sign and he wouldn't have been rear ended.

I told the parties that I would take ten minutes to consider their case and arguments and make a decision. I stepped down from the bench as Tom said, "All rise."

Dad walked into my chambers and asked if I wanted his opinion on fault.

I replied, "Absolutely not. I am the judge and it is my duty to be fair and impartial and make my own decision after hearing both sides. You taught me that. It wouldn't be fair if someone, even my Dad, told me what my decision should be."

Dad hugged me and said, "I knew you would answer me that way. I was just doing an ethics check."

I returned to the courtroom and Tom remembered to say, "All rise". I summarized the case and found that equipment failure was not the contributing cause of the accident. Therefore, the accident couldn't be considered unavoidable. I find in favor of the plaintiff for $7,500 plus court costs.

I looked across the courtroom and my Dad just smiled. I turned to Tom and said, "Call the next case please."

My next case was for a breach of contract. There were no lawyers which allowed the case to proceed much faster. I called on the plaintiff to make any opening statement or proceed with proving his case.

He testified, "My name is Ralph Sanders. I am retired and I hired Mr. Scott to build a wheelchair ramp into my home. My son was injured overseas and is coming home. My son won't be able to get into my home without a ramp. Mr. Scott said that he had built numerous wheelchair ramps and promised to have the ramp ready for when my son got home. Mr. Scott had two full months to properly build the ramp. He finished on time and he built a beautiful ramp that I walked on and it was sturdy for me. I paid Mr. Scott and even gave him a small bonus for doing such a nice job.

My son came home and his electric wheelchair couldn't get up the ramp. It wasn't built wide enough for my son's model of electric wheelchair. I didn't know there was a difference. Mr. Scott said that he would have made the ramp wider if he knew about the electric wheelchair. I think Mr. Scott needs to redo the ramp."

I called Mr. Scott and asked for his opening statement or he could proceed with his defense. He testified, "A typical ramp approved by the

Americans with Disabilities Act (ADA) is 36 inches wide and has 12 feet of run for one foot of rise. I built the ramp according to ADA standards. Mr. Sander's son is a very big man and his chair is four inches wider than a standard wheelchair. I didn't know that Mr. Sander's son used a special size wheelchair. Had I known; I would have built the ramp wider. There was plenty of room to make it wider."

I asked Mr. Scott if the existing ramp could be used and added onto. He replied, "No. The entire ramp would need to be removed and a new ramp constructed."

I asked if the new ramp had resale value.

He replied, "I didn't think of that. If Mr. Sanders would agree to let me sell the existing ramp, then I would rebuild his ramp wider to meet his son's needs. I do thank him for his service to our country."

I turned to Mr. Sanders and he agreed. I entered judgment in favor of Mr. Scott with the understanding that Mr. Sanders would pay him to rebuild the wheelchair ramp and then Mr. Scott would sell the existing ramp and give the proceeds to Mr. Sanders. The parties signed off. I looked towards my Dad and he nodded his head indicating his approval of my decision.

I turned to Tom and said, "What do I have; one or two more?" Tom replied, "You have four more cases today."

I said, "Please call the next case."

My next case was a neighbor dispute. A six-year-old accidentally threw a ball through the neighbor's window. I ruled no liability because it was a real accident.

The next case was another accident case from my neighborhood. Mary Ann and Ellen were brushing the hair of one of Mary Ann's porcelain dolls when the doll slipped out of Ellen's hands and fell to the floor. The face shattered and the doll was ruined. Mary Ann said that Ellen needed to replace the doll. Ellen said it was an accident and she told Mary Ann that she was sorry.

I ruled that the case was an accident. Ellen was handling the doll with Mary Ann's permission when it was dropped and damaged. I denied relief to Mary Ann.

My final case was a dispute over who owned trees on the property line. Mr. Colson and Mr. Stevenson planted a row of trees along their property line 48 years ago. Mr. Colson was planning on moving and his buyer wanted to remove the trees. Mr. Stevenson refused to allow the buyer to remove the trees so he didn't buy Mr. Colson's house.

I asked if the trees were on both sides of the property line.

Mr. Stevenson said, "The trees are approximately 50% on each side of the property line. As such, we both own the trees together. I wasn't sure of the actual law on trees located on boundary lines so I winged my decision and applied good old common sense.

I replied, "I find that both parties own the trees and neither party has the right to remove the trees unless first receiving written and signed permission from the other owner."

At home, I asked Dad about the tree laws. He said that my decision was spot on the law. The law says that you need your neighbor's permission if you are going to take out a tree that is on both properties. I felt so good.

My Dad told me that he was surprised that adults were actually coming to my court.

I replied, "I'm not. My Kourt is a reasonable alternative to the regular court system. I am only 13, almost 14 by the way, and I think I am making good decisions."

My Dad said, "I know. I watched you and you looked like a judge on the bench.

My next full court day was Saturday. I had a surprise visitor. Judge Rodgers had been hearing about my Kourt from his clerks and even some parties in his court that said they should have tried my Kourt. Judge Rodgers asked if he could observe my Kourt. I welcomed him into my judicial chambers and offered him water or orange juice.

Judge Rodgers said, "Amy, it appears that you are doing a wonderful job. I see your knowledge growing weekly as you sit with me in my courtroom. Now I would like to sit with you and see if I can learn more compassion when sitting on the bench. I mention this because my father- in-law was Mr. Sanders who appeared in your Kourt with Mr.

Scott and the wheelchair ramp. Mr. Sanders had nothing but praise for your effort as the judge. I liked the outcome. If they had appeared before me, the only thing I could do is enter judgment against someone. You resolved their problem while entering judgment. I am truly impressed." My little red light blinked telling me that the first case was ready. I asked Judge Rodgers if he wanted to sit next to me or sit on the public pews.

He replied, "Do you have room next to you? I brought my judicial robe."

I banged my gavel and called the court to order. I introduced Judge Rodgers and let everyone know that he was observing and would not be commenting on any cases. I reminded everyone to direct their testimony to me.

I looked at Tom and said, "Call our first case."

Two women sat down at the two tables. I asked for introductions. I learned that the plaintiff was sitting at the defendant's table. I asked them to switch so I didn't get them confused. I asked, "Do either of you have witnesses?"

Ms. Shore, the plaintiff replied, "I have two witnesses.

Ms. Johnson, the woman that owned the dry cleaners said, "I might have a witness if he shows up today."

I asked Ms. Shore to make her opening statement or make her offer of proof of her claim.

Ms. Shore was the first to testify. She said, "I bought a beautiful cashmere sweater and I took it to Johnson Dry Cleaners to have it cleaned. When it was returned to me, the sweater was falling apart. My sweater was worth $174 and I want the value of my sweater."

I said, "You may call your first witness."

Ms. Brown testified that she saw the sweater being worn by Ms. Shore. It was beautiful. Look at it now; as she pointed to the sweater in evidence."

I asked for any other witnesses that had something different to say. There were no more witnesses for the plaintiff. I asked Ms. Shore if the Plaintiff rests.

She replied, "I haven't rested since my sweater was ruined."

I smiled and asked Ms. Johnson to make her opening statement or explain what happened.

Ms. Johnson testified, "I was asked to clean the sweater. It had no cleaning instructions on the garment so I used standard dry-cleaning methods. I noticed that the sweater was damaged and I pointed it out to Ms. Shore. She told me that the sweater was cashmere. I explained to her that when the sweater was checked, I learned that the sweater is fake cashmere and not worth what she paid for it."

I thanked Ms. Johnson and asked her if her witness had shown up yet. She looked around and said, "No, he isn't here."

I said, "I will review the facts in my chambers and give you my decision in ten minutes.'

Tom announced, "All rise" and I left for my chambers. Judge Rodgers followed me. Judge Rodgers said, "I won't make any suggestions, but I am curious of your thought process right now."

I replied, "These are hard cases to decide, but it is my job to make the best decision I can under the circumstances. The woman claims she lost the value of her cashmere sweater. The laundry operator says it isn't cashmere, but she did destroy the sweater. She should not have proceeded with cleaning the sweater if it didn't have a product label telling her about the sweater. I believe she should have asked more questions. I believe the dry cleaner is at fault for negligence, but I am stumped on the value of the sweater. I felt it and it didn't feel like my mother's cashmere sweater."

Judge Rodgers simply said, "Good luck Judge Amy."

I turned on Tom's light and he said, "All rise." I entered the Kourtroom and addressed the parties. I said, "We have a case of a damaged sweater. Ms. Johnson was responsible for making sure that her cleaning process would work on Ms. Shore's sweater. The fact that the sweater didn't have a product label put Ms. Johnson on notice to ask more questions before agreeing to clean the sweater. On the other hand, Ms. Shore has failed to produce a retail sales receipt or the product label proving the sweater is cashmere. I find both parties were negligent and contributed to the sweater damage. I therefore…

Excuse me Judge Amy, but my witness just arrived. May he talk to the court?

I swore him in and let Ms. Shore ask him questions.

Mr. Reed testified, "I have been in the clothing business for 36 years and I know the difference between cashmere and fake cashmere. I looked at the sweater that was damaged. It is made from plastic fibers which dissolved when typical dry-cleaning solvents are used. If I may show the court?

Mr. Reed looked up and asked, "Which one of you is the judge?"

I replied, "I am the judge. Please show me what you are talking about. Everyone gathered around the bar in front of my bench and he showed how the fibers shrunk and dissolved."

I asked, "Is the value of the sweater different if it wasn't cashmere?" He replied, "Yes, this is a knock off of the original cashmere. You can buy this sweater on sale in many stores for $22.99 or less. It is not worth much more."

I thanked the witness and entered judgment against Ms. Johnson for $32 for the loss of her sweater.

I talked with Tom and asked him to call our next case.

Tom called Monica and Sheryl. Both were in tenth grade. He introduced the complaint as Monica alleges that Sheryl was spreading false information about her on her Internet social media webpage. As a result of the information, other students were calling Monica names and causing her to fear for her personal safety. Monica wants Sheryl to remove the information and issue an apology and admission that the information was false.

I swore both parties and then asked Monica to present her side of the case. I reminded her that she was under oath.

Monica testified, "I went to a party with Sheryl. While we were at the party I danced with Sheryl's boyfriend. He started kissing me and he dumped Sheryl. She said she would get even with me. I began receiving phone calls mentioning the statements being made about me by Sheryl." I asked Monica if she could tell the court what the statements were.

Monica began to cry and said, "I will try, but it hurts to even think that Sheryl would treat me this way. Sheryl told everyone on her site that I was pregnant with David's baby and I got what I deserved. Sheryl warned her other girlfriends to guard their boyfriends because I would do anything for love. Sheryl put my phone number on her site and put underneath it, "Just call me for a good time. I don't know how to say no to anything and I mean anything." I began receiving phone calls from boys asking me for a date and suggesting things we could do on the date. I couldn't even answer my phone anymore. I screamed and threw my phone in the toilet so it wouldn't work anymore."

I asked if Monica had any witnesses.

She replied, "The entire school knows about what Sheryl wrote about me."

I asked Sheryl to take the witness stand. I reminded her that she was under oath.

Sheryl testified, "I did most of what Monica said. She stole my boyfriend and embarrassed me so I embarrassed her. I only did the one posting which I felt was fair enough for what she did. I liked hearing about boys calling her for a date. She deserved the attention she is now receiving."

I asked Sheryl, "Do you have personal knowledge that Monica is pregnant from relations with David or anyone?"

Sheryl replied, "I have no idea. I just made it up because that is the type of girl she is."

I asked her if she wanted to call any witnesses.

She replied, "No. I don't need witnesses. I was there."

I reminded both parties that they are subject to the jurisdiction of my court. They agreed. I said, "I am ready to enter judgment.

I said, "This case arises out of anger and bullying between to former friends. Monica ended up with Sheryl's boyfriend at a party attended by both of them. Sheryl retaliated using social media and entered defamatory information about Monica which was wrong and lacked any truthful element. The act of publishing the facts on the social media page caused Monica damage and affected her standing in the school. Sheryl is liable for Monica's damages. I order Sheryl to do the following. (1) To put an apology on her social media website explaining to the readers that what she wrote about Monica was not truthful; (2) That Sheryl remove the defamatory information from her social media website within 24 hours of this decision; (3) Sheryl apologize to Monica in front of the student body at the next school assembly; and (4) Sheryl purchase Monica two movie tickets for her and a friend. The tickets are to be purchased and delivered within 48 hours of this decision."

"I will point out that this is a school case and falls within the student bullying rules. If you fail to perform your obligations under this judgment, then I will recommend a suspension from school for one week. That suspension will remain on your school records and could affect the college you choose in the future.

Is there anything in my decision that either of you fail to understand?" Both girls said, "No."

I looked at Tom and said, "I am declaring a ten-minute recess. Tom said, "All rise."

Judge Rodgers and I talked about my two cases. He said that I was a remarkable judge. I offered him cold water and we enjoyed our drinks as we talked about the law.

Judge Rodgers asked what my last case was about.

I replied, "I don't know. Each case is new to me when I take the bench. I listen very carefully to the parties so I understand the facts. If I have a question, I ask it. As we talked, Tom came into my chambers. I said, "Tom. Next time knock first before entering."

Tom replied, "Sorry Amy, I mean Judge Amy." I introduced Tom as my brother.

Tom then interrupted and said, "I have two attorneys that heard about your court and want to know if you will do a jury trial in your court.

I looked at Judge Rodgers and he shook his head and said, "No, don't do it. Keep your trials as bench trials and you will do fine. Jury trials are more than you are ready to deal with. You will need jury instructions, etc." I replied, "I have sat through more than fifty jury trials in your courtroom. I think I can do it. The attorneys are responsible for jury instructions; not me."

Judge Rodgers laughed and said, "You don't accept the word 'No' very well." I laughed and said that the word 'No' is not usually in my judicial vocabulary. Tom, schedule the jury trial for two weeks out and ask the attorneys if they care if the jurors are teenagers, adults or a mix." Judge Rodgers said, "Amy, please hold this jury trial on a Saturday so

I can sit in. It sounds like it could be a lot of fun and I can be a general resource."

I said, "I would love to have you sitting by me."

My final case of the day was another school case. It was referred by the high school principal. The school was represented by the school lawyer and the student and her parent were represented by a lawyer.

I swore all parties and two witnesses. I looked at the school's attorney and asked, "Do you want to make an opening statement?"

He replied, "No. I waive opening."

I asked the student's attorney if he wanted to do an opening statement. He also waived and said, "Let's get this over with. This is got to be a joke."

I explained to the lawyer that I am the recognized judge for the school court. Your case wouldn't be here if your client didn't agree to me hearing the case. The alternative is to face suspension or expulsion under the student rules. I will give your client a couple minutes for you to decide if you want to withdraw your petition and face suspension or deal with my court."

He replied, "My client consented to this court so let's proceed." I told the school lawyer to call their first witness.

I swore in Melody. She testified, "I caught Elizabeth smoking weed in the girl's bathroom. She seemed upset about something. Elizabeth threatened to hurt me if I told anyone. I reported the incident to the principal." She doesn't scare me."

I swore in Rudy. He testified, "I have seen Elizabeth smoking weed. At least two times I have seen her selling baggies of marijuana to other students.

The school rested.

I directed Elizabeth's attorney to present his first witness. He called Elizabeth. I reminded her that she was under oath and would be punished if she lied in court.

Elizabeth acted tough and testified, "I smoke pot; so, what. I'm not hurting anyone and they should leave me alone. The anti-pot school rules are unfair. Pot is not harmful to me or anyone."

Her attorney asked, "Have you sold pot to other students?" Elizabeth answered, "Yes. I sell pot for spending money; so, what!" He asked her, "Did you sell or deliver pot on school grounds?"

Elizabeth said, "I think I was off school grounds, but I can't be positive."

He asked, "Why do you sell pot."

Elizabeth replied, "My dad is dead. My mother is a drug addict. I have a little sister that is six years old. I use the money I make from the pot to buy us food. I can sell pot and receive a 50% profit. I get so depressed that I began smoking pot. However, I am always clear headed when I pick up Jenny from school. I am fifteen and don't have any means for a regular job. I could sell pot or prostitute myself. I chose pot. I'm sorry, but that is my life. I won't let child services take away my little sister."

The lawyer called Jenny as a witness. I asked her some questions about telling the truth and she understood the difference between a truth and a lie. I gave her a cushion to sit on.

The lawyer asked Jenny, "Who takes care of you at home?"

Jenny testified, "Liz gets me up and dressed in the mornings. She always tries to find us food before we go to school. If she finds a little bit, she gives it to me for breakfast and my lunch. Liz won't eat anything until I have eaten. Sometimes we leave early and get free samples at the grocery store. Liz asks Mr. Templeton, the store man, if he has any bread that will be thrown out for pull dates as well as any other foods. Liz tries to make sure that I have food. I know Liz does bad things with drugs, but she tells me she had to do it to keep us fed. Liz picks me up after school and we walk through the store before going home. I don't think Liz tries to do bad things. I think she is just trying to protect and feed me. Liz is always waiting for me when I get out of school. She holds my hand as we walk home. I know that Liz loves me. She gave me her warm blanket when my blanket had holes in it and didn't keep me warm. Many times, Liz and I sleep together and our bodies keep us warm when there is no heat in our house."

I had tears in my eyes after hearing Jenny testify. I asked the attorney if he had any other witnesses.

He replied, "Defense rests."

I said that I needed to take this case under consideration. I would return in ten minutes with my decision. I walked off the bench and began crying in my chambers. Judge Rodgers comforted me and asked if I wanted help with this case. It is a tough case for him. I can imagine how you are feeling.

I replied, "I am the judge and my job is to make a decision that follows the law as I understand it."

Judge Rodgers asked me, "What is your decision?"

I replied, "I'm not sure. I will have my decision before I return to my bench." I flicked my ready light and Tom announced, "All rise."

I entered and asked everyone to be seated. I explained to Elizabeth that what she did was a criminal act and violated Section 22(b)(3) of the school code. The willful violation of the code is grounds for expulsion from school for the remainder of the school year. The key in the school statute is the word 'Willful'. I am asked to determine if your conduct of using, distributing and selling drugs on school property is a willful event given your obligations to your younger sister Jenny. After hearing the testimony, I find that your conduct was willful, but justified for the limited purpose of providing food and support for you and your sister. I am ordering you expelled from school in accordance with Section 22(b)

of the school code for the remainder of this school year; however, I am suspending enforcement of my judgment and allowing you the opportunity to cease using, distributing and selling drugs on and off school grounds. If you are caught using, distributing or selling drugs over the next twelve months then my judgment will be entered and you will be expelled. In the meantime, I want you to contact Youth Services.

The agency can help you and Jenny to have food and if needed a safe and secure place to live until your mother gets off of drugs. I expect that you will report to Youth Services within 72 hours of this order and judgment. If you fail to contact Youth Services, then I will enforce my order and judgment. Do you understand my decision?"

Elizabeth politely replied, "I thank you for the opportunity and I promise that I will check in with Youth Services. I hoped that there would be a means to have food and shelter for Jenny and me until my mother quit using drugs. I have never wanted to sell drugs, but I will do whatever is needed to protect my little sister."

The Kourtroom cleared out and Thomas said, "That's all for today Judge Amy. I told Tom that court is over and he can call me Amy.

Judge Rodgers asked if we could talk. He was amazed at how I approached my cases. He said that I was evolving into a wonderful judge. He asked me how old I was and I said fourteen, going on fifteen in five months.

He asked me about school plans, like law school.

I smiled and said, "I would like to go to law school and be a judge. However, what would I gain? I am a judge now and I see my private court system growing in the future. I may hire two or three retired judges to work with my Kourt system. I'm not sure. All I have ever wanted was to be a judge.

CHAPTER TEN

My First Jury Trial

The lawyers for the jury trial notified Tom that they would accept anyone over the age of sixteen years to serve on the jury. I asked Tom to solicit volunteer jurors from the high school while I asked for neighborhood volunteers. I was shocked that no one wanted to serve on jury duty. I walked from door to door asking for volunteers. I arranged for 10 adults to serve on my six-person jury and Tom found 10 juniors and seniors that would take the job seriously. I asked Tom for the Kourt registration slip. The complaint was simply a breach of contract. No details were given. I scheduled the trial for Saturday and Judge Rodgers sat with me as planned. Tom let me know that the case was ready to proceed and Judge Rodgers and I entered the Kourtroom and I asked everyone to be seated. I asked for introductions from both parties and their attorneys.

I called in the prospective jurors. There were 20 volunteers. I explained to the lawyers that voir dire questions were to be limited to disqualifying type questions. I will allow very little general questioning. If the lawyers move to slowly then I may take over voir dire like is done by the federal courts. Judge Rodgers smiled at me. I explained to the lawyers that they received two 'preemptory challenges', which means you can get rid of two jurors without any reason, and any juror could be challenged for good cause.

The lawyers must have heard what I said. We had a seated jury in ten minutes. What was exciting was that my jury box was actually being used. I swore the jury in and trial began.

I asked Plaintiff's attorney if he wanted to do an opening statement. He replied, "Yes."

He said, "This is a simple case of a breach of contract. The defendants were hired to remove and replace a three-tab shingle roof on plaintiffs' home. We will prove that the defendants' workmanship was shoddy and they were damaging plaintiff's property. My clients are entitled to the benefit of their bargain and to recover the difference in cost between the defendant's quote and the final cost to finish the roof."

I thanked the lawyer and then asked the other lawyer if he wanted to make an opening statement. He also said, "Yes."

He started out, "These people, them there hired my clients to do a job. My clients were doing their job when the owner kicked us, I mean my clients off the property. They owes us the rest of the money for the job."

Mr. Tolt, the plaintiff, testified, "I received an excellent price to have my existing roof torn off and new three-tab shingles installed. The defendants arrived in a new truck with a sign that read, "Tolsted Roofing Company since 1958. I didn't know what a three-tab shingle meant. Judge Rodgers noticed my confusion and handed me a note that said, "It is like the roof on your Kourthouse." I passed back a note saying, "Thank you."

Mr. Tolt continued, "I hired Tolsted Roofing Company to do my job. I watched their crew arrive in beat up trucks. There had to be ten men on my roof removing shingles and throwing them onto my yard and in our planters. I stopped them and demanded that they get a dumpster before proceeding. They refused and walked off the job. I had paid them one-half of the price and they never returned. I sued them and they asked to have the case heard in this court for some reason. I agreed and our lawyers worked out the details.

I asked, "What is the status of your roof today?"

Mr. Tolt replied, "I had to hire another company to do the roofing. I had to pay twice."

I asked, "How much did you pay Tolsted Roofing Company?" He replied, "$6,430."

I asked his lawyer if he had any other witnesses. He replied, "None and we rest your honor."

The defendant's lawyer said, "We done good work. I mean my clients done good work until that man kicked them off the roof."

I stopped the lawyer and asked if he was testifying instead of his clients. He replied, "I don't think so. What did I say that sounded like I was doing testimonial?"

I replied, "Please call your first witness."

He said, "Jeff, get your lazy butt in the witness chair."

Jeff got up and I said, "Stop right there. Please raise your right hand and repeat after me, "I promise that the testimony I give in this proceeding will be the truth."

He replied, "Like you said."

I asked, "Are you agreeing that you will tell me the truth and only the truth?"

He looked at his attorney and whispered, "Am I to tell her the truth or what we talked about. I'm confused."

I reminded him that perjury is a criminal act and I would prosecute him if he didn't tell the truth in my court.

He replied, "I will say the truth to you."

His attorney said, "Tell the little girl that we got kicked off the job and we was doing good work."

He replied, "I am to tell you that we got kicked off the job when we was doing good work."

"And tell her that we didn't plan for a dumpster in our bid. We would clean up what we could when we were done and paid."

He replied, "I am to tell you that we didn't plan...

I interrupted and asked if Mr. Turk was a lawyer licensed by the state bar association.

He replied, "The what, Association? Which bar are you talking about? There is Sam's and Lakeshore and Roosters. Which one does you want me to talk about?"

I asked if the defense had any other witnesses. I looked over the Kourtroom and there were 23 hands raised with each waiting on giving testimony. I asked the plaintiffs' attorney and the defense attorney if either has a problem with me conducting voir dire of the potential witnesses.

Both agreed to let me proceed.

I asked, "Of those of you in this Kourtroom that want to testify, how many of you will say the same thing already said by Mr. Turk and Jeff. Every one of them said they would say the same thing.

I asked if the defense rests.

Their attorney said, "We does that most of the time."

I turned to the jury and explained that the attorneys had a verdict form for them to follow. You are to answer the following questions.

1. Was there a contract between the plaintiff and the defendants? Yes _____ No _____
2. Was the contract completed? Yes _____ No _____
3. If the contract wasn't completed, did the defendants have justification to walk off the job before the job was completed? Yes _____ No _____
4. Do you find that the contract was breached; Yes _____ No _____ and if so, which party breached the contract?
5. For any breach, what do you find as damages to be awarded and to whom should damages be awarded?
   PlaintiffsAmount: $ _____
   DefendantsAmount: $ _____

I directed the jurors to the jury room which was the kitchen area. There was a large table and eight chairs. I told the jurors to pick a 'foreperson', meaning a head juror, and then decide the case. I needed five out of the six jurors to agree on the 'verdict', which is the jury's decision.

The jury left for the jury room, had a bottle of water, and I could hear laughing coming from the kitchen area. Tom blinked my light and let me know that the jury had made a decision. Judge Rodgers looked at his watch and it had been 33 minutes. I walked in and asked everyone to stand for the jury. The jury entered and I asked them to sit down. I then asked, "Has the jury come to a verdict in this case." A sixteen-year-old girl was the foreperson and she said, "Yes your honor, we have."

I asked her to please publish her verdict to the court. I asked the parties to stand up and I stood out of respect for my jurors. I learned that from Judge Rodgers.

The foreperson read, "We the jury find in favor of the plaintiff and award him damages of $6,600."

I asked, "Did at least five jurors reach the decision." She replied, "It was unanimous."

I excused the jurors and my Kourtroom was empty except for me, Tom and Judge Rodgers. We retired to my chambers and had a good laugh about my first jury trial.

CHAPTER ELEVEN

What are Conflicts of Interest?

M r. Burns stopped by my Kourthouse and congratulated me on a job well done. He had been following my Kourt in the news and he regularly heard from people he knew that were familiar with my court.

Mr. Burns said, "Amy, I have a friend in the concrete business that has been a trusted friend of mine for forty years. We have built thousands of residences and some office buildings. He is the best there is. He is being sued by a homeowner who claims that he didn't follow the job specifications and the work is substandard. I want you to hear the case. I don't want to tell you how to decide the case, but I do want you to know that he is one of my best friends and I would appreciate your special look at the facts. He used my contract format so venue is in your court."

I thanked Mr. Burns for my Kourthouse, but explained that I must avoid the lack of impropriety and remain fair and impartial in all cases. I said, "I owe you my sincere gratitude. You helped make me a judge. I can only hope that you will now want me to be a good and fair judge because that is all I can be."

Mr. Burns gave me a hug and said, "I would expect nothing less from you Amy."

Tom was contacted by the homeowner and he set up the trial for a Saturday. The parties objected, but understood that we were in school during the week. The homeowner, Mr. Jewel told Tom that he heard nothing but praise coming from my Kourt and he gladly agreed to have his case heard before me. He told Tom that I was known as Judge Amy, the ultra- fair and impartial judge.

I told Tom that I was excited to receive such praise, but I wondered if Mr. Jewel was trying to grease the skids before getting to trial. I refuse to be unduly influenced by anyone when I sit as judge. The parties should be aware that they can trust me and my decision making without worrying about biases.

I talked with Judge Rodgers while visiting him on Tuesday. He explained about ethics and the problems judges can get into by favoring one side over another. "If a judge loses his or her impartiality, then the person should quit as a judge. If the judge can't be trusted to treat both sides fairly then that person should quit as a judge. You are now being seduced by the parties to like one party over the other before the trial. Your job is to keep them at arm's length and be fair and impartial. You understand this because you are talking with me about what happened. When you get into trial, look at both parties equally and treat them both fairly. I felt like I handled the situation correctly. I loved hearing Judge Rodger's feedback. He always made me feel so good and so grown-up."

Our judicial conference time arrived and I scheduled the trial for after the conference. I checked with Mom and Dad and asked if I could go to the conference with Judge Rodgers and his daughter Patricia.

Mom replied, "Is Patricia going for sure this year. Last year she went to cheer camp."

I replied, "She is no longer cheerleading. She is taking running start and will start college two weeks after the conference."

Mom said, "I don't know. I still have problems with you going with a man anywhere. Ask your Dad."

I sat on Dad's lap and asked if I could go to the judicial conference again this year. I explained that I would be going with Judge Rodgers and his daughter Patricia like the first year I went."

Dad asked what Patricia would be doing while I was in the conference. I replied, "I have no idea. I will be with Jerry; Judge Rodgers attending the convention. That is all I have an interest in. Patricia and I will be sharing a room next to her dad's room."

Mom said, "I am still uncomfortable with you going out with a married man."

I replied, "Mom! We are not going out. We are going to a judicial conference. I have been accepted by the judicial community as a real judge and I have been invited to attend on my own merit. I am not going as Judge Rodger's guest. I am my own person. If you don't want me staying with Patricia, then rent me a hotel room for the four days or come with me. You know that I am underage and can't rent a room myself. Send Tom with me if you are concerned."

Dad replied, "Amy, you are a straight A student. Tom is a C & D student. He can't afford to miss school."

I said, "How about I begin tutoring Tom in exchange for his help in my Kourthouse; and in escorting me to the judicial conference?"

My parents weren't happy, but allowed me to go with Tom. We arranged for two beds in the room and to have adjoining rooms with Patricia and Judge Rodgers. That was fine with me. I wanted to learn.

Jerry and I checked into the conference while Tom and Patricia discussed what they could do during the day. After the first day of the convention, Jerry and I returned to our rooms. I found Tom and Patricia kissing. I got mad at Tom and went into Jerry's room to talk, but he wasn't there. I didn't want to watch Tom and Patricia so I sat on Jerry's bed waiting for him. Jerry arrived with two pints of ice cream and asked where Patricia was.

I said, "In my room kissing my brother."

Jerry handed me Patricia's ice cream and said, "Enjoy." Jerry and I ate the ice cream until my tongue froze and I couldn't talk. Jerry said, "Can't have that" and he began tickling me. I felt him come a little too close to my personal space and I backed off and said I needed to go back to my room.

Jerry apologized if he did something that scared me or offended me. I replied, "No you didn't. I really like you and sometimes I wish you were my father. You are so kind and understanding towards me. That is something that my parents rarely offer me. Your help has made me a good judge in my opinion and I enjoy being with you as often as I can. I guess it is a school girl's first crush on an older man. I hope you understand and why I have to keep my distance. Our friendship is very special to me and I wouldn't want to lose you as my friend and mentor. Jerry smiled and reassured me that my virtue would always be protected around him. He had a special place in his heart for me too. He explained that Tuesdays were his favorite court day because I was there with him.

I thanked Jerry and gave him a hug. I then said, "Let's get Tom and Patricia and get some dinner." Tom and Patricia sat together and Jerry and I sat together. It was a very nice dinner and I was glad that I told Jerry how I felt about him.

I was surprised that the convention had an ethics course that matched my circumstances for the upcoming trial. I had shared with Jerry and he suggested that I use it as an illustration affecting ethical conduct from the bench.

I suggested that I would think about it. As we sat drinking our juice, the speaker invited me up to speak about my incident to get the ethics discussion going.

I pointed out that my Kourthouse was leased to me by a very special businessman. He approached me one day and said that he had a good friend that would be using my Kourt to decide his case. He hoped that I would give the case a very special look for him. He said he wasn't trying to influence my decision, but he did want me to take a very close look at the facts. I replied that my highest duty is to be fair and impartial with the parties and the evidence. I had to maintain an appearance of fairness so I couldn't discuss any case with him before it came before me. I asked him if he would like it if I was handling one of his cases and the other side tried to influence me before trial.

The speaker said, "That's good Judge Amy Jefferies." Now let's open up the facts for discussion. I went to sit down when he asked me to remain on the stage. He asked the group, "How many of you have been faced with similar requests to subtly influence your decision in a case?" I was surprised that almost all the judges raised their hands.

He asked, "What about how Judge Amy handled herself. Do any of you have any recommendations or feedback?"

One judge said, "I would have cut him off quicker when he announced that the case was coming to my courtroom. I would have refused to talk with him further." Another judge said, "I think she handled herself in accordance with the judicial canons and ethics." Another said, "If you believe you have been tainted by the requested influence, then you have a duty to recuse yourself and have another judge hear the case. The discussion ended on my case and I was allowed to sit down. I immediately asked Jerry what were the judicial canons and ethics and where would I find them. I also asked what it meant to recuse myself.

Jerry replied, "You don't miss anything, do you?"

I replied, "I want to learn how to become a good judge." Jerry promised me that he would get me a copy of the judicial canons and ethics rules and give it to me the next Tuesday. Jerry asked if I would be more comfortable with him sitting in on the upcoming trial because of the ethical issues.

I replied, "Would you? You know that I would like that very much. I don't think there will be a problem, but who knows. Besides, I like it when you sit next to me. I feel braver and smarter."

Jerry disappeared briefly during the conference and I wondered where he went. He returned with a bag and a box in the bag. He said, "Open it later. It is the latest in fashion for judges." When we returned to our hotel rooms, I opened the box and I had a new judicial gown.

Jerry said, "I saw that your original gown was getting a little short and looked more like a coat or cover up than a robe. Please try it on so I can see how it fits you."

I modeled my new robe and I felt sensational wearing it. It was from the same manufacturer that made all of the Judge's robes. I loved it. I gave Jerry a big hug and kiss, but quickly backed off to avoid offending him or making me look silly.

Tom and Patricia arrived and I modeled my new robe for them too. Tom gave me a thumb's up sign and then took Patricia's hand again and asked if they could go to the movie being shown on the other side of the hotel.

Jerry replied, "Go ahead. Amy and I need to eat dinner yet. He asked me, "Are you comfortable going to dinner with me?"

I replied, "Of course I am. I trust you. Just because I have a crush on you doesn't mean that anything bad is going to happen. In fact, I would love to have dinner with you tonight."

Jerry chose one of the nicest restaurants in the hotel and I felt so grown up. He pulled out my chair and offered me any vintage of water and pop that I wanted. Jerry said, "I don't drink and you are too young to drink."

Jerry asked, "How old are you now Amy."

I replied, "I am nearly fifteen in three months." Jerry laughed and said, "You are fourteen."

I said, "No, I am almost fifteen." Jerry said, "OK, you win."

Jerry and I finished dinner and I took his arm as we walked back to our hotel rooms. He opened my door and gave me a hug and kiss and said, "Thank you Amy for a wonderful evening. I really enjoyed having dinner with you."

I replied, "I felt so grown up having dinner with you too. I always feel so comfortable around you." I changed into my pajamas and opened the door to Jerry's room and said "Good-night". I slept like a baby until Tom returned and woke me up. He suggested that I sleep in Jerry's room so Patricia could sleep in our room.

I looked at Tom and said, "Brother, that isn't going to happen now or ever so get the thought out of your head."

I was showering when Jerry knocked on the door to see if I was ready. I yelled that I would be ready in ten minutes. Jerry said, "I'll be back in ten minutes." When he arrived, we walked to the dining room and enjoyed breakfast before starting day three of the conference. All I kept thinking about is how kind Jerry is. I liked being treated like a young woman.

Day three and four of the conference was reviewing new case law. We heard lawyers and judges talk about the new case law. Much of it was over my head, especially when they talked about bankruptcies, divorces, land use, etc. When the conference was over, I received a participation certificate just like Jerry's certificate.

Jerry and I had one final dinner before our final night at the conference. I enjoyed dinner and being treated like a young woman instead of a little girl. Jerry was good at treating me like an adult and I liked it. On the way back to our rooms, Jerry let me hold his arm again and he acted as my escort. I wore my nicest dress and my heels to look just a little taller. When we got back, Tom and Patricia were still out so Jerry and I sat and talked. He told me that I looked beautiful and I helped him feel young.

Jerry said, "You have the difficult trial coming up. How can I help you?" I replied, "Just being at my side will be nice. Your presence gives me confidence as a young judge."

We talked about my future and my desire to make a private judicial system grow to meet more needs in the community. Jerry mentioned that he was four years from retirement from the public bench. He asked me if I would like him to be part of my private Kourt system.

I replied, "Of course I would. I hope to open a second Kourthouse within three years. You could be the judge for that Kourt. I think we could become partners in the business and even begin charging greater fees for services.

Jerry laughed and said, "Amy, you have it all worked out." I replied, "I hope so. I don't give up as you have seen."

Saturday arrived and the ethics case arrived as scheduled. I had hoped the case could have settled, but that didn't happen.

I welcomed the parties and counsel. I looked for Jerry, but he wasn't there when court started. I had no choice but to proceed without him at my side. I turned to plaintiff's counsel and asked if he had an opening statement.

Mr. Brown replied, "I do."

I said, "You may proceed. He looked up at me and asked, "How old are you? You look like a kid."

I replied, "My age isn't what is on trial. I am the judge in this Kourt and I expect that you show me respect for the position, if not the person."

Mr. Brown apologized. As he was apologizing Jerry showed up and whispered, "I heard what he said. You did well."

I then told Mr. Brown, "Please proceed with your opening."

Mr. Brown said, "I represent Mr. Pederson. He owns the home at issue. Mr. Pederson's home is built on a hillside and special concrete specifications were called out as part of the bid. Approximately one-half of this house is supported by concrete pillars and pilings driven into the ground. The concrete was to be a six-sack mix and the pads were to be twelve inches thick and thirty-six inches square. The evidence will show that the defendant used a four-sack mix and the pads are six inches thick and sixteen inches square. The house is settling because of the improper foundation causing cracking in the walls and windows. There is a good chance that this house will slide off the hillside. My client is seeking the cost to fix the problem."

Mr. Steiner said he represented Red Rock Concrete Company. My client has been in business for 55 years and had never had a lawsuit before. We will prove that my client did nothing wrong. Mr. Steiner kept winking at me. I finally asked him if he had a problem with eye control.

He replied, "No as he winked at me again." I said, "Please continue." He said, "The owner changed the concrete specifications once the house began to settle. The evidence will show that the original specifications were met by my client when the job was done. We will show the original engineering specifications filed with the county. Your honor will see that Red River Concrete did nothing wrong and if there is settling problems, it is because of faulty engineering and faulty specifications. My client denies any liability to Mr. Pederson." I said, "Mr. Brown, please call your first witness."

He replied, "First tell me who the man is sitting next to you."

I replied, "It is none of your business, but I will disclose that he is Judge Rodgers of the civil court system. He is sitting in on this trial at my request. It is for my evaluation purposes only. You will address me as the trial judge."

I then said, "Mr. Brown, please call your first witness."

Mr. Pederson was sworn and testified, "I wanted to build my dream home. Our view is beautiful and looks over the ocean. One–half of our home was designed to sit on large pillars anchored into the hillside. I hired an engineer to design the loads and develop the specifications for the job. His early design specified four sack concrete and sixteen-inch square footings for the pillars. The job was bid out at the current specification. The engineer then informed me that he made an error and the mix needed to be six-sack and the footings needed to be thirty-six inches square and twelve inches thick. I notified Mr. Roberts of the Red Rock Concrete Company of the change in the job specification. He told me that it wasn't a problem. He would bill me for the additional concrete and the mix change.

My home was only framed when I learned that there was some settling started. I learned from the men that poured the concrete footings that the pads were only sixteen inches square and they showed me the construction specifications. I contacted the concrete company and learned that the concrete was a four-sack mix and not the six sack I requested.

I spoke with Mr. Roberts and he told me not to worry about it. They would over pour the sixteen-inch square footings and turn them into thirty-six inch by twelve-inch footings. He also told me that the difference in a four sack and a six-sack mix is negligible.

The contractor finished my home and I began to notice settling cracks around the windows, doors and wherever two joints came together. My engineer has told me that my home…

Objection, "hearsay" your honor.

I asked counsel, "Is the engineer going to testify in court today?" The attorney said that he would be testifying in person.

I replied, "Objection overruled."

Mr. Pederson then finished his testimony saying, "My engineer said that my home was at serious risk of falling off the cliff."

I heard from the Engineer and saw the revised specifications for the Pederson job. The question in my mind was whether Mr. Pederson passed on the specifications to Mr. Roberts to change the work.

The plaintiff rested and Mr. Steiner was asked to call his first witness. He called Mr. Downs.

Mr. Downs testified that he owned the concrete company and he had been building houses for 55 years without a single complaint. We built the footings and ordered concrete according to the specifications given to us by Mr. Pederson through his engineer. It was after our crew had completed the foundation and poured the footings that Mr. Pederson contacted my company with a change in the specifications. I recommended we would try an over pour, but the best approach was to dig out the footings and redo the job at the new specification. Mr. Pederson refused the cost of the full tear out and paid us to over pour. I couldn't guarantee it would work and I obtained his signature on this release form. In terms of the cement mix, I can't change the sack mix once it is poured in place.

Mr. Pederson was then asked specific dates. He replied that the new specifications were given to Mr. Roberts on July 25th before the concrete was poured.

Mr. Downs was called to testify again and he denied that the specs changed before the work was done according to their paperwork. He said that he received the changed specifications in their office on the 26th day of July.

Mr. Roberts was called and he testified that they poured the concrete and then Mr. Pederson asked for changed specifications. He said, "I reported the problem to Mr. Downs and he made the over pour recommendation."

I heard closing arguments and then took the case under advisement and said that I would have a decision in thirty minutes. Mr. Steiner smiled at me and winked once again.

I became angry and asked Mr. Steiner if he was attempting to influence the court with his winks, or if his winking implied something about this trial.

Mr. Steiner denied anything except a lazy eye.

Jerry went into chambers with me and asked if I needed any help. I replied, "No, I know the right answer is here in these exhibits. I looked at the date the first concrete pour took place. I looked at the plan change required by the engineer and the delivery tickets for the concrete.

Nothing seemed to match up. I determined that the concrete company delivered concrete on July 24th. The engineer changed the specifications on the 25th and says he delivered the changed specs to Mr. Downs on the 26th. The facts supported Mr. Downs' and Mr. Robert's testimony. The concrete material and Mr. Downs' work schedule matched showing that his company delivered the concrete and poured the footings two days before the new specs were delivered. I told Jerry that I understood and I was entering judgment for the concrete company. I got up from my chair and noticed in the light that there were smudges on the concrete delivery ticket and the job sheet. Both dates had been changed.

I returned to my Kourtroom and said that I had a few questions for Mr. Downs. My first question was for clarification. I asked, "Do you own the concrete construction company and the concrete mix company?"

Mr. Downs answered "Yes."

"How is your concrete delivery ticket prepared at the mix company?" I asked.

He replied, "It's called the batch plant. The delivery tickets are prepared by our computer when the concrete order is placed into the cement truck for delivery to the customer."

I asked, "Were you on Mr. Pederson's job when the work was done?" He replied, "No. I own the company, but I haven't done any actual concrete work in more than five years. I am a dinosaur and I don't think I could do that kind of work anymore. I have several forepersons that run the different jobs."

I asked him if he would please look at Exhibit 7 which was his company load ticket.

He replied, "All right, I have looked at it like you asked. Do you have a question for me?"

I asked, "Please look at the date. Can you explain why the date on Exhibit 7 is rubbed off the computer load ticket and a different date substituted?"

He replied, "It shouldn't be changed. That is why the computer prints out the delivery date and what mix and quantity was sent for billing purposes."

I asked him to look at Exhibit 4 which was his job ticket. He said, "Same thing. Someone changed the date."

He then called Robert over and asked, "Did you change these dates before this court hearing and discussing this case with me? Don't you lie to me?"

Mr. Roberts answered "Yes."

Mr. Downs replied, "I don't care that you are my son-in-law. I have no place in my company for cheaters and liars. You are fired."

Mr. Downs told Mr. Pederson that his company would fix the problem. The two men met and discussed the matter and the attorneys said, "Your honor. Our clients have settled and the case can be dismissed."

I hit my gavel and said, "Case dismissed by stipulation."

I was again praised by Jerry, except that he said that the judge isn't to do the attorney's work in solving their problems. We hear the facts and enter a decision. However, you were remarkable. I gave Jerry a very nice hug and said, "Your comments mean more to me than anything else. Thank you for supporting me."

CHAPTER TWELVE

What Next?

I continued to learn from my experiences as an Amy's Kourt judge. During my fifteenth year, I heard 125 cases in total. I brought in $31,450.00 in revenue over the year. I used the revenue to pay for maintenance and utilities mostly. I began paying myself a salary of $200 per month. My popularity as a private judge continued to climb to my delight.

Half of my cases involved adult cases and business cases. My greatest joy was still Amy's Kourt where I could reach out to my fellow classmates. Tom graduated from high school with a B average, I think due to my tutoring him. Maybe he just cared more working as my clerk/bailiff. Tom asked to keep on as my bailiff. I agreed to pay him minimum wage which meant I needed to bring in more money.

I had no problem with demand for my Kourt services. People came to me because I promised a fair and timely solution to the backed-up court dockets. I decided to do some advertising. I put together a short flier that I sent to every attorney in our county. I explained my private court services and the cost for filing different actions. I raised filing fees for adult personal injury cases and business disputes to $100. If the other side had a counterclaim then they had to pay $100 as well. I started keeping records of case dispositions such as judgments entered. I made sure the attorneys understood that a judgment in my court was enforceable in the superior court.

I began receiving inquiries about how broad my court could reach. I would explain that participating in my court was a matter of private contract. The parties needed to sign an agreement granting my court jurisdiction over their case. My agreement said that all of my decisions are final and binding. There are no appeals from my court.

My Dad thought my notice was a little harsh, but to the point. I received at least two court inquiries daily from attorneys exploring having a case heard in my Kourt. I asked that they try my Kourt one time and then decide whether to continue using my services.

Jerry suggested that I put my picture on the flyer and my name, Judge Amy L. Jefferies. Many of the calls I received included a polite comment about how cute I was. When I told Jerry about the comments, he replied, "You are cute. The best-looking judge that I know."

I was coming up to my sweet sixteenth birthday to be followed by the judicial conference. Jerry bought me a new judicial gown, but this one was green. He suggested that my Kourt was different and I could dress differently if I chose to do so. I thanked Jerry, but I liked the black robe. It just felt right.

My sixteenth birthday brought my driver's license and a renewed appreciation of where I was and where I was headed. My parents were taking me out for pizza and I asked if I could invite Jerry, Patricia and Jerry's wife, Jenny. Mom agreed, albeit reluctantly. Mom said, "I think you see too much of Jerry."

I had learned a long time ago that you don't argue with your Mother. You never win and usually have an angry mother. I did reply, "Jerry is my judicial mentor and I am good friends with his daughter. I have only met Jenny once but she was really nice."

Mom asked how old Patricia was now.

I replied, "She just turned 18 and will graduate this year from high school with two years of college that she completed through the Running Start Program. Patricia wants to be a lawyer too.

We went out for pizza and Jerry gave me a new laptop computer with the court rules; state statutes; and jury instructions on it. My Dad objected until Jerry told him that all the judges received laptops. I already had one so I passed this one on to Amy for her use in court.

While we were all discussing, I brought up the judicial conference again. Jerry explained that this year was six days instead of four and would be held at the state convention center. I asked, "Mom and dad. Can I go to the conference again this year? I am taking Running Start and will be taking classes at the community college for my first two years of college. I am already signed up for Running Start. I am now old enough to go without a chaperone, but I would welcome either of you to go with me."

Dad replied, "I can't go this year. I have pretrial depositions and trial that will start following the convention. I just can't fit it in."

Mom replied, "I have your sister and brother to worry about. I can't sit in a hotel room for six days." I asked again, "Can I go?"

Jerry said, "Jenny and Patricia are going this year. I hope that helps in your decision making. I thought I could get two rooms and allow Patricia and Amy use one room and Jenny and I in the other."

My parents finally gave their approval and I couldn't thank them enough. When we got home, I thanked dad for trusting me.

He replied, "You I trust. I don't trust any men around you. That is always a dad's worst fear."

I was packing and mom asked me, "Why are you packing your nice clothes?"

I replied, "Just in case we go out to dinner. I want to have something nice to wear. I also need to dress nicely for the convention. You don't expect me to wear the same dress every day, do you?"

Mom replied, "No."

Jerry picked me up at my house. My mother quickly asked, "Where is your wife and daughter?"

He replied, "Jenny and Patricia are still getting ready. I decided to pick up Amy and then get Jenny and Patricia."

Mom asked, "They are going, right?"

Jerry answered, "Yes. They are getting ready."

We arrived at our hotel rooms. Jerry made sure that Patricia and I were set up and then he left for his room next door. Jenny was putting away their things when Mom called and asked me if Jenny and Patricia were with me.

I replied, "No. There is just me in my room right now."

Mom said, "I thought so. You and Jerry lied to us about you going alone with him."

I replied, "Mom that is totally untrue. Jenny is in their hotel room putting away their clothes. Patty is getting her suitcase and will be right back."

Mom said, "Let me talk with Jenny". Mom sounded like she didn't trust me. I laid the phone down and called Jenny. Mom talked with her and seemed to relax. All I could think about is how paranoid could a mother be?

I talked with Jerry and decided to tell him about my Mother's fears. He replied, "Amy, you are beautiful and smart. I know that I have a special love for you because I enjoy being around you as much as I can. I also understand relationships and I value our friendship and our future business relationship to cross the line. I want you and your parents to trust me when I am with you. I may think something like I would love

to kiss you, but I wouldn't do it. Just being friends is nice."

I thanked Jerry and I kissed him and said, "Let's get checked in." Like usual, I took Jerry's arm and he escorted me to the convention. This year was nice. I didn't have to talk. I sat with Jerry and took notes of everything the speaker said. Jerry saw what I was doing and he whispered, "Relax and just listen." Jerry showed me the course booklet that we received at check-in. The woman talking had her entire talk in the book given to us. As I listened, I read ahead and realized that everything was written out for future reference.

At the end of day one, Jerry and I returned to our hotel rooms and Jerry read Jenny's note, "Gone shopping up north. I have the car. Back late. Love Jenny."

Jerry said, "It is you and me for dinner. He showed me Jenny's note. I replied, "I should get dressed for dinner."

Jerry suggested we use room service and eat in our room tonight. We can get relaxed and talk about the different presentations and maybe

I can answer questions for you from today's lectures. I liked the idea. There was a sofa in Jerry's room next to a dining table. When we finished dinner, we sat together and talked about lots of things. We began to watch a movie on television when Jenny and Patricia returned. Patricia said, "I'm tired from shopping. Are you ready for bed Amy?"

I yawned and said, "Yes I am. See you all in the morning."

Jerry told me that Jenny asked him if he liked me. She said that I act a little too flirtatious around Jerry and she didn't like it. I apologized if I was the problem. When we returned from the seminar, I hit the problem head on like I did so many other things in my life. I said, "Jenny, I have a teenage crush on Jerry, but that is all there is. He and I have never done anything to give you worry and we never would. Please forgive me if I am a problem."

Jenny replied, "You are not the problem. I think that Jerry and I have grown apart a little, but that is expected as you get older. I am not worried about you and Jerry so please forgive me too."

I replied, "Jerry is my judicial teacher and mentor. We are just friends and colleagues."

The next day I used a little more caution to avoid any appearance of impropriety in front of Jenny. I didn't want to do or say anything that would affect my relationship with Jerry.

The conference ended and I was excited to get back to my Kourthouse. Tom already had the school cases lined up. He laughed and said, "Today we have nine school cases. We got backed up with the last business case." I replied, "Then let's get going. I may need to use my Tuesday for these cases and not sit in with Jerry."

Tom called the first case. A ninth-grade student struck another student. In short, they were fighting. I gave them both garbage clean up around the school for one week. One of the boys said, "I won't do it."

I replied, "Do you want a one-week suspension instead?" He replied, "No. My parents would kill me. I'll do it."

Tom called the next case. It involved two first graders that got into a fight over who had the biggest doll collection. Under school rules, fighting was a one-week suspension regardless of the grade.

I called Susan and asked her if she understood truth from lies. Susan said, "I do. We talk about being truthful in my Bible study class on Sunday.

I replied, "Thank you. Please tell me why you were fighting with Kenzie." Susan testified, "Kenzie came to my house and we were playing dolls.

I have a lot of dolls in my bedroom and we counted 121 dolls. Kenzie told me that she had more. I asked her to prove it. She said she didn't have to prove anything. I got mad and Kenzie went home. When I got to school on Monday, Kenzie told me again that she had more dolls than me and yelled out to our classmates that I am a liar. I got mad again and told Kenzie that she wasn't my friend any more. Kenzie pushed me down in a mud puddle and I got my shoes and dress muddy. My mom says my shoes may be ruined. I didn't fight Kenzie. She fought me.

I swore in Kenzie after confirming that she understood what the truth is. Just to make sure, I pointed out to Susan and Kenzie that if they lie in my Kourt, that I will give an additional punishment.

Kenzie testified, "Susan bragged about all her dolls. I got mad and said that I had more than her. She got mad at me and told me to go home unless I wanted to prove that I had more dolls. I refused. Susan asked me at school if I was ready to put up or shut up about the size of our doll collections. I got mad and she kicked me so I pushed her down. It was her fault.

I asked if there are any witnesses. Kennedy, a kindergarten boy was introduced by his mother. She told me that Kennedy saw what happened. I confirmed that Kennedy seemed to understand the truth. I said, "Kennedy, please tell me what you saw."

Kennedy testified, "I heard the girls arguing about how many dolls they had. That girl, pointing to Susan said, "Put up or shut up about your dolls. That girl over there, pointing to Kenzie shoved the other girl into the mud puddle."

I asked, "Did you see Susan kick Kenzie?"

Kennedy said, "No", but I might have not seen her do it."

I issued a three-day suspension to Kenzie and Susan for fighting. I told them that the suspension wouldn't happen if they didn't get into trouble for the rest of the school year. Both girls promised that it wouldn't happen again. As the girls prepared to leave, Kenzie apologized to Susan and said, "Susan, you have more dolls than me. Can we play again at your house?"

I asked Tom to call our next case. Tom explained that the case involved theft of school property. The school wanted a one-week suspension.

I had developed a system where the school could send in a fact sheet and if the student agreed to the general facts and charge, then no one from the school needed to testify. The trial was left to the student's explanation.

I read the complaint. It read, "Gerald (11th grade) removed a laptop computer from the school without checking it out first. When asked about it, he denied having the computer. School security found the computer at Gerald's house."

I asked Gerald, "Please tell me your side of the story."

Gerald testified, "I will be honest. I took the computer home to get caught up on some school assignments over the weekend. I don't have a computer at home and I have to wait and share the computers in the library with many other students. I told the security people that I didn't take it because I was scared. I can only apologize. I am working hard to keep my 4.0 GPA, but my teachers keep giving Internet assignments. I told security that I would have brought the computer back to school on Monday.

He said, "Likely story. I don't believe you and he wrote me up."

A mother was sitting with her daughter waiting for her case to come up. She stood up and asked if she could address the court.

I asked, "Do you have something to add to this case?"

She said, "Maybe. I have an extra laptop that I was going to donate. I would like to offer it to Gerald. He will need to get his own Internet connection, but I understand that most of the Internet providers have free services for those that qualify."

I asked Gerald if he would like a computer.

He replied, "Yes. My school work would be so much easier having access to my own computer. Thank you."

I entered judgment against Gerald, but waived enforcement if he kept out of trouble for the remainder of the school year.

I was getting tired and asked Tom to call the final case of the day. He explained that Sara was being harassed by David at school and over the telephone. She wants him to stop. Both are in 12th grade.

I swore in the parties and asked Sara to tell me her complaint.

Sara testified, "I was dating David, but we broke up almost a year ago. Since then, he stops me in the halls at school and tries to get close to me. One day he kissed my nose and told me that he still loved me. I pushed him away and he called me some names that I don't want to repeat. I told my parents and they told the school. David stopped for a little while, but recently has been calling me at home and following me around the school. I just want to be left alone.

I asked David to tell his side of the story.

He replied, "We were dating like she said. One day she cut me off without an explanation. I have been asking her since then why she broke up with me. She refuses to discuss it with me. I follow her in the halls asking her why she broke up with me. All she does is talk to her girlfriend Angela. I got Sara's cell number and I began calling her at night. I told her several times that all I want is an answer as to why she broke up with me.

I asked if either party brought witnesses. Both said, "No."

I explained that not knowing why they broke up is not relevant; nor is it justification to harass Sara. The fact is that your relationship ended and you following Sara and calling her at all times of the night is unacceptable behavior. That is called harassment.

I am entering judgment suspending you for one week. I am withholding enforcement on the understanding that you have no further direct or indirect contact with Sara for the rest of the school year. That includes off school grounds. This is an Amy's Kourt restraining order. If you violate my order, I will enforce the punishment. Do you understand my order?

David replied, "Yes."

On David's way out of the Kourtroom he turned to Sara and said, "You haven't heard the last from me."

I recalled David and his mother. I asked him why he violated my order and judgment by talking with Sara.

David replied, "I thought you meant after court is over. That is when your order started."

I replied, "Wrong and you are smart enough to understand that. Because I just heard you threaten Sara, I am adding one additional week of suspension. You are hereby suspended for two weeks starting next Monday."

I heard David's mother tell David, "Shut your mouth next time. That judge means business. You had better not violate her order or who knows what might happen."

I thanked Tom and said Kourt is over for the day. There are four cases that we can hear tomorrow or I can have my bailiff reschedule. All four wanted rescheduled.

My family was going on vacation. I didn't want to go, but I had to go according to my mother. I closed Amy's Kourt for one week and rescheduled all trials. We had to go because my grandpa died and we were going to his funeral. I was upset that I didn't get to sit with Jerry on Tuesday.

We returned in one week and I was excited to get Kourt up and running again. I opened the door and found that someone had vandalized the Kourt while I was gone. Mr. Burns had four security cameras installed and the police quickly identified Gerald as the vandal. When Gerald's parents were contacted, they agreed to restore my Kourthouse. The damage was nearly $4,000.

I couldn't wait to talk with Jerry and fill him in on our vacation and what happened at my Kourt. When I arrived, Jerry welcomed me like usual, but explained that I may need to recuse myself from one of the cases he was handling.

I asked, "What case is that?"

He explained, "I have a young man named Gerald appearing before me for arraignment on a charge of vandalism. I know that it was your Kourt. He is also here as a girl named Sara is seeking a restraining order against Gerald to stop his on-going harassment. I am concerned that since you were involved in both matters that you shouldn't be sitting next to me when I hear those matters."

I asked, "Can I sit in the pews and watch?"

Jerry said, "Of course. This is a public courthouse. Once Gerald's matters are concluded, you can put on your robe and join me at the bench." I heard Gerald's case get called. His lawyer pled him not guilty to vandalism of my Kourthouse. Jerry set trial for six weeks out. Jerry then called Sara's harassment case and her request for a restraining order. Sara looked at me and smiled.

Judge Rodgers, my Jerry, swore in Sara and Gerald. He asked Sara why she wanted a restraining order against Gerald. She explained the same facts that she presented in my school Kourt. Gerald denied that he was harassing her and said, "All I want to do is get her to answer why she broke up with me."

Jerry ruled, "I am granting the restraining order which requires that you do not come within 100 feet of Sara. You may not directly or indirectly contact Sara in any manner from in person, telephone and Internet. You shall not publish or ask another to publish anything derogatory about Sara on any social media website or anywhere else. If you violate this restraining order, you will go to jail. Do you understand the scope of this restraining order?"

Gerald replied, "You sound just like her. She told me the same thing." Jerry replied, "You are here because you violated her restraining order.

I am entering a public order restraining your conduct. If you break either order you will go to jail. Do I make myself clear?"

Gerald replied, "Yes."

I sat with Jerry through the rest of his calendar and I learned more and more about the practice of law and serving as a judge.

I was intrigued when Jerry heard a motion for summary judgment on a civil case. I read the pleadings and learned that a 'summary judgment' allows the judge to enter judgment on non-disputed facts.

Jerry explained, "Trials are for the judge to resolve disputed facts. If the facts are undisputed, then there is no need for a trial and the judge can make a decision applying the law to the undisputed facts."

I asked Jerry if I can do summary judgments in my Kourt.

He replied, "I would think so. Your court is a private court and you can make your own court rules."

Jerry's words opened up a whole new part of my Kourt that I hadn't explored. As we were wrapping up, Jerry asked me what I knew about mediation.

I replied, "Not much. I know that the courts are beginning to make parties try to mediate a settlement before going to trial."

Jerry asked me if I would like to attend mediation training with him. It was an all-day seminar to be held two Saturdays in a row from 7:30 am to 4:30 pm. Jerry reminded me that I would miss Kourt both days.

I excitedly said, "I will reschedule. I would like to add mediation services to our Amy's Kourt services."

Jerry said, "I think you would be a very successful mediator. Check with your parents and let me know if you can go with me. I will pay the seminar fees for both of us if you can attend."

At this point in my life, I was pushing seventeen and was mostly grown up. It was also a day program without overnight hotel stays. My parents agreed to let me participate. I was very excited to tell Jerry that I could go with him.

I saw Jerry the next Tuesday, like always, but he was different. He was quiet and seemed to be lost in his thoughts. I had been around Jerry since I was a little girl and I knew him very well. I asked, "Jerry, what's wrong?" He replied, "Jenny has stage four breast cancer. She didn't even know that she had it and the doctor says it is inoperable because the cancer had moved throughout her body. Jenny is starting aggressive chemo-therapy and radiation therapy and we can only pray that she beats it." I replied, "Jerry, I am so sorry. Is Jenny in the hospital?"

He gave me her room number. My Mother and I arrived and brought Jenny flowers and a get-well card. I held Jenny's hand and said that I had been praying that she recovers."

Jenny replied, "If I die from this cancer, then please take care of Jerry for me. Jerry and Patricia will be devastated and I know that both of them love you."

I replied, "Jenny. You will beat this cancer. I know it."

The following Tuesday, I arrived at Jerry's court and he wasn't there. I called him and he explained that he had been trying to reach me. He explained that Jenny died overnight. The doctor said that she had a heart attack and died instantly. Apparently, her cancer had entered her heart as well.

I attended Jenny's funeral, as did my entire family. My Mom put out a buffet for the reception. I walked through Jerry's house and I felt creepy knowing that Jenny was dead. I looked around when Patricia offered to show me around. I let Patricia know how sorry I was that her mom passed.

Patricia's only reply was, "At least it was fast and she didn't suffer." I gave Jerry a big hug and told him how sorry I was as well. He said,

"Life goes on. Are we still on for the mediation seminar next Saturday?" I replied, "I am looking forward to it and spending the day with you. Please let me know if you want to talk about Jenny's death or not. I don't want to offend you. I care too much about you and I just want to be supportive." I wondered to myself why Jerry didn't seem to be very disturbed about Jenny's death. I thought he would be devastated.

CHAPTER THIRTEEN

What Is Mediation?

Jerry signed both of us up for mediation training. When we arrived, I was asked my age. I told the registrar that I am seventeen.

The registrar replied, "I'm sorry miss, but this mediation training is for judges only."

I replied, "I am a judge of Amy's Kourt and I would like training as a mediator."

She replied, "Nice try, but I can't let you in. This is serious training." I said, "There is my name tag right there." I was becoming frustrated and looked for Jerry. He was registering under his name at the other end of the room. When he looked up, I waived and he came to my rescue. The woman saw his name tag and Jerry explained that I am a recognized judge by the state Supreme Court and by legislation. There is no reason to deny her entry into this training seminar.

The woman apologized, but said, "If she isn't an elected judge, then she cannot attend. There are many mediation training centers through regional dispute resolution offices."

As she talked, I noticed that Jerry had disappeared again. I heard his voice over the speaker system. He asked the judges in attendance if any of them had an objection to Judge Amy participating in mediation training."

The "No" sound was impressive. What was more impressive was when the Chief Justice took to the microphone and personally welcomed me as the judge from Amy's Kourt.

The woman handed me my name tag and Jerry and I sat down. I asked Jerry if he wanted something to drink. I brought us two coffees and two Danish pastries.

Jerry asked, "Drinking coffee now? You are growing up before my eyes." The seminar was fascinating. We did numerous role plays with each of us acting as a mediator. Two judges received a script covering a dispute and then we used our training skills that we learned to try to settle the case. I thought to myself that I do mediation in my Kourt all the time. I just never called it that.

On our way home, Jerry told me how well I did. He pointed out how tenacious I was in expecting effort from both sides. Jerry then asked me if I was hungry.

I replied, "I am starving."

He said, "Will you join me for dinner tonight?" I replied, "I would love to have dinner with you."

We went to a Mexican restaurant. Jerry pulled out my chair and ordered for me. We toasted our day of mediation training and then talked about our future when he retired from the bench.

Jerry explained, "I wasn't kidding before. I am looking forward to building Amy's Kourt into a large private judicial system that can serve as an alternative to regular courts. You and I can be partners and serve as judges. I envision hiring retired judges to become our judges and mediators."

I replied, "I can't wait to get started."

I began working on a mediation program for Amy's Kourt. From what I learned so far, mediation could be used for any kind of case where there are two parties in dispute. The technical term was 'Alternate Dispute Resolution' or 'ADR'. For any dispute exceeding $500, I added a requirement that the parties participate in mediation before scheduling a trial date. I could not mediate a dispute and be the judge as well. That is because what is said at mediation is for settlement purposes only and cannot be used at trial. Mediation could influence my job as the trial judge. I began the task of preparing my own Kourt Rules. For any case over $500, I would require a formal complaint be filed. The defendant would file an answer. I set a date when each party was to disclose their witnesses and trial exhibits and set a deadline for mediation to be completed. The final date was the trial date.

Neighborhood disputes were all subject to mediation and I offered my services for disputes where the parties would accept mediation instead of trial. I wanted the experience. Over a period of six months, I mediated 29 neighborhood cases. I had 22 civil cases where I would be the judge. Each of those cases mediated and 18 settled before trial. Unfortunately, the remaining cases didn't settle for any number of reasons.

One of my trial cases was noteworthy. Ben's Diamond Sales sold a diamond engagement ring to Bill Porter to give to his fiancé. Bill alleges that the diamond was a fake. Ben's Diamond Sales said that they sold a real diamond. If the diamond was a fake, then it is because Bill removed the real diamond and had a fake put on the band. The parties tried mediation, but couldn't settle. I swore in the parties. Neither had an attorney representing them.

I asked Bill Porter to make his opening remarks and then tell me what happened.

Bill testified, "It's quite simple. The most important act in my life is getting married. I bought an engagement ring and my fiancé accepted my proposal. Her mother noticed that the diamond didn't sparkle very well and they had the setting checked by a local jeweler. He looked at the ring and said, "This is not a real diamond." The Jeweler asked me how much I paid for the setting. I said, "$1,486". He told me it wasn't worth much more than $125. I went back to the store and they denied they sold me a fake diamond and refused to refund my money even though they advertise a 30-day money back guarantee on all sales. The explanation for the denial was that I removed the real diamond."

I asked if he had any witnesses.

He replied, "My fiancé is here to testify."

I swore her in. Lisa testified, "My mother and I thought the diamond wasn't right. We went to the store the next day and learned that the diamond was a fake. I returned Bill's ring and called him a loser."

I called Ben from the Diamond Store. He testified, "I personally sold a beautiful diamond engagement set to Bill. It was one of our best engagement settings. I have no idea how a fake diamond ended up on the ring. I apologized to Ben, but said, "We didn't do anything wrong." I wasn't sure how to rule on this one. I said that I would take the case under consideration and give my decision in the next half hour. I wanted to review the testimony. I returned to the Kourtroom and told myself that I needed to make a decision. I was about to speak when a uniformed police officer and a woman in a business suit entered my Kourtroom.

The officer apologized for interrupting court. They walked over to Lisa and placed her under arrest for theft and fraud.

Bill stood up and asked, "What is going on here. She is, or was my fiancé."

The woman detective replied, "She was yours, and she has been the fiancé of seven other men. In each case, she removed the diamond from her engagement ring and replaced it with a fake diamond. Her mother is her accomplice and is also under arrest."

Bill asked, "What about my diamond? Did you find it?"

She said, "We have it in evidence. It will be returned to you once her trial is completed."

I shrugged my shoulders and asked Ben if the Diamond Store would take back the ring and diamond once they verify there is no damage. Ben agreed to a full refund when the ring was returned to their store.

Bill replied, "Thank you. I will purchase my next ring from you."

I was asked to mediate a dispute between a seventh grader and an eighth grader. Eric the eighth grader bought Grace a beautiful Orchid for their school dance. She promised to go with him. When Eric arrived, Grace took the Orchid, but explained that she couldn't go to the dance with Eric. Eric wants the value of the flower he paid for her to wear.

I asked Eric how much he paid for the Orchid. He replied, "$10.50." I asked, "Did you ask Grace to return the Orchid or pay for it?" He replied, "Yes and she said, "No."

I asked Grace why she believed she could take Eric's' expensive corsage and then not go to the dance with him.

Grace replied, "I got a better offer. When I saw the corsage, I grabbed it because it matched my dress perfectly."

Do you feel that you should have kept it knowing that you were not actually going to the dance with Eric?

"I didn't think about it that much. I put the flower on my wrist and Tom's mother arrived and picked me up. I went to the dance and didn't think about the flower."

You now have had time to think about it. Do you believe that what you did was right?

Grace admitted that what she did was wrong. I asked her how she could make things better.

Grace replied, "I suppose I could pay him for the flowers." I asked, "Are you agreeing to pay for the flowers?"

Grace said, "Yes. That would be the proper thing to do. I will give Eric payment tomorrow at school."

It was that easy. I saw Grace the next day and she gave me a thumb's up sign and said, "All paid. Thank you, Amy, for keeping me honest."

My next Tuesday arrived and I was seated in court with Jerry. He explained that he had two criminal cases to deal with and then we would get on with the civil calendar. I adjusted my robe and smiled.

A police officer entered the courtroom and Gerald was in handcuffs. The prosecutor explained to Jerry that Gerald violated the court's restraining order and assaulted Sara. He is charged with violation of a restraining order and simple assault.

Gerald's attorney argued that Sara caused Gerald to violate the restraining order. She talked with him and flirted with him. Gerald is not a threat to the community and lives with his parents. We seek a no bail release.

Jerry replied, "This is Gerald's third run in with the courts over the same restraining order. I am setting bail at $20,000 and trial in four weeks."

I learned that Gerald couldn't make bail and he sat in juvenile hall until his trial. Jerry told me that Gerald was lucky. He turned 18 next week and I would have tried him as an adult and put him in jail.

When court was finished, Jerry asked me if I had any dinner plans for tonight.

I replied, "No. I would need to check with my parents, but I am sure that I can go to dinner with you if that is what you would like. After all, I will be eighteen in nine days and then I don't need parental permission to go out."

Jerry said, "I was thinking of dinner at my house. I made spaghetti and meatballs, salad and garlic bread."

I asked, "Where is Patty?"

Jerry said, "Patty is spending the night at her friend's house. It would be just you and me if that is all right with you."

I wasn't sure, but said, "OK. I would love to have dinner with you tonight." I was nervous and wondered about having dinner with no one around us. Do I sit next to Jerry or across from him? Will he pull out my chair at his home or what? Was I taking my first step into adulthood?

We arrived at Jerry's house and he kicked off his shoes and told me I could kick off my shoes too. We walked into the kitchen and he had the spaghetti sauce heating in a crockpot. He offered me a drink of ice tea, water or pop while he put the spaghetti noodles into the boiling water. I asked what I could do to help.

Jerry replied, "You could make our salads while I put the bread in the oven."

I was feeling so grown up and I was enjoying my private time with the man that I had a crush on since I was nine years old.

When dinner was ready, we filled our plates from the stove and sat on the sofa using TV trays. Jerry said, "You mentioned wanting to see this movie. I rented a movie for you and one for me." We watched my movie while eating our delicious dinner. Jerry could really cook spaghetti and meatballs. We cleaned up the dishes when the first movie ended. Jerry then gave me a hug and asked, …My heart began to race and I wondered how I would answer his question. Jerry finished his statement, "Would you like to watch the second movie or are you ready to get home?"

I replied, "Let's watch your movie too." We sat on the sofa and I fell asleep leaning on Jerry. He woke me up; kissed me on my forehead; and said, "I need to get you home. You are sleeping and it is getting late."

I thanked Jerry for a very special night. I kissed him one time in the car and thanked him for being such a good friend. He squeezed my hand and thanked me for being so caring and understanding.

My eighteenth birthday arrived and I had a party at my house. I invited Jerry and Patty, my brothers, sister and parents. Not much of a party, but I was surrounded by those people that love me and whom I loved in my own special way. We had a bar-b-que and I took great joy blowing out my 18 candles wiping out my childhood. Today, I became a woman who was independent, self-determined and ready to grow my court system. My sister Cynthia was eleven and I tickled her and asked when she was going to let me train her as an Amy's Kourt judge.

She replied, "Maybe soon. I do want to work with you Amy." Jerry commented that Cynthia and I looked like twins.

I replied, "Twins separated by seven years of age."

My Dad commented, "You seem so much more mature today than yesterday."

I replied, "Dad. I am now a mature adult and I am at the helm of my destiny. I am excited to move forward with my court system and my life as an adult."

Jerry helped me pick up some more hot dog buns from the kitchen. When we were safely inside, I kissed Jerry and for the first time, he kissed me back. I held him tightly, but Jerry said, "Amy this isn't right. I am old enough to be your father. I want to be your partner, but in a business sense. I'm not ready to have a wife or whatever you would like our relationship to evolve into."

I began to cry and apologized for being so arrogant and pushy. I said, "I thought you loved me. I guess I read the facts incorrectly. I am so sorry."

Jerry replied quietly, "The problem is that you read me correctly. I have fallen in love with you. I just don't know how to deal with our ages. I don't want to disappoint you. You are brilliant and beautiful. I just want to be close to you."

I suggested that we take things slowly and see if we can be more than business partners. I would like to date you when you have time to be with me. Our dates could include more dinners at your house. I love how you cook.

Jerry kissed me and said, "Let's move slowly and learn about the other side of each other. When you learn about me, you may not want me around."

I laughed and said, "I doubt that, but let's see where we go from here. Just know that I do love you." Jerry replied, "I love you too."

Later that night Cynthia curled up with me and said, "I saw you kissing Jerry. He is so nice and cute too. Are you going to marry him?" I replied, "Only time will answer that question."

CHAPTER FOURTEEN

On Becoming Partners

Jerry finished twenty years on the bench and decided to retire. His retirement income was enough to support him while we redeveloped the Amy's Kourt system into a private court system.

Jerry explained, "We need a name change to reflect the changing focus of the court system. Instead of being a judge focused business, I think we should develop a mediation and arbitration service."

I asked, "What is arbitration?"

Jerry explained, "Arbitration is just like a trial. The decision maker is called an arbitrator instead of a Judge. That avoids confusion between the public court system and our private court system. The arbitration hearings would flow just like a trial and we would still be a faster method to resolve disputes. You and I would also be mediators making ourselves available to the mandatory mediation requirements imposed by the public court system. You and I could make a very decent wage as well." I asked, "What about Amy's Kourt. That is where everything started." Jerry replied, "We will keep Amy's Kourt as is. We will still hear neighborhood disputes and school disputes. We will limit those schedules to gaps in our schedules and one day a week. The important thing is that we remain flexible and meet the needs of everyone seeking our services." I held Amy's Kourt and heard eight cases while Jerry was drafting promotional literature for our new court system. I began having Cynthia sit with me in court. I gave her my short robe to wear. Cynthia enjoyed being with me, but her interest seemed to substantially less than I had thought it would be. Cynthia would listen carefully, but had a bad habit of tickling me when she became bored.

Jerry and I decided on the name Professional Arbitration and Mediation Services or PAMS. I liked Arbitration and Mediation Your-way or AMY. Jerry suggested that we needed to sound professional if we were going to attract quality work. I agreed and deferred to his judgment. Jerry and I met for dinner and he let me know that we had a limited liability company set up under the name Arbitration and Mediation Your-way. I smiled when Jerry said the other name was in use. He then said, "Why not use your name. You are the founder and people seeking an alternative to the public courts want it their own way. Our acronym was "AMY".

After dinner, Jerry and I worked on promotional literature informing the public and law firms of our services and what we charge and the time frame to have matters heard. Jerry said, "We are going professional and our rates must increase for regular cases. You can keep your rates for neighborhood and school disputes if you would like."

I replied, "How is a six-year-old girl or boy going to come up with our scheduled fees. I have to be accessible to them. That is where I started." We finished our brochure and my name "AMY" was stated on the front cover with my picture and Jerry's picture. We each listed our judicial experience. I had eleven years acting as a judge and Jerry had twenty years on the bench and another seven as an attorney. Jerry said, "Let's send it out and see what happens. To accommodate calls, we hired a secretarial firm to answer our phones and take initial case information. Jerry and I decided on a slow, but steady movement in a forward direction.

Jerry and I heard cases together at Amy's Kourt. I still had my full complement of cases from the business community. I now had nine businesses that listed my, I mean our Kourt, as the stated venue. Any disputes heard against those companies had to be heard in our private judicial system. I suggested that Jerry send each of the businesses updated information with our name change, fees, etc. I was afraid that I would lose customers, but they seemed to like the forward progress and changed their contracts to include AMY as the required venue.

Jerry told me that we needed another courtroom. We have outgrown our current building. I contacted Mr. Burns and asked if we could add on to our existing building.

He replied, "If I can do the job for you. Amy, you are doing a terrific job and I will support you any way I can."

Mr. Burns showed up a week later with plan revisions adding two additional courtrooms to the existing building. He added five large conference rooms as well for arbitration hearings and mediation. Next to each conference room was a small office.

I told Mr. Burns that I loved the building layout, but how much will it cost us?

He replied, "I will do all the work for you at my expense. You agree to pay me 10% of your annual earnings as rent and I will be happy. Jerry and I said, "Done!"

It took five months, but Mr. Burns delivered and built us a beautiful building with courtrooms, conference rooms, and small offices. He made sure that the courtrooms had judicial chambers. I kept my original Kourtroom and Jerry took the courtroom next to me. We had plenty of room for growth and grow we did.

It took a little more than six months from when we sent out our promotional literature for a return on investment to occur. Our calendars began to fill up and Jerry told me over dinner that we need to hire one or two court clerks to help process cases, get mediation and arbitration agreements signed, schedule deposits and collect fees. Throughout all of our business growth, I kept Mondays to hear school cases and Saturday mornings to hear neighborhood cases. I refused to turn my back on the very purpose for becoming a judge. Everyone including little children need access to a decision maker when needed and I pledged to always be there to help.

I was in a conference room wrapping up a successful mediation. I found that men won't argue as much when a young lady is present. I used my age and apparent good looks to engage more settlement efforts and it worked. Many times, I heard parties saying, "I never thought this case would settle." The men noticed children entering my courtroom and asked if I was doing a school tour or something.

I replied, "No. This is Amy's Kourt day. Those children have a problem and they are here to have me help solve it. It is a community service. We don't make any money on their cases, but that is all right. The kids don't have any money anyway."

Mr. Knowles asked me how long I had been taking care of neighborhood disputes. I pulled out my photo album and showed a picture of my original Kourtroom. I was seven at the time. I have been doing this as a community service for eleven years.

He replied, "I am truly impressed with you." I received a thank you card from Mr. Knowles along with a check for $5,000 to help with expenses related to my community service work. When Mr. Poole heard what Mr. Knowles did, he sent me $5,000 as well. I mentioned this to Jerry and he smiled. Jerry asked me, "Do you know who Mr. Knowles and Mr. Poole are?"

I said, "A little. I successfully mediated a case for them."

Jerry said, "Mr. Knowles and Mr. Poole are multi-millionaires. Between the two of them, they own most of the business high rises in town."

I began receiving referrals from Mr. Poole and Mr. Knowles. We received word that business people were being strongly urged to use our service to resolve disputes. The word was, "see AMY". Over the month, we brought in a second retired judge, Jeanette Stewart to serve as a judge, arbitrator and mediator and within thirty days, we brought in Judge George Roxy, another retired judge. Both judges were highly regarded when serving on the bench. Their presence brought even more business to AMY.

On my twentieth birthday, Jerry and I reviewed our business and we were now taking in over $38,000 per month and going up monthly. Jerry and I each took a salary of $5,000 per month. By the time I reached twenty-one, Jerry and I had seven retired judges working for AMY along with nine clerical support staff.

I cornered Jerry in my chambers on my twenty-first birthday and I kissed him and told him that I truly loved him and hoped he felt the same about me.

He replied, "I do" and that led to him telling the minister, "I do." We were married and both of us were so very happy. I moved in with Jerry and completed my childhood fantasy of falling in love with my knight in shining armor. Jerry was everything to me and had been since I was nine years old. He had taken me under his wing and taught me to be a real judge.

AMY began receiving requests for arbitrations and mediations across the state resulting in Jerry and I exploring opportunities to open branch AMY offices. We located a very nice business complex across state, but the monthly rental was nearly as much as we brought in. I suggested we find some land and consider building a complex similar to our existing complex. I found the perfect location with freeway access and local access from four major business regions. I asked Mr. Burns if I could use his building plans to construct at least one or possibly two more complexes for AMY.

Mr. Burns replied, "Have you located the land yet?"

I replied, "I have found one nice parcel with easy access. I was going to contact a real estate sales person to make some sale inquiries. I am looking for another parcel in the eastern side of the state."

Mr. Burns offered to look at property with me and Jerry. He arrived in a large limousine. When we got in the car, I could smell food. Mr. Burns had a catered breakfast waiting for us along with hot coffee. When we arrived at the first property, Mr. Burns laughed and said, "I already own that one. Amy, it is yours now. Let's look to the east side. I have many lots there too." Mr. Burns showed me four parcels that could be used for our purposes and asked which one I wanted.

I said, "I like this one, but you can't be giving me your properties. It isn't right."

Jerry was looking at the local map as I talked with Mr. Burns.

Mr. Burns replied, "Amy, I have no wife or children. I don't have any living relatives. I am worth approximately 540 million dollars, but please keep that tidbit quiet. What am I supposed to do with my money when I am dead? Giving you some of it pleases me because I see nothing but goodness coming from you. You have volunteered for 14 years of your young life trying to make others feel better, or at least to bring resolution. Please let me give you the land and build your buildings for you. You would honor me."

I didn't know what to do. I had tears in my eyes and I hugged Mr. Burns and told him thank you.

He replied, "When are you going to start calling me Ted. It is so much friendlier than Mr. Burns."

True to his word, Mr., I mean Ted built two more beautiful AMY complexes. He held the title, but the buildings were ours to use forever. We had certain start-up costs to get the facilities open. I was shocked when Mr. Burns, I mean Ted sent me $500,000 to help with our expenses. His note said that he could send more if and when needed. I put a placard inside each AMY building that the facilities were donated by Ted Burns in service to our community.

I remained at home and kept our original facility moving forward. I continued to hear the neighborhood and school disputes and let the other judges handle the arbitrations and mediations. Jerry hired five retired judges for each facility and we hired retired court clerks to work in each AMY facility. Within 60 days of our grand opening, we were scheduling arbitrations and mediations at three months out.

Jerry asked me how I was getting so much business.

I replied, "I think Ted Burns, Mr. Poole and Mr. Knowles have a lot to do with it. They all like me and they go out of their way to promote our business.

Our accountant let me know that our monthly net income after expenses was $38,500 and climbing. She projected after expense earnings of $50,000 for the current year and next year she expected it would double if demand for our services continued. I thought not bad for a young woman's dream. Jerry and I were each taking $10,000 per month as a salary for running AMY. We owed no money so we kept our salaries low.

I walked into my first courthouse and immediately saw a picture of me on a placard. Under my picture was the word "Founder". Next to the placard was my story from my first Kourthouse to present day. I asked, "Who did this?" My Mom and Dad came out from my office with a cake to celebrate my 22nd birthday and fifteen years of service to the community. The newspaper and television representatives were on hand along with my childhood friends and school principals who all made this happen for me and now for Jerry too.

I talked with Jerry that night and I said, "My love, my husband, we have so much more to do."

The following morning Cynthia was dropped off by dad so she could visit me. I hugged my little sister who was now fifteen years old. I kissed her on her forehead and said, "Kissing you is like kissing me in the mirror. We continue to look alike. I asked Cynthia if she wanted to join me in changing the world.

Cynthia replied, "I did back when and I could find nothing of more interest than being with you and helping others to help themselves. When do we start?

CHAPTER FIFTEEN

There's More To Amy Than Courts

I was thrilled that our AMY businesses were doing so well. I had a lot of free time to think about other community needs that might go unfilled if I didn't do something. Mediation was good for settling disputes, but what about those children that needed counseling and personal assistance. I remembered fondly Elizabeth who sold drugs to get money to feed her little sister. How did they fall through the cracks? How many other children suffer quietly to avoid being taken from their homes by a system that thought it was helping the children by destroying their family?

I explained to Jerry that I was going to take a diversion from legal matters and explore the needs of children that are suffering and are fearful of where to turn. My sister Cynthia is walking with me on this adventure. I want a program in place for kids to be rescued on a temporary basis, be it to receive food or a place to sleep; lunch money or clothing. I must reach out to the children in our community.

I did an analysis of the general needs in the community. I checked with food banks and with the schools to determine what needs may exist and are not being filled.

Principal Peters explained to me that the truly poor children receive family expense and food assistance. The hungry children are from those homes where the parents are in debt paying for large homes, motor homes, cars and boats, etc. and can't afford to feed and clothe their children. Those are the true lost children. You will find them in the nicer homes in town and often see them eating samples at the grocery store. Their shoes are too small, or worn out and the parents can't afford new, and have too much pride to take from charity. Pride leaves many children hurting and without assistance, and they are afraid to ask for help out of fear that they will be taken from their parents.

I wanted to focus on K through 8th grade to start. I asked Principal Peters if I could talk with the children in an assembly. I wouldn't name any names or embarrass any student. What I want to start is a 'HELP BOX".

I was given the opportunity to talk with the students at a full assembly. I had Cynthia at my side. Through her enthusiasm, I felt strong and empowered to reach out and help others.

I said, "Welcome. My name is Amy and this is my sister Cynthia that most of you probably know. I went to school at this same school. When I was seven years old, I started a community service called Amy's Kourt. I resolved disputes between my neighborhood kids and later adults. My ability to help solve problems brought me into the schools where I sit as a school judge and determine punishment when appropriate. There are times when we do things for reasons that shouldn't be punished. Those times are when someone does something to help someone else. I remember fondly a student that appeared before me because she sold drugs on school property. Now that's bad, isn't it?

The students all said, "Yes."

Let me tell you a little about that girl. She had a mother that was sick from taking drugs. She had a little six-year-old sister that would go hungry if she didn't make money selling drugs. Sometimes she would take her little sister to the grocery store to get free samples, or ask for expired food for her and her sister to eat. At one point, she even took food from their neighbor's garbage can. That same girl always made sure that her little sister was fed before she ate anything for herself. When her sister's blanket fell apart, she gave her blanket to her sister and she used the tattered blanket. This is what love and caring is all about.

I know that none of you are hurting like the two girls I mentioned. You eat daily and so do your friends. You wear nice clothes and have a safe home to live in. But what if you knew one of your classmates was hungry just like the girls I mentioned. Would you turn your back, or reach out to them? I am not saying you need to do anything personally. Instead, "I am putting this box in your school cafeteria to remind you about the little girls and hopefully you will think about those around you. If you see someone that does need help with food, shelter, shoes, coats or clothing, but won't ask, then I ask you to please write their name on a piece of paper and drop it into the box. I ask each of you to look into the mirror and put in your own name if you are someone that needs help. No one will know who put in a name or that your name was put into the box. You see, I have the only key. The important thing is that the named person receives free help. Help could be new clothes; shoes; coat; food; lunch money; or even a safe place to live if there is nowhere to go. I am asking you to take care of your friends, and even yourself, and take the first step in helping another student. Please do not hesitate to give help and to ask for help. Thank you.

I thanked Principal Peters and said that I would pick up the box daily. I could only hope that it would work. I stopped by the next day and there were eleven slips in the box. Some had just a name while others had specific references such as shoes and coats or food.

I checked with Principal Peters and he said that he didn't realize that he couldn't give out information on students without the family's permission. I had names, but no way to contact the students and get them the help they needed.

I decided to try it differently. I put in seven boxes labeled coats, shoes, clothes, lunch money, food, and shelter. Principal Peters allowed me to talk with the students a second time. I explained the problem and asked the students that need something to quietly place their name in a box representing their need. I need your mother or father's signature on the form authorizing me to contact them. Also put on a phone number so I can call to set up an appointment. I received two names over a four-week period.

I became frustrated and took a break to figure out the problem. I decided that the best approach might be to have a school clothing fair. I advertised, "If you have good clothes that are not being worn, bring the clothes to the fair. If you would like to swap clothes, come to the fair. If you know of someone that has an unfulfilled need, come to the fair. There will be confidential assistance provided. We will have many cash prizes and food baskets for those who come. People could win a year's worth of basic food with our several raffle drawings.

Principal Peters arranged the fair for all three K-8 schools in our district. I set up tables for everything from hats, shoes, coats, gloves, shirts, pants, dresses, underwear, sweaters, purses, raincoats & umbrellas. I tried to think of every kind of clothing needed. I reserved one table for possible job openings that might come together within 30 days.

I set up one booth that I labeled "Questions". I prayed that my idea might work. My booth sat in the background and when a person entered my small area, they could see signs that said, "If you know of a need, fill it or ask me how it may be filled."

I arranged to collect donations for three weeks. I was amazed that we had such a terrific response. I received hundreds of coats, shoes, etc. Many of the clothing and shoe items looked brand new. To have fun, on fair day, I used pairs of shoes as a guide for visitors to follow as they walked around the fair's clothing tables. My sign said, "Please follow the shoe line and feel free to stop and look at any time." Cynthia was wonderful taking people and making them feel welcome. She doted on children needing basic clothing items. I could hear the laughing and giggling as Cynthia would tickle kids while they tried on shoes and coats. I heard often that my twin sister was wonderful and so kind.

The fair started at 9:00 am on Saturday and would run until 4:00 pm on Sunday. I kept the fair open until 10:00 pm and Cynthia and I personally appeared at 6:00 a.m. just in case someone needing help wanted to stop by before fair hours or remain after fair hours.

The first day of fair brought 8 people in before lunch time. After lunch, I began receiving many families that would ask, "Can we pick up items for other people?"

I replied, "Yes; as long as the clothing items are used and not thrown out."

I learned that those families that Principal Peters talked about were the ones that showed up at 6:00 am or stayed past 6:00 pm. Their pride prevented those accepting help in front of their neighbors and friends. I was happy to let them shop from our tables and encouraged them to check back the next day when we would most likely have more inventory. I heard one woman say, "Jennifer, I didn't know that you needed clothing for your family. I would have gladly given Jimmy my son's hand- me-downs. I saw that Jennifer was ready to cry when Cynthia intervened and said, "Thank you Jennifer for your donation. I will see to it that your donation is put to good use."

Jennifer thanked Cynthia and me. Later, I arranged to deliver the shopping bags to Jennifer and she broke down, cried, and said, "Thank you. My neighbor can be so self-righteous."

I sold raffle tickets for our several cash drawings. I collected the $1 for each ticket and talked with the people buying the tickets. I learned from several women that they were very short on money for food and lunches for their children. The money would truly be a blessing. Each prize was $100 with one grand prize to be drawn from the $100 winners. I wasn't in my Kourt and I felt as though I could manipulate the drawing to help those in greatest need. One mother said that she had four kids that often went hungry because her husband refused to sell their motorhome. Another mother said that she just lost her job and public assistance covered the rent and utilities, but left her short for food for her three children after paying other expenses. Another father said that he was a single father and could barely afford his rent. He drove an old car and gave every extra penny he had to his children to buy milk for school lunches. I sat back and was heartbroken by the stories.

I wandered into the fair area where I saw little girls and boys looking at shoes and clothes. I watched their mothers slap their hands and say, "Leave those clothes alone."

I heard one little girl say, "My shoes have holes in them. I need some new shoes and those are nice shoes."

I walked over and asked if she knew someone that could use a pair of shoes. The little girl said, "Yes." I put the shoes in a bag and said, "Would you please take these shoes to her. These are special shoes. They need little feet to be inside of them. They are lonely on this table." The little girl beamed with a smile that warmed my heart.

Cynthia made an announcement, "Ladies and Gentlemen. If you know someone that could use any of the items on our tables, you may take the items to that person. If they don't want the clothes, then please return them so someone else can use the clothes." That was the announcement that gave everyone the ability to select clothing for their family while claiming that they were picking up items for someone else. I felt that Cynthia was a genius at helping people help themselves.

The raffle ticket drawings took place after the fair was over. I had carefully marked my copy of each ticket with a number from 1-5 with 5 being the most in need. I wasn't surprised that when I drew winners, all the fives won $100 and the single mother of four children won the grand price of $1000.

By the end of the fair, I had seven pairs of shoes, two jackets and one dress left. I had given away $2,800 in prizes. I was pleased that the fair went so well. I feared that there were so many other children that that were not being reached. I donated $1,000 to each K-8 school and

$1,000 to each high school to cover a student's lunch – no questions asked. If a student was willing to ask for lunch money, albeit in the form of a prepaid ticket, then they received it. Principal Peters said that the fund would go a long way to helping those students that didn't have a lunch for whatever reason.

I wanted to develop a full-service agency that parents and students could use as an emergency safety net when things went wrong for any reason. I explained what I was trying to do to Jerry. He suggested that we start a different business for the new program. Cynthia suggested calling the new business "Amy's Place" or "Amy's Clothing Boutique".

CHAPTER SIXTEEN

The Beginning Of Amy's Place

J erry supported my philanthropic efforts without question. AMY was working perfectly, leaving me with the time to work on my outreach programs. Jerry filed papers to create AMY'S PLACE, a not-for-profit organization. Jerry insisted that we be protected, while at the same time, allow for tax-deductible donations. Jerry and I completed our various tax registrations and my Dad help me to qualify my organization as a charitable institution under section 501 (c) of the Internal Revenue Code. Amy's Place was set up to help those in need for food, clothing, emergency money and shelter. It wasn't a food bank. We had plenty of food banks in the area. What I wanted was a place where food would be made available to children that needed lunches, meals at home or whenever. I wanted clothes to be available just like our fair. I wanted to eventually create a boarding house as emergency shelter for up to two weeks. I wanted to provide bus tokens for people to get around if they couldn't afford gas for their cars. I wanted funds available for emergency help in paying utilities so water and power was kept on.

I explained to Jerry that I needed a service where people didn't have to forfeit their family unity or pride in order to get help for themselves, or their families. I wanted Amy's Place to be synonymous with hope and understanding. I wanted an honor's jar. If you need help, take a dollar. When you are doing well, return a dollar. Always burning in the back of my thoughts were the young girls that had to beg for food because they were part of the forgotten middle-class poor.

I started out Amy's Place in the kitchen/jury room of my first Amy's Kourthouse. I visited priests, ministers and rabbi clerics to get the word out that assistance was available through confidential means. I gave out a phone number for people to call and an address to write. My motto was, "All you need to do is ask."

I began in the schools and let students know that there were emergency lunch tickets available through the school. There was no cost to get a lunch. The lunch ticket was there if you forgot your lunch; didn't have time to make a lunch; or you just need a lunch because you are still hungry. Just ask for a lunch ticket from your teacher, or the office and you will receive it without any qualifying questions asked.

I mentioned to the students that the Amy's Kourt building is the temporary warehouse for clothing exchanges and other emergency items. You are welcome to anything with no questions asked. If you have a particular need, stop by and ask for me. What we talk about is private so don't worry about asking for help for you or anyone you know. Amy's Place is your place too. Please make use of it.

Within one week, I began receiving more clothes than I knew where to store them. I had to rent a storage locker to store clothes until we could distribute them. I began receiving donations from the community with a promise that more would be coming. What I needed was money to cover storage and to fulfill emergency needs for the community.

Jerry and I were on our way to church one morning and I noticed a family of four sleeping in their car. They had blankets and parked out of the way on our church parking lot. After church, I asked Jerry to pull over so I could talk with them. They were a family of five. The parents had three children ages 11, 8, and 3. The parents both worked for the same company which closed its doors. They were evicted from their apartment for nonpayment of rent. What little money they had saved up was garnished from a judgment obtained by their landlord. Mr. Miller told me, "All we want is another job. I go to interviews while my family sits in the cold car. We can't afford to keep the car running to keep warm. I asked about the shelter. Ms. Miller said, "Two problems. (1) The shelter is limited to women and children. We don't want to be separated;

and (2) the shelter is always full. I asked where else they had tried to get help. Mr. Miller said that he asked several churches. They would give $50 towards utilities or food, but that was it.

I asked about welfare for a limited period of time. Ms. Miller explained, "I can get aid for me and my children, but my husband cannot be living with us or receiving any part of the aid. Why should my children lose their father just to get a little help? We have decided to stick together and pray that we find jobs quickly."

I talked with Jerry and explained that these are the people that I want to reach out to. They want jobs and a secure place for their entire family to live on a temporary basis. I am going to figure out a way to help those people that do fall through the cracks. I asked them to follow me to a local motel. It wasn't the nicest place in town, but it had clean beds and it was warm. I asked them to stop by and pick up some food items. I explained that I had a lot of bread, peanut butter and jelly. I had juice, milk and some treats like chips and cookies. I had more items, but those required a stove. I paid for one month at the motel and gave them my name and number to call if they had any questions. The Millers couldn't thank me enough. I said, "It isn't me. It is a wonderful man named Ted Burns that makes all of this possible."

I was sitting in Amy's Kourt Saturday morning when Mr. Burns, I mean Ted stopped by to say hi and see how things were going. He could see that I was frustrated. He asked me, "What's wrong with my little angel?" I explained the need to have a facility that could provide emergency housing, food, clothing and even financial assistance for those in need. You can see that my jury room and kitchen is full of donations and I need to find somewhere to store the items. I want to help those that are trying to help themselves, but have fallen through the cracks. I do not believe in a social welfare system that seeks to separate husbands from wives and children. My sister and I are doing everything we can to help, but we are providing inadequate services given our space limitations. Ted replied, "Is this your lovely sister?"

I introduced Cynthia to Ted. He commented, "She looks just like you. Are you twins? Do I have two angels on this earth?

Cynthia replied, "I'm no angel, but I do care and want to help people help themselves."

Ted said, "I have the perfect property for you to consider."

I replied, "No. Mr. Burns, I mean Ted, you have already been so gracious and generous. I can't take more from you."

Ted replied, "Why not, I can afford it." I asked what the perfect property was.

Ted asked, "Do you have an hour to take a good look at it?"

I replied, "I will make the time." Ted drove to an abandoned public elementary school. He explained that the school had 22 classrooms, a gymnasium, kitchen and dining area, storage galore, and so much more. Ted smiled and asked if we could see what he was talking about.

I replied, "If it were possible to turn classrooms into temporary housing; we could use the kitchen and dining area to feed the homeless and the families in temporary housing; the gymnasium could be our food bank and clothing section and anything else we might want."

Ted said, "I could convert this entire building for under $500,000 if you just say the word."

I asked Ted, "What word?"

He asked that I refer to him as my grandfather. He loved me like a granddaughter and he needed someone to love and hopefully to love him as he entered the final years of his life.

I told him that he would live forever in the community because of his generosity.

Ted replied, "I hope to live another year or two. I have cancer and it doesn't look good. I am doing everything I can do to beat it, but I'm not sure I will win this battle. I hope Amy that you don't have to become the judge or mediator between God and Satan when it comes to my soul. I pray that I have been a righteous man, but that is my perception and possibly not what God has in store for me."

I gave Ted a hug and I called him grandfather. Ted's smile made me begin to cry.

He held me and said, "Please don't cry for me. Do something to make me proud of my granddaughter. Let's make your dream a reality.

Tomorrow I will buy the school and have my construction company get the permits to rebuild the structure into Amy's Place. I asked to name it "Ted's Place", but he would have nothing to do with that. Ted said, "Amy, this is your dream. Let me fulfill it for you. I want you to call it 'Amy's Place'."

I explained to Jerry what Ted and I discussed. Jerry thought it was a wonderful gift from a great member of our community. As was usual, Ted followed through and I had a beautiful facility ready to provide services to the community. I realized that I needed employees for all of the departments in the building. When we were done, we had 26 apartments; one large kitchen and dining room; a clothing donation room; a job resource room; a laundromat; mini-market and administration office. Jerry and I obtained all of the operation licenses and all that was left was hiring people.

Ted dropped by the "Help Center" to say "Hi" and to ask if I was satisfied with the conversion. I said, "Grandfather, you did it again. I love you for what you do for me and our community."

Cynthia walked up to grandfather and hugged him. She said, "I want to thank you grandfather for your generosity and love for our community."

In the front of the office was a donation box for monetary gifts. The checks and cash slide into a secure vault. The next day I opened up the vault and found a check from grandfather for one million dollars to fund our project. I sat down and cried over grandfather's generosity. All Cynthia could say is, "We will make grandfather proud of you and me. Let's go to work sis."

Within six weeks we were up and running. Our food store was fully stocked and families employed to work in the store. Any family that was temporarily living in one of our apartments had to make one parent available to work within the system handing out clothing or collecting clothing; cooking; cleaning, etc. Everyone works to make the system work. I opened up an emergency financial center to help families with utility payments; to catch up on an apartment payment; to student lunch programs that I kept funded at all of our public schools. Principal Peters informed me that there were no incidents of students going hungry. Anyone could take a meal ticket from the box and buy lunch.

Our own food bank was overflowing with food. We parceled out our food to other food banks to make sure that everyone was fed. We opened up the cafeteria from 7-8 pm for those individuals that chose to live on the streets, or refused other assistance. I insisted that there always be food for anyone that asked.

I wondered if I would be taken advantage of with my cash assistance program. However, after the first month, I had given out $3855 in cash to help cover emergency expenses. To get cash for a utility payment, the person needed to give me the bill and I paid it over the telephone. The same held true for almost all of the emergencies. I refused to simply hand out dollar bills. That was too tempting for those that wanted money for alcohol and drugs.

Over a period of six months, Cynthia and I had Amy's Place posters up in the libraries, churches, grocery stores, post office, police office, public schools, service clubs and anywhere that they would hang a sign. The only place where I refused to put up posters was on tavern and nightclub type establishments. If someone could drink, then they didn't need Amy's Place.

I was walking through the clothing area of the facility when two little girls approached me and asked if I had size 3 shoes for one of the girls and size 5 for the other. I helped them look, but we were out. I asked the girls what type of shoes were they looking for. Rebecca held up her foot and said, "The kind that don't have holes on the bottom"

I walked through the inventory and noticed that we were quite low on children's shoes. I called the local shoe store and purchased 10 pairs of shoes of different kinds and 10 pairs of tennis shoes of various kinds. The owner asked, "What do you want?"

I said, "I want to buy 10 pairs of every size shoe you carry for children up to a size 10 for girls and a size 12 for boys. When she learned who I was, she offered to sell me the shoes at her price plus 2% for a stocking fee. I asked her how soon she could deliver me two girl's saddle shoes in sizes 3 and 5 and two tennis shoes for girl's sizes 3 and 5.

She replied, "My store is only six blocks away, I will personally deliver the shoes."

Kathy Stone delivered the shoes and two little girl's eyes lit up like it was Christmas. Kathy made sure the shoes fit the girls and let me know that she would have the rest of the order in two days at the most.

I heard Rebecca tell her sister Candice, "Wow, shoes without holes." It was this exact situation that Amy's Place was created. I asked the girls if they needed anything else. Candice asked, "Could we look at coats and maybe some school clothes for us. My mom doesn't know we are here, but we know we need help and the sign I read said you would help us. I helped the girls select five dresses and five pairs of pants, underwear, socks, jackets and gloves. Both girls thanked me and then asked, "How do we get our new clothes home?"

Jerry overheard them and offered to deliver the clothes to their home. Rebecca asked, "Can I wear my new shoes?" I replied, "Sure you can."

Jerry delivered the clothes and the mother drove in as Jerry was leaving the residence. She asked what Jerry wanted.

Jerry explained that he delivered some clothes and shoes for your daughters.

The mother screamed at Candice and asked her why she went to the help center when she was told to stay away from there.

Candice cried and said, "Mom, Rebecca and my shoes have holes in the bottom. Our feet get wet walking to school. Why can't we have some new shoes? They are not costing us anything."

She yelled, "Do you know how embarrassing this is having welfare deliver clothes to my children."

Jerry replied, "Do you understand how embarrassing it is for your girls to have holes in their shoes at school? Amy's Place is a help center. It isn't welfare."

She said, "Take the clothes back now."

Jerry refused. The mother put the clothes on the porch. We drove by on our way home and noticed that the box was no longer on the porch. The next day Candice and Rebecca stopped by to show us their new clothes and shoes. They were two very happy little girls. I reminded them that they could stop by anytime they needed help with anything.

Candice asked, "You said anything, right?" I replied, "Yes, anything that I can do."

Candice showed me the mail that she picked up from their mailbox on the way to school. Inside were final shut off notices for water, electricity and gas to their home. The bills hadn't been paid in three months. I asked Candice if she knew why.

Candice replied, "My dad left us for a girlfriend. My mom is looking for a job while we go to school. She hasn't found one yet."

I asked Candice if she understood what her mother did.

She replied, "My mother is a certified public accountant or CPA. She passed her exam and my dad left us. Mom doesn't have experience to get a job."

I asked Candice to have her mother contact me about a job. I think I have the perfect job for her.

I spoke with Janine and offered her a job as the Amy's Place accountant. We had reached the point where we needed an inside accountant to manage the programs and funds as the funds came into our system. Janine was thrilled. I received a good employee and she helped herself on the road back to family security.

I hired two people to work in the help center. I had one man and one woman. Their job was to talk to everyone and to make sure that visitors received the help they were seeking without being embarrassed. I reminded them to pay particular attention to children that are looking around. Make sure that they get help finding what they are looking for.

I noticed that those in need always apologized for having the need in the first place. I worked tirelessly to avoid anyone apologizing for their life slipping off the proverbial tracks. Our help center would get them back on track.

Within our first thirty days, we had all of our family housing filled to capacity. I decided that the housing would go to families with children first. Meals were served in our dining room from 6-8 am for breakfast; 11-1:30 for lunch and from 4-7pm for dinner. Our special needs kitchen opened up from 7-8 pm for street people. I hated to do it, but we locked down the cafeteria during this period of time so none of the street people would get into other parts of the facility. The only exception was clothing. My staff was to take coat sizes and deliver coats where needed as well as blankets. I insisted that no one would be turned away from help.

I was helping one woman when she asked me, "How can you afford to do this? Most of your items are new." I showed her Ted's picture on the wall and said, "Ted is our benefactor. He is funding this operation for me." I put Ted's name in for "Man of the Year" for our community. Ted didn't want the recognition, but he was crowned the Man of the Year.

In a television interview, he gave me the credit for the ideas. He just provided the funds to make it happen.

I invited Grandfather to dinner at our house as often as he could make it. On his therapy days, he felt poorly and couldn't eat that much. Other days, Ted was his loving, generous self. Jerry and I enjoyed Ted's sense of humor and his stories of adventures over his 78 years.

Ted would often stop by the Help Center just to say hi. He was watching children playing on the dilapidated playground equipment and he walked out to look at it more closely. He found sharp metal edges and lots of potentially dangerous items. The following day, a bulldozer arrived and removed the playground. That afternoon a very large log play structure was placed outside with three slides, four sets of swings, teeter-totters, rope swings, crossbars and so on. The ground was covered in ground up rubber from tires. It was clean and flexible if a child fell. The playground was beautiful and the children thanked Ted while he was there. I turned the playground into a neighborhood park for children up to age 14.

I received word that Ted was hospitalized. His cancer was winning the fight and the doctor didn't believe that Ted would leave the hospital this time. I would sit and hold his hand as he remembered me sitting behind my make shift court house. He told me that he was so very proud of all I had done for the community.

Ted said, "Granddaughter, I will miss you more than my life. Please never forget your grandfather. I want to be remembered by someone that loved me and cared for me. That is you Amy. You are my angel from heaven."

I squeezed Ted's hand and said, "Grandfather, I will never forget you. I love you." I felt his hand relax in my hand. His eyes glossed over as he smiled his last smile looking at me. I cried for nearly an hour when the doctor said that they needed to move Ted to the morgue.

Jerry, Cynthia and I attended grandfather's funeral. There were a lot of business people there, but he had no family except me and Cynthia. I broke into tears seeing grandfather lying in his casket. He meant so much to me and my community service. I don't know why he loved me, but I know he did.

I was contacted by grandfather's attorney after the funeral. He asked if he could talk to me in private. I walked with him over to my car and we talked briefly. He asked me to stop by his office the next day. He said he would be reading Ted's Last Will and Testament and I needed to be there. Jerry and I attended and Ted's Will was read. He left one million dollars to cancer research and one million dollars to his church. The attorney then read, "The rest, residue and remainder of my estate, after taxes, is to be given to Amy Jefferies-Rodgers in furtherance of her services to our community."

Jerry asked if there was a number. Jerry had no idea how wealthy grandfather was. I never told him. The attorney took out an asset sheet and said, "These assets are yours now."

Grandfather had $36,844,000 in properties. He had $123,540,000 in investment accounts. He had 17 businesses valued at $18,500,000 and cash, or cash equivalent accounts in the amount of $348,731,530. Ted's total estate, which was now apparently mine, totaled $527,615,530. The lawyer said, "There is more."

I asked, "What more could there be?"

The lawyer asked for Jerry's forgiveness as he kissed me on my lips one time. He explained that Ted wanted you to receive one last kiss from him. I carried his kiss to you Amy. I couldn't stop crying no matter how much Jerry tried to comfort me. Grandfather was such a wonderful man and I still couldn't believe he was gone and he gave me his estate. I looked up at Heaven and promised grandfather that I would put his money to work helping those that needed his help.

CHAPTER SEVENTEEN

Welcome Cynthia

My little sister, Cynthia, had been working with me on Amy's Court cases since she was nine years old. Like me, Cynthia liked the thought of being a fair and impartial judge over neighborhood disputes and school disputes, but Cynthia wanted to accomplish so much more with her life. I was very proud of Cynthia because she maintained straight "A" grades in school while remaining active working with me in Amy's Kourt and at Amy's Place. At fifteen, Cynthia had a knack for communicating with people. I could tell that she was loved by those around her just like I was loved by Jerry as I grew up. I enjoyed Cynthia around me. There was seven years difference in our ages, but Cynthia looked almost like my double and she was often called Amy which was fine with me. I loved my sister as much as I loved my husband. Cynthia was at that age where she needed to focus her attention on where she wanted to be in five, ten and twenty years down the road. Cynthia would often say, "Married to a wonderful man like Jerry."

Cynthia was being pushed by mom and dad to go to college before choosing a career. Cynthia would sit and hold me and ask my opinion on her destiny. I welcomed her into my world and encouraged her to take on management of Amy's Place, or try being an Amy's Kourt judge for the neighborhood and school.

Cynthia had been sitting in as my clerk for Amy's Kourt for three years since Thomas graduated and decided to join the Navy. Cynthia and I would talk about the cases we heard that day and I would encourage her to think about what she would do under the facts of the case. I had Cynthia over to our house three or four times a week for dinner. Jerry loved having her around and he would quiz her on facts and what her decision would be as judge.

On Cynthia's sixteenth birthday, I told her that it was time to take a chance. I bought her a judicial gown and her own gavel. Her eyes glowed. Cynthia looked at her black robe and asked, "Do these things come in different colors? Black is so boring." I began laughing and remembered Jerry had purchased me a green robe. I pulled it out and Cynthia said, "Now you're talking my language." Cynthia modeled her robe for me and Jerry and I confirmed her appointment to the bench as an Amy's Kourt judge.

Cynthia asked if I truly felt she was ready.

I replied, "Little sister. You were ready when you were nine years old. I have total confidence in you."

Cynthia took to the bench the following Saturday. I sat next to her and we had questions about being twins. I heard Cynthia say, "Claire, please call our first case."

Appearing before Cynthia was two neighbors in a knockdown, drag out dispute over parking cars. Cynthia called Mr. Braddock to present his case and asked him to pay particular attention to the law as he understood how the law applied to his facts.

Mr. Braddock testified, "I have five kids. My fourth child just obtained his driver's license and I bought him a car. I only have room to park two cars in my garage and one in the driveway. I can put two in front of my house at the curb. I have my last child arriving at home park in front of Mr. Smith's house. He is objecting even though he doesn't usually use the area along his curb.

Cynthia called Mr. Smith. He testified, "My wife and I live at the home. We park our cars in the garage so we don't have to look at parked cars in our driveway. We look out our big picture window and all we see is Mr. Braddock's kid's cars parked at our curb. The curb parking is not public parking. My property runs to the centerline of the road. I am not giving permission for parking and I want it stopped.

Cynthia asked, "Do you, Mr. Smith, have any legal authority that would confirm that your ownership includes out to the centerline of the roadway?"

Mr. Smith answered, "No I don't."

Cynthia asked, "Mr. Braddock, do you believe that you can park your vehicles anywhere on the road?

Mr. Braddock answered, "Yes, along the curb, but he had no authority either."

Cynthia then asked Mr. Smith, "If you own the road out to the centerline, then do you believe that you can close down the road in front of your house?"

Mr. Smith replied, "I don't think so."

Cynthia replied, "I would agree. I think that is why my dad has always called that the right-of-way."

Case dismissed.

Cynthia reached over and tickled me and said, "Bailiff, please call the next case."

The next case dealt with garbage from one neighbor on another neighbor's yard.

Cynthia called the case and asked for Tommy (8 years old) to tell his side of the story.

Tommy testified, "I had to clean up Johnny's garbage from our front yard and driveway because he didn't put it in the garbage can. Animals tore into the garbage and made a mess that I had to clean up. I asked Johnny to help me, but he refused and said that it was our garbage. I brought some of the garbage with me. These are envelopes with his parents' names on them."

Cynthia then asked for Johnny's version. Johnny (8 years old) testified, "I dumped the garbage in the can like I always do. Tommy took out the garbage from our can and kicked the bag causing garbage to fly around onto his yard. I told Tommy that he had to clean it up. He refused."

Cynthia thanked the boys for their honest testimony. She reminded them that she could tell the truth from a lie and if someone was caught lying, they would be punished twice as much. I will return with my decision in five minutes. Cynthia left the bench with me. I laughed with

Cynthia. She said, "I don't know who is telling me the truth, but I am going to find out."

Cynthia walked back into the courtroom and asked if either boy had a different story. Johnny raised his hand and said, "I'm sorry I lied. I kicked the garbage because I was mad that I had to dump the garbage. I hate dumping the garbage."

Cynthia said, "I am ready to enter judgment. I order Johnny to haul Tommy's garbage to the curb for one month."

Johnny asked, "How many times is that."

Cynthia replied, "As many times as Tommy has garbage to haul to their garbage can."

Johnny asked, "What will you do to me if I don't do it."

Cynthia said, "I will visit your parents and we will talk about something you like to do that will be taken away."

Johnny replied, "I'll do it."

That case ended Cynthia's judicial calendar and completed her interest in being a judge. Cynthia wanted to give it a try, but her love was in helping others that needed help. Cynthia asked for a responsible position at the help center.

I asked Cynthia what she would like to do.

Cynthia replied, "I want to help mothers to help themselves."

I placed Cynthia in the clothing help center. I laughed inside as Cynthia would take children's hands and get them to follow the multiple shoe road. She would sing as she taught children to dance their way through our clothing center. When children saw shoes they liked, Cynthia would grab a foot measuring device and measure their foot for length and width. If we didn't have a shoe the child wanted in their size, Cynthia ordered it. Our rule was basic shoes only since children's feet grow rapidly. To relieve some of the parent's stress of taking help, Cynthia would quickly grab their children and wander through our inventory. As she got to know the children, she learned about their needs and would then fulfill them. One afternoon, a fifth grader whispered to Cynthia, "My mom needs a new coat and some shoes and a dress to job hunt. Can you help my mom too?

Cynthia replied, "Where is your mom right now?"

Gloria said, "My mom is sitting in the car. She is too embarrassed to ask for help. But I am not."

Cynthia and Gloria walked out to her mother's car. Cynthia mentioned, "Gloria let me know that you may need a nice dress, shoes and a coat to job hunt in. We have many dresses in our center. What are you, a size 10?

She answered, "It makes no difference what size I am; I can't go into the help center. It makes me feel like a total failure."

Cynthia was as tenacious as I am. She asked, "What would it hurt to tell me your dress and shoes sizes. I will bring out some dresses and shoes for you to look at and try on."

She replied, "That is ridiculous. How am I going to try on dresses in my car?"

Cynthia said, "My point exactly. Please follow me. No one cares if you are in the help center. You could be getting clothing for someone else, or donating clothing."

Cynthia led her through the shoe trail to dresses first. Abby was surprised that there were so many dresses in her size to choose from. She tried on three that she really liked and then chose one while looking at the other two. Cynthia said, "I will put these back where they belong. Let's look for shoes. Abby found three pair of dress shoes and said, "Those look the most professional. I will get these, but I really need tennis shoes to keep up with Gloria.

Cynthia took Abby's hand and said, "Let's look at coats next. Abby found what she believed to be the perfect coat to match her dress and shoes. She turned to Cynthia and said, "I can't thank you enough. When I get a job, I will bring a donation in." When Abby got home, she found her bag had all three dresses, the work and tennis shoes, and her coat. She called Cynthia crying, while saying thank you so much. In our true passion for giving, Cynthia asked her if she had pantyhose.

She replied, "No. I will have to go without stockings."

Cynthia asked if Abby could drive by the help center. When she pulled up to the parking area, Cynthia was standing there with three pairs of pantyhose and said, "Abby, good luck with your job hunting."

Cynthia was a miracle worker around the help center. When she wasn't taking visitors on tours of our clothing center, she was helping to do scheduling and even worked in the cafeteria doing dishes or whatever was needed. Cynthia was a godsend and I loved having my little sister with me on this adventure.

Cynthia decided that the help center needed to focus on different needs on different days of the week. She focused on Mondays for women; Tuesdays and Thursdays for kids; Wednesdays for Men; and Friday/Saturday for anybody needing help for themselves or someone else. Cynthia developed a motto for the help center. It read, "Please help someone today." She discussed it with me and I understood quickly that anyone could help themselves or someone they knew that needed help. Cynthia always greeted adults as, "Welcome to the help center. How can we help you help someone today? The fact that adults could assume a role of helping someone else instead of themselves worked well in getting the help where it belonged. Cynthia would explain, when all else fails, I thank someone for their donation to avoid embarrassment.

One afternoon, a woman named Ellen came into the help center seeking a new pair of shoes. When her neighbor saw her, she walked up and asked what she was doing there. Cynthia jumped in and said, "Ellen is making a clothing donation and then Cynthia thanked her."

Sara replied, "I wish I was that well off. I am here for help. I am having trouble meeting our expenses and clothing my kids. I am at a point where I am asking for help. Ellen then admitted that she was there for the same reason. The two found great friendship that day while they shopped for their children. A common comment we heard was, "Most of their clothing and shoes are nearly brand new.

Cynthia asked to add a sign to the building. The sign would read, "Family and Children's Clothing and Shoe boutique". Cynthia had the banner installed across the front of the building and many families visited to see what we had to offer. Above all of our clothing racks were signs that read, "If you need something, just take it. If you have something you don't wear, donate it." Cynthia and I heard many women and a few men comment that it was nicer to come to a shoe and clothing boutique over a help center. They felt better about the process and appreciated the opportunity.

About two weeks later, our first little girls, Rebecca and Candice returned. Candice modeled her still new shoes and asked, "Can I take some shoes to a girl that lives by me. Her shoes have toe holes and her brother has holes in the bottom of his shoes like I did. Their parents won't come to the help center. I heard their dad say, "If they need shoes, I will buy shoes. We are not taking charity from anyone." Robbie said that his dad said that all the time, but he never buys them shoes. He does buy a lot of beer though.

I asked Candice if she could find out the shoe sizes for Robbie and his sister Jennifer. If not, then please try to bring them into the help center and we will find them shoes. The next day Candice and Rebecca introduced me and Cynthia to Robbie (Age 12) and Jennifer. (Age 10) They were dressed like street urchins and their clothes reeked of not being washed.

I had both children put on clean socks and then I measured their feet. Robbie wanted tennis shoes and Jennifer wanted warm shoes. We fitted both children for two pairs of shoes. Cynthia did some measurements and selected clothes for both children. We gave each child three full sets of clothes, including underwear. That evening, Robbie and Jennifer's father arrived and threw the clothes and shoes inside our building and yelled, "Stay away from my children."

I had never called child services before, but the conditions mentioned by Robbie and Jennifer justified an investigation. I heard on the news that the home was raided by police and aid workers. The home was unheated and the plumbing didn't work. The home was more than disgusting. The father was drunk at the time of the raid and the mother was high on methamphetamines. The children were removed into foster care and asked for their new clothes. I delivered their clothes to the child welfare office and to two very happy children that tolerated the abusive home environment for fear that they would have no home at all.

I waited for Candice and Rebecca and gave them a very special thank you for helping out someone in need. I gave each of them $10 to spend on themselves or someone else in need. I learned that each girl spent $5 and donated $5 to a charity so they could help someone else.

I was walking with Cynthia when she saw a young man looking around. Cynthia thought she had seen him at the high school before, but wasn't certain. She walked up and asked him how she could help him help someone in need.

He replied, "Hi, my name is Mike. I am looking for a pair of jeans, about my size, for my friend, Dennis. He refused to come into this place. Cynthia asked Mike, "What is your size?"

Mike replied, "I'm not sure, but he is my size."

Cynthia said, "Unbutton your jeans as she rolled back the top seam of his pants looking for his size. Cynthia called out size 32. She grabbed a tape and measured his inseam and verified that he was Dennis' height. Cynthia then took him by the hand and led him to the jean section where she found two pair of jeans in Dennis' size. Mike was so pleased. Mike said, "Is it too much to maybe get a pair of shoes for Dennis. His shoes are getting bad. We have the same size. Cynthia looked at Mike's shoes and couldn't disagree. She found him a pair of casual shoes and tennis shoes and asked if Dennis needed anything else. Mike asked if it would be too much to get a couple shirts and a jacket. Cynthia took his arm and led him to the shirt section and asked what shirts Dennis might like to have. Mike quickly identified three shirts. Cynthia asked if Dennis wore the same size shirt too.

Mike replied yes. Cynthia checked his shirt tag and Mike selected one of the shirts and a jacket.

Mike thanked Cynthia for helping him help his friend out. Cynthia smiled and said, "That is why I am here." Cynthia quietly said, "Good-by Dennis."

We had and met every demand. Mr. Peters and his wife came into the help center asking if we had canes. I took them to the cane section and they were amazed that we had over 300 canes in stock. They selected a new cane with a better grip and exchanged their present cane. That was all they needed.

CHAPTER EIGHTEEN

When Is Help Too Much Help?

learned early on that help can be misused by those looking for help. Our emergency residences were for a maximum of two weeks, except in cases where a medical emergency required a longer stay. I spent much of my day counseling temporary residents and in seeing how I could help them help themselves. Living and eating off of Amy's place was a privilege; not a right. I wasn't running a welfare system and I found that several parents elected to not work or otherwise provide time in service for a place to live. Without a good excuse, I had to ask people to move out so others could be helped on a temporary basis.

I returned to work one morning and I found a family I had evicted living on the playground inside of a climber. They had put up blankets to block the wind and keep in warmth. I heard Emily, their three-year-old, coughing and my heart broke again. This was the family that was living in their car and now on our playground. I offered up minimum wage jobs around the center, but I had nothing like an apartment for them to live in. I was told to keep my jobs since minimum wage wouldn't be enough to support any kind of housing and food. I had to ask myself if this is why the welfare laws are so convoluted. I was 25 and I was taking on the problems of the world; OK, at least my neighborhood. I took them to the local motel and paid for one month's rent to give them time to find a good job to support their family. I encouraged them to pick up food items at the help center to help out over the month. I explained to the Millers that this is all I can do. Good luck.

Cynthia was working the night food service for our street group. We had security in place and several workers for safety. I heard some commotion and ran to the cafeteria area. A man had Cynthia by her throat threatening to kill her if she didn't give him the cash box for the cafeteria collections. I screamed Cynthia's name when she signaled me to calm down. She explained to the man that the food, blankets and coats are all free services. There is no cash except what we use to purchase the food and clothing items. He asked for that cash. Cynthia explained that we keep no cash on-site. He finally released Cynthia when the police showed up and arrested him for simple assault. Like me, Cynthia gave me a hug and returned to helping those in need just like nothing had happened.

I talked to Jerry about what happened and we both agreed that we needed formal security at night to protect our employees and volunteers. We decided to hire stand-by police officers to be on duty during our food service hours. We had the police department's promise that they would be close if an emergency arose in the future.

About a week later, Mr. Miller stopped by our offices and thanked us once again. He found an excellent job and the company would hire on his wife within sixty days. He thanked me for helping them through their rough times.

I replied, "That is why we are here."

Mr. Miller asked, "Do you think we could get a cash advance to pay first and last month's rent for an apartment. We will pay you back with our paychecks. I advanced him $3,000 over Jerry's objection. Jerry had Mr. and Mrs. Miller sign a promissory note promising to repay the loan within 90 days. Sadly, I never heard back from the Millers. I thought this is a lesson well-learned.

I admitted a family of five into our emergency shelter. Our rules were very clear. To reside in the shelter, one adult was required to be actively looking for work and the other parent was required to work at least three hours of in-service daily somewhere within Amy's Place. He or she could cook, clean, handle clothing, etc. Anything could be done except handling money. That was exclusively our in-house CPA.

Our new family followed our rules and Tina Minton was going out daily for job interviews. Robert Minton helped out at our facility cooking meals. I allowed his eight and ten-year-old sons to help him in the kitchen to lessen the burden on our childcare program. Robert had a problem arriving for his shift on time resulting in a referral to me by Cynthia.

I spoke with Robert and he complained that he was expected to work without formal breaks and he wasn't being paid for his services.

I replied, "You are receiving in-kind benefits such as your free temporary housing and meals. I think you are being paid quite well thank-you."

I received a letter from the Department of Labor informing me that Amy's Place was the subject of a labor audit. I showed it to Jerry and we both concluded that we were paying our employees more than minimum wage and all taxes had been paid. Neither of us was worried.

The Department of Labor sent Elizabeth Stone to do the audit. I welcomed her into our facility. Ms. Stone asked, "Do your payroll records reflect all paid employees of Amy's Place?"

I replied, "Yes they do."

Ms. Stone quickly looked through the stack of reports and asked me where she would find the payroll records for Robert Minton.

I replied, "Robert Minton isn't an employee. His family is residing in our emergency housing. A condition of receiving emergency housing is that one parent must volunteer at least three hours daily while living in the apartment."

Ms. Stone replied, "You are a business. If someone works for you, then you are liable for the payment of wages at the minimum wage level at least. Why they are working for you is irrelevant to the department." I replied, "The three hours Mr. Minton works, when he does work, are exchanged for his temporary housing. The housing has a value of $650 for two weeks. He is getting more than minimum wage. If you calculate it, he is receiving around $15.50 per hour in in-kind value." Ms. Stone replied, "Are you telling me that you pay your tenant workers $15.50 per hour?"

I replied, "With in-kind services. They live here in exchange for their 42 hours of work over the two-week period."

She explained that I can't allow my emergency tenants to work without paying them. It is called "Voluntary suffrage" and does not excuse my obligation to pay them wages if they provide work to my business. She calculated Mr. Minton's wages at $15.50 per hour times 42 hours and claimed that I owed Mr. Minton $650 less payroll taxes. I was also assessed penalties and interest.

Ms. Stone then asked how long the help center had been open for emergency housing.

I replied, "Eleven months."

She asked, "Have you been full for all eleven months?"

I replied, "Yes, but not all people work. Single parents are not required to work at the center so long as they are actively seeking work." She asked, "Who watches a single parent's children while they are job hunting."

I replied, "Our parent volunteers do. They take turns watching each other's children and my company has nothing to do with the volunteer childcare program."

Ms. Stone said that I needed to calculate the hours due to each and every parent that worked for the center since opening our doors. I needed to pay those parents and withhold the proper taxes.

I called my favorite tax attorney. Dad explained where the Department of Labor was coming from in their audit. He contacted Ms. Stone and was able to reduce the hourly wage to minimum wage, but that still left Amy's place with a billing of $17,359.40 for wages, taxes, penalties and interest. The money wasn't the problem. What was the problem, was having temporary housing guests who did not contribute help for the center. I thanked Mr. Minton as I reminded him that his family had two days before they were required to move out.

He replied, "You can't make my family leave. What you are doing is a retaliatory eviction. My family isn't leaving. Now, please leave me and my family alone." didn't know what to do. I called Jerry and he stopped by my office to discuss the problem. Jerry asked me when Mr. Minton's two weeks were up.

I replied, "In two days."

Jerry said, "We will wait and ask him to leave when his two weeks are ended. If he refuses, then I will file for what is called an 'unlawful detainer' which simply means he is staying where he has no right to be." Cynthia chided in saying, "No need Jerry. I will boot his butt out the door. I will not be taken advantage of."

I asked if we should pay him his wages now or wait until eviction day. Jerry replied, "Let's get him paid now and maybe he will leave without a fight."

I calculated the taxes and wrote out a check payable to Mr. Minton. Jerry and I delivered it to Mr. Minton. He thanked us for the check, but said, "I am still not leaving here with my family."

Jerry replied, "You signed an agreement limiting your stay to two weeks. Your two weeks are up in two days."

Mr. Minton replied, "Sue me. My attorney says that your contract is an adhesive kind of contract and is unenforceable in court."

Jerry replied, "You mean, adhesion, don't you?"

Mr. Minton replied, "Whatever the word, you can't make my family move out. I will see you in court."

Amy's Place filed suit seeking to evict the Minton family. As evidence, we offered our two-week emergency tenancy agreement. Jerry set up a 'show cause hearing', which I understand is a hearing before the judge to explain our side and the other side. The judge then decides to do the eviction or set the case over for a mini-trial.

Jerry and I appeared on behalf of Amy's place. Mr. Minton appeared with an attorney. I asked Jerry how Mr. Minton could pay a lawyer, but he can't find a place to live.

Jerry replied, "Either pro bono or county paid."

The judge came into the courtroom and Mr. Minton looked directly at me and said, "You are going to lose big time today." He said it loudly so the judge could hear his comment.

Judge Terry called our case. He said, "Good morning Judge Amy and Judge Rodgers. I should correct myself; I remember it is now Judge Amy Rodgers."

I replied, "Good morning Judge Terry. Actually, it is Judge Amy L. Jefferies-Rodgers.

Judge Terry said, "Good enough. Good morning to you too sir. Let me see, oh yes, Mr. Minton. Judge Rodgers, please present your evidence in support of an order of eviction.

Jerry replied, "We have a two-week emergency housing program for families with children. Mr. Minton and his family accepted a two-week occupancy while they were supposed to be looking for a job. Their agreement, which I am handing to the bailiff, clearly states that the tenancy terminated after fourteen days so we can accommodate other families in need. Mr. and Mrs. Minton signed the agreement, but refuse to move out of our temporary housing. We are justified under our contract to obtain an order of eviction.

Judge Terry asked Mr. Minton to explain why an order of eviction shouldn't issue under the contract.

Mr. Minton replied, "Judge, those two people made me work while my family was in residence. I complained and the Department of Labor made them pay me for my work. The part of the contract that required me, or my wife, to volunteer three hours a day for every day we resided at the help center was not the law and the entire agreement should be thrown out. They are also doing retaliation against me."

Mr. Minton's attorney clarified the record saying, "Your honor, my client is trying to allege a retaliatory eviction."

Judge Terry asked if the attorney had some document beyond the help center agreement that permitted a stay longer than fourteen days.

He replied, "No your honor."

Judge Terry replied, "I didn't think so."

Judge Terry then responded to Mr. Minton by correcting him and explained that the help center can require non-paid volunteer help as an in-kind exchange for services rendered. The case is Wilford v. Thomas and it was decided three weeks ago by our state Supreme Court. I learned about it at the recent judicial conference. You are owed nothing and I am ordering you to return the payment to Amy's Place. I am also granting an order of eviction. If you are not out of the premises within 24 hours, I will have the sheriff physically remove you. You will be responsible for all fees and cost associated with the sheriff's duties.

We were walking out of the courtroom when Judge Terry said, "Wait. Let me give you my course book from this year's judicial conference. You were both missed and especially Judge Amy. I picked up my phone and called our CPA and had her put a stop payment on the check to Mr. Minton.

When I returned to my office, I contacted the Department of Labor and cited the recent Supreme Court case. Ms. Stone acknowledged the case and said the Department was sending me a refund of taxes, penalties and interest paid.

Jerry and I laughed over dinner about missing one judicial conference and it happened to be the one conference that had direct application to what we were doing. He said, "Judge Amy, next year you and I are going to the judicial conference together. This time we are only going to have one room which will be really nice."

CHAPTER NINETEEN

....

Training Up New Amy's Kourt Judges

My love of being a judge came from my experiences hearing and resolving disputes between kids. Maybe I was so successful because I could see the dispute from a kid's point of view instead of an adult's viewpoint. I always believed that the law should be used to help the parties and not be limited to the entry of judgments and verdicts.

I double checked with Cynthia, but she was no longer interested in being a judge. She loved the Amy's Place help center and enjoyed helping others help themselves. I needed to rethink my future once again so I could address the missing elements in our help system. I know that grandfather was watching me from Heaven and I really needed to do a good job for him. Cynthia was turning 18 and would graduate this year. She didn't want college. She wanted to be with me through life. I told Jerry that I am appointing Cynthia as Director of Amy's Place. I gave her the run of the programs and I knew that she could handle it. Jerry and I remained as executive directors and always available to assist when and where needed.

Cynthia was happy beyond belief. She would dress as a fairy or princess on children's days and walk children through the clothing and shoe center. On occasion, she wore overalls and a straw hat and walked around bare footed. On men's day, Cynthia wore a man's suit with a fake mustache and walked around showing the men where things were. Cynthia found that men were uncomfortable around young women; especially cute young women. On the woman's day, Cynthia wore the

Amy's Kourt latest fashion from our boutique from dresses to shoes. She knew how to make her job fun. I had complete confidence in Cynthia's abilities. Cynthia was like a chameleon and could change quickly to fit whatever environment she was engaged in from cooking in the kitchen to working with the center's accountant. Cynthia was also brilliant and loved by everybody.

I next focused on Amy's Kourt and School Kourt. I continued to hear cases in both Kourts, but I felt that our AMY's centers were exceeding the practical reach for the kids. I located a piece of property near our existing Amy's Kourt building and I built a new Amy's Kourt. I lowered the bench and the counsel tables, all to fit kids more than adults. I used an architect to help design the height of tables and chairs and the bench. I wanted the building to look like an AMY's courtroom, but more kid friendly.

Once the courthouse was built, I had slogans painted on the walls. "Be Fair"; "Play Fair"; "Treat others like you want to be treated"; "Help – don't hurt"; "Truth is better than a lie" and so on. I had a sketch of the courtroom in the entrance. Each seat in the courtroom was labeled so a kid could see where they should sit when their turn arrived. If someone was confused, they could push a button and the diagram would speak explaining who the plaintiff and defendant were; the judge and bailiff.

When done, the new Amy's Kourt was beautiful. I heard that kids developed disputes so they could see inside the new Kourthouse. I decided to have an open house for the public and the schools. My judicial services were routinely accepted by the community at large and I felt honored to be the Amy's Kourt judge.

I put out an announcement that I would be looking for two straight 'A' students wishing to train to be Amy's Kourt Judges. I was surprised that I received 14 requests for interviews. Each request was to be accompanied by the latest school transcript. Eight of the fourteen applications didn't have transcripts attached and were disregarded. I arranged interviews for the six candidates. I had one nine-year old; one ten-year old; two eleven-year old's; one twelve-year old and one fifteen-year old.

I decided to establish a two-part interview process. The first part would be a group interview to explain the job of an Amy's Kourt judge.

The purpose was to discuss responsibilities like being fair and impartial regardless of who the parties are; the ability to wait until you hear all the evidence before coming to a decision; and the obligation to be in the Kourtroom when scheduled to hear cases.

I held a general discussion with the six applicants and I felt comfortable that each had a good understanding of the volunteer judicial positions. I explained that they would intern with me or Jerry for one year before taking the bench on their own. I also explained that there would be two positions created.

Matt, the fifteen-year-old asked if he would be paid.

I replied, "Not in Amy's Kourt. However, if you serve five years as an Amy's Kourt judge, you could be eligible to serve in one of the AMY centers as an arbitrator or mediator. Our arbitrators and mediators make over $100,000 annually. Matt apologized for wasting my time. He needed a paying job now.

I had five applicants left. I met personally with each applicant and learned that one of my eleven-year old applicants had been found guilty of theft of property. I thanked her for her application and then let her go. I had four applicants left. I developed three written scenarios that I had dealt with as a judge. I presented each scenario to the applicants and asked them to carefully read each scenario before writing out what their judgment would be under the facts.

The first scenario was, "John is sitting on his porch using his laptop computer. His friend Steve stops by and visits. John excuses himself and goes to the bathroom. When he returns to his porch, Steve is gone and so is his computer. John accuses Steve of stealing his computer. Steve denied he stole anything. What is your decision?"

The second scenario was, "Kim and Sally are playing with Kim's porcelain dolls. They were brushing the hair on the dolls when Sally accidentally drops her doll and the face shatters ruining the doll. Kim wants Sally to buy her a new doll. What is your decision?"

The third scenario, "Kelly was selling candy at school. The school rules said that no candy can be sold on school property. Kelly was caught selling her candy. She could be suspended for one week. Does it make any difference that Kelly was selling her candy at school to feed her younger sister?"

The purpose of the scenarios was to test each applicant's ability to think and process information before making a decision. I sat the applicants down and read the first scenario four times and then asked each applicant to write out their decision on the facts.

Cassandra was the nine-year-old. Roberto was the ten-year-old; Kaylie was the eleven-year-old and Susan was the twelve-year-old.

In response to the first scenario, Cassandra indicated that she didn't have enough information to make a final decision. Roberto said that he would award judgment against Steve for computer theft. Kaylie concluded that under the facts, it could have been Steven, but she couldn't be certain. Susan believed that the only logical person to have taken the computer would be Steven.

The applicants were given the second scenario. Cassandra said that it was an accident, but Sally should offer to replace the doll if she can afford it. Roberto concluded that Sally had to buy a new doll for Kim. Kaylie concluded that it was an unfortunate accident and if Kim didn't want her dolls damaged, they shouldn't have been playing with the porcelain dolls. Susan felt that Kim should get a new doll paid by Sally.

The final scenario resulted in all of the applicants concluding that Kelly broke the school rules and should be punished. However, Kaylie suggested that the punishment should address the reason for the bad behavior. Is it really so bad when she is trying to feed her little sister? Cassandra thought she might give a strong warning and punish her if she broke the rules again. Roberto suggested she be kicked out of school and Susan felt that a smaller suspension was warranted under the facts.

I called the group together and gave what my decision would be for each scenario and why. Under the first scenario, there is no evidence to support that Stephen took John's computer. All the facts give is subjective speculation which is unacceptable as a fact. In the real case, John's mother saw the computer sitting on the porch and she brought it into the house. No one had stolen the computer. I commended Cassandra and Kaylie for their thought process. I gave each of them a positive mark on my sheet.

I reviewed the second scenario. This is clearly a matter of two girls playing with porcelain dolls. What happened was an accident – nothing more. We cannot hold Sally responsible for replacing the doll. I again commend Cassandra for her insight. We can't make Sally pay, but we could encourage her to do so if she could. I also commend Kaylie because she recognized that this was a simple accident. I gave both girls a second mark.

Roberto stood up and said, "Screw you. I can see where this is going. You are going to choose two white girls instead of a Latino boy."

I explained to Roberto that his nationality had nothing to do with the selection process. If it had, he wouldn't have made it to the final selection round. I thanked him for applying and let him know that attitude is as important as knowledge when you sit in judgment over someone else.

I reviewed the third scenario and explained that it was a tricky one. I wanted to see if you could demonstrate some compassion from the bench. I believed that Cassandra's and Kaylie's decisions showed compassion where Susan only sought to minimize the punishment.

For these reasons, I hereby appoint Cassandra and Kaylie to serve as interns under Amy's Kourt. If you stick with me until you are eighteen, I can assure you that you will receive training and jobs in the AMY judicial system. I explained that the first day of learning would be Saturday. You will be hearing school and neighborhood cases.

I hired an experienced bailiff/clerk for Amy's Kourt. I didn't want to be training judges and the bailiff at the same time. Our bailiff was named Sandy. I introduced my two interning judges and let her know that Kaylie was nine and Cassandra was eleven. I presented them with green judicial robes and I wore my black robe. If they survived the internship, then after one year they can begin wearing a black robe to court.

Under the new Amy's Kourt rules, cases were scheduled in advance. A complaint form was filled out indicating the parties and the nature of the complaint. We had twelve cases on the docket for Saturday and I let Sandy know that we were ready to go. I flipped on my ready light and heard Sandy say, "All rise. Amy's Kourt is now in session. The Honorable Amy Jefferies-Rodgers presiding with judicial trainees, Cassandra and Kaylie. I took center chair and my trainees sat to each side. The news media was on hand for the grand opening of Amy's Kourt. Our picture seated in Kourt was on the front page with a nice story about the history of Amy's Kourt. When the media was through, I asked Sandy to call our first case.

Sandy said, "This is docket number 1 for this court. Allison vs. Rebecca. I directed the parties to sit at the table's marked plaintiff and defendant. When they were seated, I verified that Allison was the plaintiff, or the one with the complaint. Rebecca was the defendant. I swore in both parties and they promised to tell me the truth.

I asked Allison, age 12, to explain her complaint that she had against Rebecca.

Allison testified, "Becki, age 12, and I are friends. We were going to the school spring dance. I was trying on my dresses with Becki watching me. She didn't have a nice dress to wear to the dance and I agreed to share one of my dresses since her mom couldn't afford to buy her one. My only condition was that she takes care of it because it was one of my favorite dresses. We had fun at the dance until Becki spilled punch on my dress. The red punch stained my dress and the stain won't come out. I want Becki to buy me a new dress. My dress cost $58 on sale. Here is the receipt.

I asked Rebecca to explain her side of the story.

Rebecca testified, "It was like Allison said. I borrowed her dress and wore it to the dance. It was a beautiful dress and I felt so pretty wearing it. I was drinking some punch when a boy ran into me causing my punch to spill onto the front of the dress. I didn't do anything to cause the spill and I don't think I should have to buy a new dress since it wasn't my fault. I thanked the parties and said that the Kourt would take a brief recess and return a decision. I asked my interns to follow me to my chambers. Once inside, I asked Cassandra what she thought. Cassandra said, "Becki accepted the dress and promised that she would take care of it. The punch spilling was an accident and not Becki's fault. However, she did promise to take care of the dress. I believe that taking care of the dress includes replacing it if it was stained."

Kaylie said, "I mostly agree with what Cassandra said. I think that there is always a risk of having something special damaged when you loan it to someone else. Allison knew that the dress could be damaged. That is why she asked Becki to take care of it which she agreed to do. I would enter judgment for Allison for one-half the value of the dress.

I said that my ruling would be that the damage was an unavoidable accident not caused by Becki. As such, she has no liability to Allison. Allison assumed the risk of damage to the dress when she lent it to Becki. I gave my ruling and I could tell that Allison was upset with my decision. She looked at me with a scornful face and both girls remained in my Kourtroom.

I said, "Sandy, call the next case on the docket."

Sandy said, "Docket No. 2. Robert vs. David. This is a theft case." I had Kaylie swear the plaintiff Robert who was seven years old. She did well to make sure that he understood what the truth was. I smiled at Kaylie and said, "Take over Judge."

Kaylie asked Robert to explain his complaint.

Robert testified, "I received some new toy soldiers and I was playing with them in my front yard when David came by. David liked the soldier with the cannon. I let him play soldiers with me. When David left for home, I was putting away my toy soldiers and saw that the solder with the cannon was missing. I think that David took my toy soldier."

Kaylie thanked Robert and asked David to testify. He started to talk when Kaylie remembered that she needed to swear him in.

David testified, "I didn't take his stupid soldier with the cannon. I don't know what happened to it, but I didn't take it."

Kaylie asked for any other witnesses. There were none and she announced that she would take a brief recess and then give her decision.

Kaylie walked into my chambers and said, "That was so much fun. I did it by myself too."

I replied, "You did well so far. The hard part is making a decision for the case. What is your decision?"

Kaylie replied, "I'm not sure. There is no evidence that David took anything. All we have is a missing toy. I can't enter judgment against David just because he was there."

I asked Cassandra her opinion.

Cassandra replied, "I agree with Kaylie. We have no evidence that David took the toy."

We hit our ready light and Sandy said, "All rise."

Kaylie said, "You may be seated. This case deals with the unfortunate loss of a special toy that was owned by Robert. He believes that his good friend David took it. The evidence doesn't support any claim against David and the case is ruled for David. I just hope and pray the solder and cannon can be found quickly."

I tickled Cassandra and said, "You are up next." Cassandra said, "Sandy, please call the next case."

Sandy said, "This is a school case. The student is being accused to copying off the Internet instead of doing her own work."

Cassandra read the school report and statement from Ms. Bolt, the seventh grade English teacher. The assignment was a reference paper. The student could cite an Internet story, but the paper was to be mostly original thought. Any references to the Internet story required quotations and sourcing.

Cassandra was very familiar with reference papers. She called Stephan to step forward. She swore him in and asked him to take the witness stand.

Cassandra stated, "Stephen, your teacher has accused you of using an Internet resource article in your paper that you did not reference. That failure is called plagiarism. Please tell me how you prepared your report." Stephen testified, "I did copy from the Internet article. I quoted the article as my reference and it is in my report. I didn't know that I had to document every word that I used. I thought the one reference was sufficient. My teacher refused to hear my explanation."

Cassandra said she would be at recess and then enter her opinion, I mean judgment.

I asked Cassandra, "How do you intend to rule?"

Cassandra said, "He did reference the Internet article. His report all came from the article. Although he copied much of the article for his reference report, I believe that he did identify his reference. I don't think that a couple quotation marks should ruin his school career. I would order him to fix his paper and properly quote everything that he took directly from the Internet source."

Kaylie replied, "I would do exactly the same thing. This is a case where he didn't do a very good job quoting and using quotations. It is a learning experience. He should revise his paper and turn it in."

Cassandra returned to the bench and said, "Plagiarism is wrong. If you use the thoughts of another author, you need to set off those thoughts in quotations and then identify your reference material. You did identify your reference source, but you failed to attribute those parts of your report that you copied with quotations. I am entering an order directing you to redo your report properly quoting from your reference source. You have one day to turn in your paper to your teacher."

Before I could say something, Kaylie said, "Sandy, please call the next case. Sandy replied, Docket No. 3. Anthony vs. Stone. Anthony is complaining that Stone's trees are dropping leaves on Anthony's yard and he wants Stone to clean them up.

Kaylie swore the parties and asked Anthony to testify.

Anthony testified, "Our yard has no trees. Stone's yard has six big Maple trees with gigantic leaves. Every fall his leaves fall on our yard and I have to clean them up. That should be Stone's job."

Stone testified, "My parents have large Maple trees. I can't control where the leaves go. If the wind blows toward Anthony's yard, he gets leaves. It is natural and not my doing. I should not have to clean up his leaves."

Kaylie said, "I will take a brief recess."

I discussed her opinion and both intern judges agreed that there should be no judgment. Kaylie returned and said, "Judgment for the defendant."

Anthony asked, "What does that mean?"

Kaylie explained that there is no responsibility owing by Stone for leaves that fall into your yard.

Cassandra asked Sandy to call our next case. Sandy said, "Docket No. 4 –School case/fighting on school property.

Cassandra asked, is Jeffrey here?

Jeffrey stood up and said, "Yah, I'm here. So, what do you want?"

Cassandra kept her cool and said, "Jeffrey, age 14, you are charged with violating Rule 78(a) fighting on school property.

Jeff testified, "Some kid from another school came onto our school and was calling kids names. I told him to stop or I would pound his face. He refused to stop and I hit him in the mouth. He took off running, but a teacher saw me hit him. I was defending our school."

Cassandra said that she was ready with her decision. I asked to talk briefly with Cassandra and Kaylie. I explained that so long as they were interns, all decisions will be discussed before delivery of the decision. Both agreed. I then asked Cassandra what her decision would be.

Cassandra said, "I am going to suspend him for one week for fighting. However, I will not carry out the suspension so long as Jeff has no further fights during this school year."

Kaylie laughed and said, "That was what I would have said." I replied, "Good decision. Proceed."

Cassandra gave her ruling and asked Jeff if he understood the seriousness of her decision.

He replied, "I promise, no more fighting."

Our final case of the day was also the most interesting. My interns flipped a coin to see who would take the case. Kaylie won the toss and asked Sandy to call the next case.

The case was a harassment case. Shelby was harassing Celia. Both girls were twelve.

Kaylie swore both parties and asked Celia to explain what the harassment was about.

Celia testified, "Shelby and I are friends. I have a 13-year-old brother that took Shelby to a movie one time and Shelby loves my brother, but he doesn't want to have anything to do with Shelby. I told her how my brother, Randy felt about her. She calls me in class, after school, at night and all night long asking me to talk to Randy for her. I have asked her to leave me and Randy alone, but she won't listen to me."

Kaylie called Shelby and asked for her side of the story. Kaylie smartly said, "Please make sure to tell me why I shouldn't grant the anti-harassment order."

Shelby testified, "I love Randy. I think he loves me, but Shelby won't let me near her brother. I heard what she said about Randy, but I don't believe her. All I want to do is talk with Randy once and I know that he will love me too."

Kaylie said, "Do either of you have any witnesses to call?" Celia said, "My brother Randy will testify."

Randy walked up to the bench and he was gorgeous. Kaylie smiled and I pinched her and told her to get on with the trial. Kaylie laughed and swore in Randy.

Randy testified, "I took Shelby to the movie one time. That was it. She won't leave me alone and won't take no for an answer. I have a girlfriend and I am not looking for another."

Kaylie gruffly said, "I will take a recess and give my decision." Kaylie and Cassandra said, "Dang. Too bad he's taken. Randy is

really cute."

I replied, "That's all fine, but what is your decision?" Kaylie said, "I want to marry Randy."

I asked her to get real. He had a girlfriend.

Kaylie said, "I heard him. I am going to find that Shelby is harassing him and enter a restraining order.

Cassandra and I concurred. I handed Kaylie our restraining order form. She read, "I am granting the restraining order or anti-harassment order as requested. Shelby, you may not directly or indirectly through any person or by electronic, verbal or written means, communicate in any manner with Celia and her brother Robert for the next twelve months. If you violate this order, then this matter will be referred to the police department for enforcement. Herein fail not at your own peril. Do you understand my order?"

Shelby said, "I do understand."

Kaylie then asked her to step up to the Bailiff and she will give you a copy of our restraining order. The other copies will be given to the police department and to Celia and Robert.

We returned to my chambers and Kaylie and Cassandra were so excited. They began jumping up and down thanking me for the opportunity. Both said that they loved being Amy's Kourt judges. As we began to leave the courthouse, Robert rode up on his bike. He found his solder and cannon. My young judges had twinkles in their eyes as they concluded that they believed the toy would show up.

Over the next year, either Jerry or I would work with the judicial interns. I was amazed at how quickly they were picking up on the law and how they treated their job seriously. The schools signed off on both interns and allowed them to begin hearing school cases once I released them. I let the girls know that graduation day was coming the following Saturday. Jerry and I will be evaluating you for each step in the process of holding court. You will be seated on the bench by yourself. Remember all you have learned.

I flipped a coin and Cassandra was the first to be tried and tested. I watched her flip her ready light and I heard Sandy announce, "All rise. Amy's Kourt is now in session. The Honorable Cassandra Wicks presiding." Jerry and I were sitting in the back of the court observing Cassandra.

She looked at Sandy and said, "Please call our first matter on the docket." Sandy called School District vs. Jerry Dolan."

Cassandra asked if Jerry Dolan was in the Kourtroom. He stood up with his father. Cassandra asked him to step forward and be sworn. She politely invited his father to sit with him at the table. Once seated, Cassandra read, "Jerry Dolan, you violated school rule 35(a) for being absent without an excuse three times in one school year. Do you admit or deny this charge?"

Jerry replied, "I admit it, but I did have a legitimate reason." Cassandra asked, "What was your reason for missing school?"

Jerry replied, "My little brother is in second grade. He has skipped school more than ten times this year. When I learned that he was skipping school, I began missing school to force him to go to school. By the time I got my brother to school, it was already so late that I didn't go myself. I couldn't tell my parents and get a written excuse because I would be turning on my little brother. I refused to tattle on him and decided to deal with the problem myself."

Cassandra asked, "Is your brother going to school now?"

Jerry answered, "Yes he is. He doesn't dare skip school again or I will pound him into sand."

Cassandra said, "I am ready to make my ruling. Jerry, you violated School Rule 35(a) by skipping school without permission. That carries a suspension of three days. I am waiving the suspension with the clear understanding that you have no more unexcused absences this year. If you do, then the suspension will be imposed by the school without a further hearing. Do you understand my ruling?"

Jerry replied, "Yes, I do."

Cassandra said, "Court will be at recess for five minutes."

I heard Sandy said, "All rise" and Cassandra's first solo was near perfect, or what I called a textbook case.

I looked at Kaylie and asked, "Are you ready to go?"

Kaylie smiled and flipped her ready light. Sandy said, "All rise" and I watched Kaylie enter the Kourt like I did at age nine. Kaylie had control and I thought of myself sitting at my makeshift court and wondered if I looked as focused as Kaylie and Cassandra did.

Kaylie asked Sandy to call the next case. Sandy said, "This is a neighborhood dispute. Sinclare vs. Thomlinson. Mr. Sinclare claims that Mr. Thomlinson rerouted water drainage onto his property and he wants it stopped."

Jerry whispered to me, "That is a land use trespass case. Our interns don't know about that law. I think we need to refer this case to the superior court."

I replied to Jerry, "No, I don't think so. The case involves issues of common sense and common decency between neighbors. They chose this forum and I think Kaylie will do a good job with the case."

Kaylie looked out over the Kourtroom and asked if the parties were prepared to present their cases. Both men indicated that they were ready. Kaylie quickly recognized that the men sat in the wrong chairs and asked them to switch so she didn't confuse them.

Mr. Sinclare said, "I don't see what difference it makes where I sit." Kaylie replied, "Sir, it is Kourtroom protocol. Thank you for moving tables."

Kaylie asked both men if they brought witnesses. Neither did. She swore both of them and confirmed their agreement that Amy's Kourt hear and decide their dispute.

Kaylie said, "Mr. Thomlinson please present your case."

Mr. Thomlinson testified, "My home is downhill from Mr. Sinclare's home. He was getting a lot of water runoff from his gutters and he redirected the water into a shallow dry well. I mentioned to him that if the well filled up, it would overflow onto my property. Mr. Sinclare told me to mind my own business. The first heavy rain and the dry well overflowed and washed over my rockery and onto my lawn and planter beds. I brought pictures of the water damage."

Mr. Thomlinson went to hand the pictures up to Kaylie when she said, "Mr. Thomlinson, please show the pictures to Mr. Sinclare so I can see if he has an objection to the pictures being seen by me."

Jerry looked at me and smiled. He asked, "Did you teach her that?" I replied, "Who else. I learned that from you when I was eleven years old."

Mr. Sinclare looked at the pictures and said, "I object to you seeing these pictures."

Kaylie asked, "What is your objection?"

Mr. Sinclare replied, "The pictures show water damage, but the pictures don't prove that the damage was caused by my water."

Kaylie said, "Objection overruled. Please hand the bailiff the pictures."

Kaylie looked at the pictures and asked if Mr. Thomlinson had anything further.

He replied, "The cost to fix the water damage will be $425. I have a written estimate for the repairs."

Kaylie said, "Thank you. Mr. Sinclare, let me hear your side now." Mr. Sinclare testified, "I did build a dry well, but I deny that it overflowed during the last rain storm. The pictures don't prove that the water damaging Mr. Thomlinson's planter and yard came from my dry well."

Mr. Thomlinson asked if he could askMr. Sinclare a question.

Kaylie said, "I will allow a limited voir dire of the witness." Mr. Thomlinson replied, "A limited what?"

Kaylie replied, "I will allow limited questions."

Mr. Thomlinson showed Mr. Sinclare a picture that showed a stream of water coming from his dry well to his property. He asked, "Doesn't that show that it is your water coming onto my property?"

He replied, "Not in my opinion, it doesn't."

Kaylie thanked both parties and indicated that she was prepared to rule on the case.

Kaylie stated, "Mr. Sinclare redirected water from his roof downspout into a drywell that overflowed onto Mr. Thomlinson's planter and yard. I find Mr. Sinclare's water trespassed onto his neighbor's property causing the damage. I award the sum of $425 plus court costs in having to bring this claim in the amount of $50.

Kaylie looked to Sandy who said, "All rise" and Kaylie left the bench. Inside my chambers, I had two very excited graduating judges that Jerry and I believed were ready to hear neighborhood and school cases. I presented each judge with their new black robes and gavels.

CHAPTER TWENTY

Amy's Place Two

was very pleased with the forward progress of the AMY'S judicial system and Amy's kid/school Kourt. My sister, Cynthia had AMY's Place working well and meeting the immediate needs of our small community. I was confident that I was making grandfather's money work for the benefit of our community. I said a prayer daily for him and all he gave to our community.

I recognized that there were individuals with specific housing needs that didn't qualify for other assistance programs. Providing two weeks of emergency housing for many families was more than enough to pull their lives together and get back on track. However, there are those families that needed a greater level of assistance. The typical example would be a family of five that need a place for the entire family. Present welfare rules made it fraudulent if both parents received any benefit from welfare services.

Jerry and I took a drive looking for an apartment complex that we could buy and convert to subsidized housing limited to one year maximum. We found an older complex that had 128 units broken down as 50 one bedroom and 78 two-bedroom units. I wanted to convert 30 of the one-bedroom units into two-bedroom units and convert 30 two-bedroom units to three-bedroom units. I contacted Gary Stewart, our construction manager for the construction company I inherited. Gary looked over the complex and indicated that it would be cheaper and faster to build a new complex. He provided me with specifications showing that the conversion would cost just under $59,000 from new construction. Jerry and I decided on new construction.

We decided to build 30 single bedroom units; 75 two-bedroom units; and 75 three-bedroom units. We provided a swimming pool, exercise room and office complex that included a computer room for residents needing access to a computer for job hunting, work and school. Our permits were obtained and construction was to be completed within fourteen months. Jerry insisted we hire an architect to supervise the construction and inspections. I resisted at first, believing that I could handle it. I now recognize that the architect was a time saver for me.

I decided to name the apartment complex "AMY'S PLACE TWO". It sounded nice and tied in nicely with our other ventures. Once again, Jerry set us up with a not-for-profit limited liability company and Dad helped me again with qualifying the company as a non-profit.

Jerry asked me what the rate structure would be for the apartments. I wasn't sure, but I wanted an ability to pay scale so people paid what they could realistically afford while receiving subsidized housing. Jerry drew up our rental agreements which clearly stated that this was a one-year residency only, as temporary housing. There would be no 'holdover tenancies', which I understood to mean when the year is through, you had to move out and make room for someone else.

Jerry and I did a walk through the complex and we were proud of our small apartment complex. Jerry said, "Enjoy this because it is going to get much more difficult as we interview tenants and start renting apartments." We decided that we would not rent to anyone that had been forced out of their last rental through an unlawful detainer or eviction action. It was a good indication that they would not leave our complex at the end of their year of residency.

Jerry and I selected an apartment manager and assistant manager and began the painstaking job of interviewing families for temporary housing. We set a sliding fee scale that would be adjusted quarterly to keep up with our tenant's employment changes. One of our conditions was that one or both parents had to be looking for work. We also put together a day care for children in residence while their parents were looking for work or working. Jerry and I decided to fully furnish ten of each apartment size for those families that didn't have furniture, etc. The furnished apartments were limited to a six-month lease.

We sent out our public notice that we were accepting applications for occupancy. The applicants needed to provide us with their employment and financial information if they were seeking a discounted rate. My goal was to provide affordable housing for those that were working jobs, but not making enough to afford a full apartment payment.

I was shocked that within the first group of applications I reviewed was the Miller family that we had helped several times in the past. The most recent help was a $3,000 loan to pay first and last month's rent on an apartment. The Millers promised to repay the loan, but never even made an attempt.

I scheduled an interview with the Millers, mostly out of curiosity as to why they never repaid our generous loan. I had already made up my mind that I would not rent to them under any circumstances. I then remembered my judicial training and decided to keep an open mind. I learned that the employer that hired Mr. Miller was shut down by the IRS for failing to timely deposit employment taxes, or what my dad referred to as trust fund taxes. The employer deducts the taxes from the employee's paycheck and is supposed to pay the taxes to the IRS. I asked Mr. Miller why he didn't tell me about what happened.

Mr. Miller replied, "I was so angry that we had just made our first and last month's deposit on a two-bedroom apartment when the IRS shut down the company. We had to move out of our apartment because we couldn't pay the rent. We have been living at my parent's house sharing one bedroom while looking for work."

I asked Mr. Miller what the name of his former employer was. He replied, "It makes no difference now. It is out of business."

I asked him the name of the apartment complex he paid first and last month's rent to.

He replied, "I don't remember the name."

I explained that we verify all application information before entering into a rental agreement.

He replied, "Then just forget it. We will stay living with my parents." I replied, "Thank you". I later learned that Mr. Miller was lying about having rented an apartment or being employed. I learned that he was hooked on methamphetamines and used our loan to purchase drugs.

I talked with Jerry and asked if we could make drug testing a part of our apartment qualification program.

Jerry replied, "I would think we could establish any condition for rentals so long as we didn't discriminate on the basis of race, creed, color, national origin or gender."

I replied, "We only rent to families and young couples so I am not worried about any of that."

Within one week of our announcement, we had three hundred and thirty-seven applications submitted. I decided to set up fifteen-minute interviews and my first day failed miserably. I was still interviewing at 9:00 pm. Most of the applicants were eligible for a tenancy. However, several applicants walked out when I handed them our overview questionnaire that asked:

Will you consent to a urinalysis testing for drug use?

Have you, or anyone in your family that intend to accept residency at Amy's Place Two ever been convicted of drug usage or selling drugs.

Have you, or any member of your family been accused, or found guilty of domestic violence or assault. Please explain.

Have you, or any member of your family been previously evicted from a tenancy.

My first interview was a nineteen-year-old girl that was seven months pregnant. Her parents were making her move out of their home before the baby was born. She needed help until her baby was born. After that, she had assistance available. I allowed her to move into a furnished one-bedroom apartment with a six-month cap.

I had a family of seven apply for a three bedroom. I learned that they had been renting a home from his mother. She recently died leaving the home to him and his four siblings. He couldn't get financing to buy out his siblings and the oldest daughter sold the house and distributed the proceeds. Each child received $32,850 from the house sale. The money wasn't enough to make a down payment and they needed help saving some money to purchase a home. I allowed them in for a one-year residency in a three-bedroom unit. There were as many stories as there were people seeking residency.

Over a two-week period, I completed all interviews and filled each apartment except for two furnished one, two- and three-bedroom units that I held out for emergency needs. I was to be the only person to determine eligibility for these units. The tenancy could be from two weeks to six months depending on the need. My purpose was to reach those people that needed more than two weeks, but possibly less than six months or a year to get back on track.

My first emergency application arrived. Shelly had five children less than ten years of age. Her husband abandoned them and Shelly wasn't employed at the time. She couldn't make the house payment. She needed time to complete her degree and get a job to support her children. Her husband was ordered to pay child support, but the amount awarded barely covered the cost of food, clothing and utilities for her family. I could tell that she was a remarkable woman with a lot on her plate. I granted her a three-bedroom furnished apartment and let her know that Amy's Place had funds to pay for her last two college courses. If she needed food or clothing, she could go to Amy's Place for that too.

She asked, "Who is this person Amy?"

I replied, "I am Amy. My grandfather left me a lot of money to help our community. That is exactly what I am doing. In the future, if you find that you have an excess of food, clothing or money, then please donate back to Amy's Place."

I met a family of four. David and Carol Daniels had two twin sons that were five years old. David had a respectable job in St. Louis, but was lured by a local company to accept their job offer. When the family arrived, the company had changed its' mind and no longer had a position available. David had already quit his previous job and needed help until he could re-establish himself and his maintenance business.

I asked David what type of maintenance he did.

He replied, "I had a contract doing apartment maintenance for my last complex."

I asked for references and offered him a job subject to qualifying references. I would offer an apartment as part of the compensation package. Fortunately, he checked out with fabulous references from his former employer. I let Jerry know that we had a full-time maintenance person. I intended to make him our maintenance manager if all worked out. I anticipated a full crew of five maintenance people once the apartments had been in use for a while.

I was genuinely pleased with the apartment rentals. I believe we were fair in our pricing and we would review rental rates in three months. I left the remaining emergency apartments open until needed.

I grabbed Jerry and we made an inspection visit to our AMY sites. I was pleased that we were doing bookings for arbitrations and mediations at four months out. I checked with my Amy's Kourt judges and bailiff and found that Cassandra and Kaylie had everything under control. According to Sandy, the bailiff, both judges were doing a remarkable job. I let both of them know that they would be eligible for positions in AMY after five years of being on the Amy's Kourt bench. I checked with Cynthia and she had everything under control. No surprise there. The facility was nicely decorated and welcoming to people that needed to help someone.

Cynthia was turning eighteen years old and I wanted to give her a very special present. She had fallen in love with a townhome not far from Amy's Place. Cynthia showed me the townhome and said, "Someday I am going to make enough money to buy a townhome for me." I had a surprise for Cynthia. I bought her the townhome and raised her salary to $90,000 a year. Parked in front of the townhome was a new car that she had her eye on. After work, I let Cynthia know that one of my employees lived in the townhome and was hosting a birthday party for her. Cynthia was excited for her birthday, but disappointed that she was only a visitor to the home that she hoped to own one day.

I picked up Cynthia and drove her to the townhome. When we entered, everyone shouted, "Surprise and Happy Birthday". Cynthia looked around and saw living room furniture like she had selected for her future home. The dining room table and chairs was what she wanted as part of her dream home. She ran into the bedrooms and found the bedroom sets that she wanted and the bathrooms were decorated with towels that she had identified. The kitchen was fully stocked with dishes, pots, pans, silverware and glassware. Her pantry was full of foods that she liked to eat. Cynthia grabbed my hand and asked, "Who lives here. This is eerie. She has the same taste as I do."

I gave Cynthia a kiss and said, "You do little sister." Cynthia asked, "All of this including the furnishings?"

I replied, "Everything including the car in the driveway."

Cynthia was so excited that she had to sit down and cry for five minutes just to release her emotions. She was a lot like me in that way. I remembered sitting on the steps to my Kourthouse and crying. Cynthia grabbed my hand and asked to see her car. I handed her the keys and we took a quick trip.

Cynthia asked me, "Why would you do all this for me?"

I replied, "Because I love you and all you are doing for Amy's Place. There is more. I have set aside ten million dollars for you. I just have to figure out how to give it to you without a bunch of taxes. Until then, the money is yours, but please keep it a secret from everyone and especially anyone you are dating. You don't need a boyfriend that only wants access to your money. I loved Cynthia's hugs and kisses."

After taking care of Cynthia, Jerry received word from Patty that she was engaged and planned to marry in less than two months. Patty met her future husband in college. He was studying prelaw like Patty and both wanted to pursue law school. As a wedding present, I offered to purchase Patty a townhome or condo near the college. I also offered to pay her college tuition for law school if she was accepted. To help them off with a good start, Jerry and I decided to give her a wedding present of $50,000.

Jerry asked Patty, "Why the rush to get married. I just learned about Michael and you dating. I like him, but you don't need to rush things." Patty replied, "Dad, I kind of put the cart before the horse. I am pregnant and we want to get married. I'm sorry about this and I hope you understand that I love Michael and we are both excited to get married."

Jerry replied, "I wasn't expecting that. You have my blessing. Are you sure that you don't want to explore any other options like adoption?"

Patty replied, "No. We want this baby. I am only seven weeks along and I can't wait until the baby is born."

Jerry asked, "What about your law school plans?"

Patty replied, "Michael will go and I will take care of the baby. When he graduates, he will take care of our child and I will go to school. We can use daycare when Michael is working."

I let Patty know that she could ask me for help whenever she needed it.

CHAPTER TWENTY-ONE

··

Time Out for Amy

Jerry and I had been going without a break for nearly four years. Much of the time we were apart. It was time for us to have a break. We scheduled a two-week cruise to get away from everything; Well, almost everything. I purchased a satellite phone just in case I was needed. Jerry and I relaxed and talked about all we had accomplished in such a short amount of time. Jerry was curious about my next project, or even if such a project existed on the horizon. I let Jerry know that I had some ideas, but I wasn't ready to share them yet.

I was twenty-seven and Jerry was forty-eight. We talked about a family, but Jerry was a little hesitant. He mentioned Patty's pregnancy and the thought of becoming a father and grandfather at the same time was just a little weird to him.

I asked, "Why would it be weird?" Jerry replied, "No particular reason."

I replied, "So what. You are not old and I am still quite young. I would like to start a family. This vacation would be a good time to get pregnant since we are relaxing and everything is going well back home." Jerry replied, "When I agreed to marry you, I wasn't thinking about starting another family. I was just caught off-guard. Things have been going so well for us that I didn't think you wanted children. I'm not sure I want to start over with more children. I just want to be with you. We have been good business partners. I don't think I could handle starting a new family."

I was upset and replied, "Well, I do want two children. I will have two children with or without you."

Jerry replied, "And what does that mean?"

I replied, "Just as I said. You are my husband and we will have two children; or, well, I will figure out what later."

Jerry replied, "That sounds like you are threatening me with divorce if I don't agree to have children. Why can't you accept how things currently are? We are great business partners. Why ruin our successful relationship?" I refused to reply. I had learned over the years that silence often speaks more loudly than words can convey. I told Jerry that the topic was closed and he wasn't to bring it up again on the cruise. I was so disappointed that Jerry was being selfish. He liked our lifestyle, but didn't want any more responsibility for a second family. I had a lot to think over while on our cruise. Over the two weeks, I felt Jerry and I drift further apart. Somewhere, we lost communication with one another and it led to me seeking a divorce when we returned home. I was heartbroken, but I saw a side of Jerry that I didn't like and couldn't live with. Jerry made his position clear that he didn't want more children in his life. I began to realize that Jerry confused our marriage with a business arrangement. He wanted me as a business partner more than a wife. I agreed to pay him five million dollars and he returned his interest in our businesses to me. Sadly, our marriage and my fairy tale romance ended.

I turned to Cynthia for moral support. Cynthia was wonderful and supportive. I felt like a loser following my divorce and a complete failure in life. Cynthia grabbed my hand and we skipped through the clothing center and throughout Amy's Place. When the tour was finished, Cynthia said, "Amy, look around you. All of this is because of you and giving to our community. The last thing you are is a loser. You are a wonderful big sister and a champion among those in need of help."

I was feeling the need to get away. I asked Cynthia if she could clear her calendar for one week and we would do something together. We chose a theme park and acted like little girls having fun for the first times in our lives. We held hands, laughed and giggled at the silliest of things. I enjoyed one woman when I heard her say, "Those girls are nuts." Being with Cynthia was what I needed to regroup and energize my mind, body and soul.

I returned to work and decided that I would start at my roots. I visited Amy's Kourt to see how Cassandra and Kaylie were doing as judges. I sat in the visitor's section until the girls saw me. On recess, they handed me my judicial robe and asked me to sit in with them. Cassandra announced to the parties and witnesses that I was Amy, the founder of Amy's Kourt. She will be here to review our work as judges. Please ignore her and pay attention to the judge assigned to your case.

I was so impressed with both girls. Their courtroom demeanor was wonderful. They commanded respect and handled the parties well. Their decisions were accurate and thoughtful. I couldn't say enough for Amy's Kourt operations. I confirmed with Cassandra and Kylie that they would have jobs in the arbitration and mediation services. Based upon their performances, I also assured them that they would start out at $100,000 per year. I had two very happy judges.

I visited our three AMY locations and verified our calendars and the success of each center. I could do nothing more for the centers. The judges and staff had everything under control.

I went through Amy's Place and worked with Janine, the CPA. She reviewed the books with me and showed me how she accounted for donations, expenditures, etc. I was surprised that with donations, Amy's Place was almost breaking even. The two-week tenancies were all doing well and were properly managed under Cynthia's direction.

My last stop was Amy's Place Two. I stopped in and talked with the apartment manager. She was excited to inform me that we were maintaining full occupancy and we had a waiting list. When I set up the initial tenancies, I put each apartment and the associated rent on a spread sheet. I used that as my baseline assuming that some rental rates may go down at the quarter while the majority would hopefully go up.

I asked Margaret, the manager, for her accounting records for monthly rentals and security deposits. Margaret was hesitant, citing that the records were not up to date yet and she would get the complete records to me in a week.

I pulled our banking records and compared our scheduled collections to deposits for months two and three since we were closing in on our first quarter adjustment period. I found an immediate red flag. The rent collected for month two was nearly eleven thousand dollars less than the original rent. I verified with Margaret that we had no move outs or delinquent accounts in the first quarter so rent collection should match the first month's collection. It didn't. I checked for month three and we were short nearly fourteen thousand dollars from scheduled collections. I asked Margaret if I was looking at the data correctly. She agreed, but couldn't understand how we would be missing over twenty-five thousand dollars. She said, I make out the deposit slips and Kelly takes the deposits to the bank on her way home at night. I asked Kelly to come into the office and I explained the missing money. Kelly had no idea what I was talking about. She just took what Margaret gave her and did the deposit.

I asked to meet with Kelly privately. I asked Kelly if she collected cash for rent payments.

She replied, "We get paid in cash all the time."

I asked her if she could guestimate how much cash.

She replied, "That's easy. We write out a cash receipt for any cash payment. The receipt book is in Margaret's office."

I asked her how frequently the deposits she makes include cash. Kelly thought about it and said, "I don't think our deposits include as much cash as we collect. I would have to compare the receipt book to the deposit slips. I make deposits every day the bank is open."

I asked Margaret for the receipt book. Margaret replied, "Here you go."

I opened it and there were only blank receipts in the book. I asked, "Where are the cash receipts for the first three months of operations?"

Margaret replied, "I was auditing our books and I took it home. I couldn't find our receipt book so I bought a new book."

I indicated my understanding. The next day I ordered a copy of all of our deposit slips from the bank. When I received the slips, I noticed that Margaret had deposited a total of first quarter cash to the account of $3,540. I asked Kelly how much cash she would estimate she collected on a weekly basis. She thought approximately $2,500 to $3,000 per week.

I confronted Margaret with the deposit slips and Kelly's information that we collect about $3,000 per week in cash. I asked Margaret if she took the missing $25,000.

Margaret quickly denied any wrongdoing. I mentioned that if I had to prove that she took the money, it will be twice as bad because I will prosecute for theft.

Margaret asked that I please don't get the police involved. She admitted taking $26,400 from cash receipts.

I replied, "How are you going to repay the money you stole?" Margaret replied, "I don't know. I will stay here and work for free until my debt is paid to you."

I replied, "That will not work. I am giving you 24 hours to move your things from your apartment. I will decide if I am going to prosecute you for first degree theft."

I turned to Kelly and asked if she felt capable of being the resident manager.

Kelly smiled and said, "I was born ready to do this job and I promise that I will account for every dime."

I replied, "You are the new manager. I am increasing your salary as well. Let's get an ad out for a new assistant manager. You can hire anyone that you believe is competent to do the job."

I tried to talk with Margaret, but she avoided me and wouldn't return my calls. I had no choice. I referred the matter to the police and Margaret was arrested for grand larceny. Margaret was found guilty and was sentenced to three years in jail and ordered to pay restitution. I felt sorry for her, but she left me no workable options.

I finished up on my whirlwind tour of the Amy businesses and then felt an empty spot inside me. I missed Jerry, or at least the Jerry that I had a crush on since I was nine years old. I had never dated except with Jerry. I had been so busy through my childhood that I wasn't even familiar with dating protocols.

I was having dinner with Cynthia when she suggested that I go to church with her on Sunday. She had been attending a new church and the pastor was really good. He inspired her to keep going to church. I believed in God, but didn't like churches that much. However, for Cynthia, I agreed to go one time. After the service, Cynthia grabbed my hand and said, "Come with me. I want to introduce you to Pastor Stevens."

I met Richard Stevens and complimented him on his sermon. He invited me and Cynthia to stay and join the church group for Sunday dinner. I reluctantly agreed to stay at Cynthia's urging. It was pleasant and I really enjoyed talking with Pastor Stevens.

Cynthia hit me up on Friday and asked if I was going to attend church with her again on Sunday. I agreed. Pastor Stevens was standing by the entry greeting people as they arrived. His sermon was on helping those who need help. He mentioned the church's outreach program to the inner-city youth and his desire to provide food and clothing where needed. He asked the church attendees to dig deep and donate. I wrote out a check for $10,000 and put it in the collection plate.

I received a call from Pastor Stevens the following Monday. He couldn't thank me enough for my generous donation. He asked if we could meet for lunch. I replied, "Sure. Where do you want to meet?"

He replied, "How about the Rectory behind the church. I live there. I would love to fix you lunch and we can talk about your mission to the community. Cynthia filled me in on your life story and your unfortunate divorce. I would like to learn more about you and where you are headed next."

I accepted and Pastor Stevens was an excellent cook. I felt a little uncomfortable eating with a Pastor and he recognized my discomfort and asked me to call him Rick. I found that I was having dinner with Rick after church every Sunday. On occasion, Cynthia would join us with her boyfriend, Taylor. I felt myself being drawn to Rick, but I continued to resist the word called 'love' for fear of being hurt again.

Cynthia stopped by my house and curled up next to me. She said, "Taylor asked me to marry him."

I replied, "What did you say."

Cynthia said, "I haven't said one way or another. I told him that I would love to be married to him, but I had to think about the commitment and talk with you."

I asked, "What is there to talk about. Just don't make the same mistake that I made. Make sure that Taylor is interested in a family if you plan on having children."

Cynthia replied, "I already discussed that. We both want two or three children."

I asked, "Do you love him? By that, I mean do you think about him all the time and want to be with him?"

Cynthia cuddled closer and said, "All the time." I said, "Then say 'yes' and get married."

Cynthia said yes to Taylor and asked Rick to do the marriage ceremony. I was sitting with Rick the following Sunday and we talked about Cynthia's upcoming wedding. I was a little surprised when Rick took my hand and asked me if I would like to consider a dual wedding.

I replied, "Who else is getting married?"

Rick replied, "I would like to marry you if you will accept my hand. I don't make much money as a pastor, but we will do all right."

I had to swallow and tell Rick that I am a little afraid of commitment.

I asked him what he thought about children.

He replied, "I love children and I would love to have two or three children; and I would love to devote myself to you as my wife."

I asked to talk about it with my family. I stopped by Cynthia's townhome and curled up with her and asked, "What do you think about me and Rick getting married?"

Cynthia screamed in excitement and when she finished hugging and kissing me, she asked if we could have a dual wedding.

I replied, "I would want it no other way." I asked Cynthia if she told Rick anything about my money.

She replied, "No. That is no one's business except yours."

I asked that it remain confidential for now. Cynthia promised.

I accepted Rick's proposal. Cynthia and I chose identical wedding dresses. As sisters, we looked like twins anyway and we decided to dress that way.

Our day arrived and we were married just like that. I booked a cruise for all four of us and we had a wonderful two-week getaway. I found Rick to be very loving and understanding. I realized that I loved Rick for what was inside him, where I loved Jerry for what was on the outside. I prayed that my marriage would be a good one and that Cynthia's marriage would be good as well.

CHAPTER TWENTY-TWO

On Becoming Mothers

Our honeymoon cruise brought more than rest and relaxation. Cynthia and I learned that we were both pregnant with approximately the same delivery date. When the doctor confirmed our pregnancies, I held Cynthia and cried briefly. In the back of my mind I kept thinking how selfish Jerry had been. Cynthia would make me face reality and I was excited for her and me.

I spent much of my time at Amy's Place, if for no other reason than Cynthia was there for me to talk with. I would have lunch with Rick daily and I would fix dinner for when he was off work. Much of Rick's time was spent at baptisms, funerals and interventions. Rick was a very caring individual and he was very pleased with Amy's Place. At the time of our marriage, Rick knew nothing about Amy's Kourt, AMY centers and Amy's Place Two. I didn't hide the information. It just never came up that I owned everything.

Rick asked me if we should consider a larger home since we were starting a family. I thought that might be a good idea, but I wanted to build two homes, one for us and one for Cynthia and her family. I want us to be next door neighbors. Rick thought it was a wonderful idea. He then asked the big question, "How are we to pay for the land and construction of the two houses?"

I replied, "Rick, sit down. We need to talk." Rick removed his jacket and cleric collar and said, "I am all ears. What do you want to talk about?"

I said, "Money."

Rick replied, "Good idea. We need to figure out how to qualify for a construction loan. We could sell your existing house and apply the proceeds to the construction loan."

I replied, "I don't think we need to go to that extreme. I haven't told you before now, and I am sorry. I inherited a lot of money."

Rick asked, "How much is a lot?"

I replied, "Oh, about $534,000,000 in total holdings. Rick asked, "How did you acquire such a fortune?"

I replied, "From my grandfather that loved me as a granddaughter. He left me all but two million dollars of his estate. In addition to these funds, I also own AMY, which is comprised of three arbitration and mediation centers across the state. I also own Amy's Kourthouse and Amy's Place Two Apartments. My total net worth is $552,448,000."

Now, do you think that we can afford to build two homes side by side for two sisters that love each other and want to live close to each other?"

Rick simply said, "Praise God."

I hired an architect to design two homes that were connected by an indoor swimming pool. Cynthia and I sat with the architect for hours discussing what we wanted. Cynthia and I thought alike and we decided to make our houses identical. Each home would be 4,700 square feet on a single floor. We would have four bedrooms and five full bathrooms. Each bathroom would have double sinks and a large walk-in shower and Jacuzzi tub. The kitchen would have granite counters and all appliances would be stainless steel. We selected dark cherry as cabinet wood for kitchen cabinets and vanities. Each home would have an office, theater and exercise area. Our homes were designed to allow access through an inside corridor that connected both homes without having to go outside. Each home could access the swimming pool.

The architect put together the building plans and I instructed my construction company to start work once the permits were issued.

Rick asked, "You own a construction company too?"

I replied, "It was grandfather's company that I inherited."

Cynthia and I would drive by the site daily and get excited as the buildings were taking shape. It took the contractor six months to finish the job because of the many changes that Cynthia and I made as the job progressed. My construction superintendent said, "Amy, it's good that you own this company. Your changes would have cost a regular customer a fortune in time loss, etc."

I replied, "Then let's be thankful that I own this company."

The superintendent said that we were three weeks from final inspection and occupancy. That was the news that Cynthia and I had been waiting on. We began shopping for our new homes. Our tastes were identical on most things. We disagreed on some lamps and Cynthia wanted love seats in her theater room where I wanted vibrating single chairs.

Our timing was near perfect. Cynthia and I were in our ninth month of pregnancy when we moved into our new homes. We invited mom and dad to our homes once they were fully set up and had a really nice house warming party. After that, it was counting the days and minutes before we would deliver. The doctor told Cynthia that she would deliver on June 9 and I would deliver about June 11 based on his best estimate of our pregnancies. We joked about delivering at the same time.

Cynthia called me on June 7th and said, "Amy, my water broke and I can't reach Taylor. He is on a jobsite and is not answering his phone." I replied, "Stay there. I will be over to get you in two minutes." I ran as best I could to get to Cynthia. I grabbed her suitcase and figured that Taylor could bring the infant car seat when he came to the hospital. I was carrying

Cynthia's suitcase and helping her to my car when my water broke. Cynthia asked, "What now?"

I replied, "We are going to make it to the hospital. I am wet, but no bad contractions. I can drive us." Cynthia and I arrived at the hospital and valet parking took our car and promised to deliver Cynthia's suitcase to the hospital front desk. I wasn't worried about my suitcase. I wasn't going anywhere too quickly myself. I began calling Rick and finally reached him at the cemetery. He said that he would get my suitcase and both infant car seats and meet us at the hospital.

I requested that the hospital put Cynthia and me in the same delivery room. We laughed and occasionally screamed when contractions hit. Cynthia's contractions were much worse than mine and made me wonder if I might not be ready to deliver. The nurse checked both of us for dilation and let us hear our babies' heartbeats to reassure us that all sounded fine.

At 4:40 pm Rick showed up and let me know that he reached Taylor and he was on his way. Taylor arrived at 5:24 pm. At 5:54 Cynthia began to deliver her child and at 5:59 my child decided to depart. Our children were both listed as being born at 6:03 pm. Cynthia and I both had little girls. I decided to name my daughter Cynthia and she decided to name her daughter Amy. I looked at Cynthia and said, "We did it!"

In anticipation of our births, I had Cynthia hire a manager for Amy's Place until she was ready, if ever, to return to work. I wanted her focused on being a mother and spending more time with me and my daughter. I guess I was a little selfish that way, but I loved having Cynthia around me. We were having a bar-b-que one evening when Taylor mentioned that they were living on his paycheck which was fine. He was concerned that his check covered all expenses, but didn't allow any retirement savings.

I looked at Cynthia and said, "You haven't told Taylor yet, have you?" Cynthia replied, "No, you said to keep it quiet for now and that is what I did."

Taylor asked, "Keep what quiet?"

Cynthia asked, "Do I tell Taylor now or when?"

I said, "Feel free to tell him now if that is your desire." Cynthia said, "Taylor, sit down please."

He asked, "Why?"

Cynthia said, "Because I don't want you to fall down. That's why?" He asked, "Are you pregnant again?"

Cynthia replied, "No. I want to talk with you about money. You need to understand that I have a kind of trust fund that is being held for my benefit by Amy."

Taylor asked, "What is the trust fund for?"

Cynthia laughed and said, "Silly, it's for me. Amy is holding ten million dollars for me. I can have more at any time I want it so don't worry about how much you make. Work because you enjoy working. I am going to enjoy being a mother for a while."

Taylor asked, "How did Amy get ten million dollars to give to you?" I replied, "From my grandfather. I inherited close to $540,000,000 dollars."

Taylor asked, "Is that how you were able to establish Amy's Place and Amy's Place Two?"

I replied, "Yes; from grandfather's estate. He entrusted me to use his money to help those that need help. That is why we have Amy's Place and Amy's Place Two."

Taylor asked, "Do Cynthia and I have access to the ten million dollars?"

I replied, "Only through me. I am holding the funds in trust for Cynthia. The money is hers, but I am keeping it under my protection as her trustee."

Taylor appeared somewhat irritated and asked, "Are you keeping Cynthia's money because you don't trust me?"

I replied, "Absolutely not. If I give her the money outright, I will have to pay approximately 55% in taxes which is ridiculous. I would rather give it to her as she needs it and avoid the taxes. I think Cynthia is well-cared for and she doesn't need the money."

Taylor replied, "Still, it would be nice if she could have her own money if it is hers."

Cynthia replied, "Taylor, drop it. I don't need or want the money right now. Besides, you should understand that it is my separate property that I owned before our marriage."

Taylor replied, "Fine. I will drop it, but it doesn't seem very fair to me that Amy won't let you have your money."

Cynthia replied, "Taylor, that's untrue. I told you that I don't need or want the money right now. Drop it please – Now!"

Taylor changed after learning about Cynthia's money. He seemed to be fixated on getting his hands on at least part of the money. He would ask Cynthia to ask me for one million, or five hundred thousand, etc. Cynthia refused, and the more she refused his suggestions, the angrier he became on the subject. He threatened Cynthia with a divorce if she refused to get part of the ten million from me now. He said, "If I divorce you, I will get half of the ten million since we are a community property state." Cynthia came to me crying. She let me know about what Taylor said about divorce and I explained that it might be the best answer. He has changed because of the money and I am so sorry that this has happened to your marriage.

Rick promised to talk with Taylor about his divorce threat. Taylor threatened Rick to stay out of his business. When Rick pushed, Taylor threw Rick out of their home and threatened him if he returned.

The following morning, Cynthia was carrying Amy and ran crying into my home. Her lip was bleeding as well as her ear and eye. Taylor struck her because she refused to demand her money from me. I apologized to Cynthia, but said, "I am calling the police for domestic violence."

Cynthia said, "No or he will be worse the next time. He promised me that he would hurt Amy next time. He was talking about our daughter; not you."

I called the police anyway and then I called Dad. Dad entered a temporary restraining order against Taylor and the police did the same thing. Taylor was charged with third degree assault and domestic violence. He was warned by the court that if he disobeyed the restraining order that he would be put in jail.

Taylor was released on his own recognizance and that night he showed up and beat Cynthia breaking a tooth and her jaw. He broke her left arm and dumped Amy's crib over causing Amy to fall onto the floor. Cynthia screamed for help and I heard her. I asked Rick to call 911 and I went into Cynthia with my pepper spray as a weapon. Taylor heard me coming and tried to grab me from behind. I turned quickly and sprayed the pepper spray directly into his eyes and mouth. He was screaming. I looked at Cynthia and I planted my foot into his groin and then helped Cynthia and Amy over to our house while Rick remained with Taylor.

The police arrested Taylor and charged him with second degree assault on Cynthia and little Amy and me. He was held without bail this time and at trial he was convicted of second-degree assault and was sentenced to eighteen years behind bars. I took care of little Amy while Cynthia was getting her jaw and teeth fixed. Cynthia was looking in the mirror with me and she began to cry because she no longer was pretty like me. I promised Cynthia that she would recover and we would look like twins once again.

Cynthia filed for and was granted a divorce from Taylor. The judge ruled that all of Cynthia's property from her house to the furnishings and money belonged to Cynthia as her separate property and Taylor received nothing except his last paycheck and his half of the tax return for that year. Cynthia spent most nights living in our home. She felt safe with me and our children could play together while we visited. I loved having her with me daily. She filled my life with happiness. Besides, she was a great shopper and we both loved to go shopping.

The young lawyer that handled Cynthia's divorce asked if he could take her out to dinner now that the divorce was over. Cynthia thought about it, but decided to not date anyone that knew about her trust funds. It just seemed a little safer to her.

Rick announced one evening that his younger brother just graduated from divinity school and would be taking on the job of associate pastor at Rick's church. I knew that Rick had a brother, but I didn't know that he was in the divinity education program. Rick asked if he could invite Jason to dinner.

I replied, "As always, the more the merrier. I would like to meet Pastor Jason."

Rick replied, "Just call him Jason."

Jason was twenty-two years old and was as charming and thoughtful as Rick was. He became a regular guest at our home. Over a year, I could see Cynthia and Jason moving closer to each other. They began dating while I babysat Amy."

Almost a year to the first meeting, Jason asked Cynthia to marry him. He said, "I don't make much money, but I will love you from morning light to night fall and through all of the tomorrows yet to come in our lives if you will marry me."

Cynthia told me, "I cried and accepted Jason's proposal. I thought if Jason is half the wonderful man that Rick is, then I will have a future full of happiness."

I hugged Cynthia and told her that she would have a wonderful marriage. I joked, "Two sisters marrying two brothers. It has got to be a good mix."

Jason asked Cynthia, "Where would you like to live once we are married. We can't continue to live with your sister and my brother."

Cynthia replied, "Did you see the identical house next door to my sister's home?"

Jason replied, "Yes, why?"

Cynthia said, "That is my home. I have been living with Amy and Rick since I was assaulted. I didn't want to live alone so I have been living with them. When we are married, we will occupy my home. It is exactly like's Amy's house if you are wondering."

Jason asked, "How can you afford such an expensive house at your age?"

Cynthia replied, "Amy built the house. Technically, she owns it, but it is my house to use forever."

Jason replied, "I think we will enjoy living next door."

Cynthia and I took Jason on a tour of her house while Rick watched our children. All Jason could say was, "You're right, it is nearly identical."

I replied, "We are sisters and we think alike."

Jason commented, "The two of you look like twins"

Cynthia responded, "Do you really think so. I was afraid that I would never return to being as cute as Amy is."

I hugged Cynthia and said, "You look like my double or I am your double. Just call us double trouble."

CHAPTER TWENTY-THREE

Cynthia Is Getting Married & More

Jason and Cynthia set June 3rd for their wedding date. There was nothing magical about the date. It just happened to be a date that the church had an opening for a wedding. Rick agreed to do the ceremony and Cynthia wanted a very small wedding. She invited mom and dad, Gary, Tom, Steven, me, and Jason's parents. I was Cynthia's bridesmaid and dad escorted her down the aisle. I did all of the flower and reception arrangements with Cynthia. Her wedding went beautifully and she and Jason took a three-week cruise for their honeymoon. I offered to watch Amy, but Cynthia said, "We are a family and she is going with us on our honeymoon."

While Cynthia was away, you could say that Rick and I played. I wasn't sure, but my suspicion was that I was pregnant again. I needed to wait and see if I had my next cycle. When Cynthia returned from her honeymoon, she acted like something was up with her. I hugged her and said, "Spill it sister."

Cynthia laughed and said, "I am not sure, but I may be pregnant. I should have had my cycle a week ago, but nothing. I am waiting to see if it comes this month."

I replied, "Can I wait with you? I think I might be pregnant too." Neither Cynthia nor I had our cycles the next month. We scheduled OB/GYN appointments and the doctor confirmed that we were both pregnant. She wasn't exactly sure, but estimated both of us between six and seven weeks. The doctor asked us if we had this planned.

I replied, "No, it just happened this way."

The doctor replied, "I remember you both from your first pregnancy and delivering at the same time. It looks like you are shooting for a repeat matchup. I would estimate that you will be delivering around June 5."

Cynthia said, "I truly hope so. Just think if our kids have the same birthdays again."

The doctor asked, "When the time comes, do you want to know the sex of your babies? I recall last time you didn't want to know."

We both said, "No, let it be a surprise."

Cynthia and I spent most every day together. We would walk through our various business holdings to keep everyone honest, and then enjoy the rest of our day as pregnant women. Our first-born daughters were approaching two years old as our delivery date arrived. Cynthia and I kept the phone on quick dial to the church just in case our water(s) broke. It would take our husbands less than ten minutes to get home and take us to the hospital.

We sat through June 5th, but no action. I expected something at night and we were sleeping on plastic absorbing pads just in case our water broke at night. We sat through June 6th and nothing so we went to bed expecting another day. At 11:40 pm my water broke. I called Cynthia and she got so excited that she jumped up off her bed and her water broke. We were both in the hospital on June 7th when we delivered our second children. Cynthia and I had a boy this time. We decided to name my son Rick and Cynthia's son Jason. All of our children were born on June 7th. I thought that would make for an interesting birthday program in the future.

Cynthia and I were talking and she asked me what I thought about Jason adopting Amy.

I replied, "I thought it was a good idea, but you will need to get Taylor's consent before the adoption can be approved."

Cynthia asked, "How am I supposed to do that. He is in prison and I can't talk with him."

I suggested we have Dad talk with him. Dad agreed, but found that Taylor wasn't interested unless he got something for doing the release.

Dad told him that he couldn't pay him anything to facilitate an adoption. It was against the law. Dad asked him to do something decent for his daughter and quit being such a jerk. Dad started walking away when Taylor replied, "I will sign it. The kid will be in high school before I get out of here anyway." Dad had the form and had the prison notary witness Taylor's signature. Dad handled the step-parent adoption for us and in no time at all, Taylor was out of our lives for good.

I wasn't so lucky. We were having a three- and one-year old birthday celebration when Jerry showed up asking to talk with me for a moment. Rick asked him to leave, but he insisted he had to talk with me. I agreed to sit on the porch and hear what Jerry had to say.

Jerry stated, "In short, I need more money from you."

I asked, "What happened to the five million I gave you in our divorce?" He replied, "I made some bad investments and then tried to make up my losses gambling. I not only lost all of my money, I am in debt to loan sharks that are threatening to break my legs or worse if I don't come up with the $700,000 that I owe them. Interest is about $10,000 per day and I need help now. Will you help me Amy? I treated you well over the years. I wish I would have agreed to a family with you. I have regretted my position ever since."

I said, "If I give you this money, then the next time you mess up you are going to be back for more. I am not feeding your bad habits. I'm sorry, but you need to live with the consequences of your own actions. You know that as a former judge. Maybe you can borrow the money from some of your friends or your old law firm."

Jerry replied, "I have tried everyone before coming to you. I never wanted you to know that I screwed up my life so badly."

I agreed to pay the debt directly to the loan shark. The full debt was $750,500 and I paid it in full and told the lender to make no more loans to Jerry because he lacked the ability to repay it and I am not helping him again. I turned to Jerry and said, "Understand me clearly. This is it. We are finished. Please never contact me again. If you do, I will obtain a restraining order."

Jerry replied, "You ungrateful little bitch."

I felt some remorse for Jerry, but I made my point clear to him. I didn't want him in my life beyond that point.

With our children, Amy and Cynthia, turning three years old, Cynthia and I decided that we would start them in a preschool setting. We visited five different preschools that appeared to be nothing more than daycare with a little education thrown in. That was not what we were looking for. One of the day care directors suggested we try the Montessori school at the other end of town. We checked it out and the education program appeared interesting, but the center had a waiting list. The only other dedicated preschool in town also had a waiting list.

I decided that our community needed another private school that would start with preschool and go through eighth grade for now and possibly high school later on. I put a half page ad in the newspaper explaining that I planned to start a new private school and I was soliciting the interest of our community. I asked, "If you would be interested in a private school setting for your children, preschool through eighth grade, then return the expression of interest form or email us at Amy@ Amyschools.org. I let Cynthia know that if we get a good response, then we will build a private school.

The responses to our newspaper ad were almost immediate. We were receiving interest by email and regular mail daily. At the end of the data collection period, we had 127 interested families. I forgot to ask for the children's ages and grades. I hired a woman to telephone every person that submitted an expression of interest form and determine the number of students, their ages and grade in school this year.

I remembered the abandoned elementary school and I had Gary, my construction superintendent, walk through the building with me and determine if the school could be upgraded as a school, or should we build a new structure. He believed that the plumbing was old and had been sitting unused; the roof was leaking and needed replacement; the gymnasium hardwood needed replacement; the boiler needed rebuilding and the kitchen was in total disrepair, etc.

I replied, "OK, I will get plans drawn for a new campus and find the land for the school." According to our interest results, we would need three preschool classrooms through fifth grade and several classrooms for sixth through eighth for required course subject matter. I decided to build forty classrooms of different configurations depending on the age slated for the room. For example, small toilets and vanities in the preschool through second grade rooms. Lower chalk boards and smaller desks. I wanted all of the classrooms carpeted with indoor/outdoor carpeting for comfort and sound reduction.

The lot I chose was next to Rick and Jason's church. The owner had been hoping the church would buy it to construct additional church facilities, like classrooms. When the owners learned that I was buying the lot, they quickly sold to me. The lot was five acres which was all that I required to construct a school under the state licensing rules.

Cynthia asked me, "Will the school be called Amy's School or Amy's Academy to be consistent with the other holdings?"

I replied, "Not this time. I plan to call the school "The Theodore Burns Academy and Pre-school. None of this would have been possible without grandfather's gift to me."

Cynthia asked, "What will we be charging for tuition?"

I replied, "Our school system will be a not for profit enterprise and we will charge families on an ability to pay tuition. I want to make quality education a part of every family in our community regardless of their ability to pay. If that means building one or two more schools in the future then I will do that too."

Cynthia asked, "What about teachers. When do we begin interviewing teachers?"

I replied, "When the curriculum is established. I am not looking for run of the mill certified teachers that read out of a text book or canned curriculum. Especially in grades five through eight, I want teachers that have specific degrees and work experience in the field of study. For math, I want engineers and accountants as teachers. In writing and grammar, I want published authors, lawyers and writing consultants that put into practice what they teach. I want public speakers, such as press spokesman teaching speech. I want our military men and women and historians teaching history and I want actual scientists to teach biology and chemistry and physics. Finally, I want someone that loves art and has worked with art and created art professionally through multi-media outlets. I want illustrators and draftsman teaching mechanical drawing and architectural studies and lastly, I want musicians that live their music to teach music appreciation."

Cynthia said, "Sounds very nice. Won't those types of teachers cost a lot of money to get on staff?"

I replied, "I will pay what I need to pay to have the best and the brightest teachers on staff. In terms of cost, just think about our children and the cost to their education if we hired mediocre certified teachers. I want teachers that are alive and excited about educating children. We have ten months to put together our curriculum and select teachers. Little sister, you and I have a lot of work to do."

I wrote out job information and posted it at the colleges and everywhere that I could garner the right type of teacher. I sent a news announcement to the newspaper and local television news. Cynthia and I appeared on television and talked about the school and the type of teachers we were soliciting. I made it a point of saying that we would pay a teacher commensurate with their training and ability. I let potential applicants know that they didn't need to be certified teachers to apply.

I immediately received expressions of interest from five certified teachers looking for work. All five had a degree in elementary education and were certified. None of them had any specialized training and as far as I was concerned, they would contribute little to the school. They were looking for a canned education program that they would teach their little piece of the puzzle.

My first professional applicant was a lawyer that retired after thirty years of practicing law. He had thirty years of professional writing of legal briefs, correspondence, demand letters, etc. He was willing to work for $5,000 a month which was wonderful. I tentatively hired him, subject to a second interview. He would be available when the school year started and he was excited to teach writing to any grade in the school.

I received word from a retired math professor that she would like to be considered for employment. I wasn't sure given the fact that the college professors were all accustomed to teaching out of a course book. I took her information and let her know that I would be doing interviews shortly and I would contact her.

I received an application from an architect that had thirty years of work designing buildings. He was a licensed structural engineer and taught engineering and math previously. He asked me what text he would be using.

I replied, "I'm not sure. I want original thought taught to our students. I want them to understand math and how to use it in real life situations. As an example, Johnny is told to clean out the gutter on the front of his house. He has to select a ladder to do the job. His father has a six-foot, eight foot and ten-foot ladder. The gutter is eight feet off the ground. Which ladder would be best for Johnny to use?"

Gary, the engineer said, "I would teach that Johnny use Pythagorean's Theorem - $a^2 + b^2 = c^2$. We already know that the vertical distance to the gutter is eight feet. If the base feet of the ladder was moved back six feet for safety, then the formula would be $6^2 + 8^2 =$ square root of 100 or the ten-foot ladder. You would use Euclidean Geometry for many practical applications arising daily. I would teach the students how to use math instead of just learning about math."

I asked what he would want in terms of compensation. He replied, "Would $70,000 a year be too much?"

I said, "No it wouldn't. You are exactly who I am looking for. I need two more math teachers. Do you know anyone that is looking for work?" He replied, "I have a very close friend that just retired and is already bored. He is an actuary and has a master's degree in physics and math."

I asked him to make the referral.

I received an application from a woman that had been doing volunteer teaching through the local community center. She taught art, drama and music appreciation. She said that she didn't have a teaching degree, but she had been teaching her courses for the past seventeen years. She would like the opportunity to teach at our school. Once again, she was the type of teacher I was looking for. I asked her what she would like to teach full time.

She replied, "Would $30,000 be acceptable?"

I hugged her and said it would be fine and I welcomed her on board for the fall.

Rick let me know that our church had a historian that lived in our district. She had been the church historian for thirty-six years and had a master's degree in history and geography.

I interviewed her and she was such a wealth of historical knowledge, both from her life experiences, and from what she studied for thirty-six years. She knew U.S. History forward and backward and followed world history as it changed on a daily basis. She had one of those pleasing personalities that endeared the listener to keep listening. I asked her how much she would ask to teach history on a full-time basis. I reiterated that I don't expect you to teach from a text book. I want the children to learn history and government in a real practical life setting. I just want accurate history taught.

She replied, "I have never worked for money before. I really don't need much. How about $1,000 a month?"

I laughed and said, "$2,500 a month it is."

Cynthia and I were walking through town and decided to take our children into a "paint and bake" ceramic store. While there, I watched this amazing man and woman running around teaching their visitors about color, balance, and style. They were wearing aprons covered with paint and dried clay. They had a sculpture section and a mold section. They taught drawing with pen, pencil and chalk and taught still life drawing once a month at the local community college. They taught the history of art from cave drawings through the Renaissance to impressionist art, to cubism and modern drawing.

I asked to talk with one of them. They asked that we come back after their class was finished. He explained that we don't get that many students so when we have them, we take care of them.

Cynthia and I grabbed lunch and returned to talk. The shop was empty and they were cleaning up. I asked about their backgrounds. He had been a sculptor and painter. She had taught art at the college level before relocating to our community. She explained that there were no teaching jobs at the college.

I asked if they would be interested in teaching art at our school. We had planned a full art department from painting to sculpting. We will even have a kiln oven to finish off pottery. You will be teaching preschoolers to eighth grade students. I want art appreciation. I want our students taught about art and how it has changed. If someone asks one of our student's what cubism or expressionist art is, then I want our students to be able to answer. The younger children should learn color, shapes, contrasts and whatever you believe will enrich their appreciation for art. I want planned creativity, but please no textbook lectures.

He asked, "What would the job pay. We have a lease on this shop for one year. I told them that I would buy out their lease if needed, but the school won't be ready until fall anyway. I would pay each one $50,000 a year to teach art full time.

They gladly accepted, but then remembered that they were not certified teachers.

I replied, "That is exactly why I want you to teach. I want open minded teachers that are not afraid to teach and challenge students."

They replied, "You have your teachers."

It took Cynthia and me five months to locate our teachers. I was pleased because only one of our teachers was a certified teacher and she had been a school principal for the last fourteen years. I hired her as the school Administrator. She was very open minded and believed in learning objectively through application of knowledge and not being limited to what the textbooks taught.

As we began to accept enrollments, we began receiving questions about the philosophy of the school; was it a religious institution, etc. I explained that our school was eclectic and we incorporated many educational theories that worked in the real world. I would explain that our teachers were practitioners in their subject before becoming a teacher. I was astounded that so many parents were concerned that we didn't have certified teachers on hand. I had to explain why so many times that I felt like I was giving a speech. Cynthia tired of the question and would kindly let parents know that the public school was full of certified teachers and they could enroll their students there. My favorite saying was, "Those that can't do; teach." I employed doers and I was proud of our school.

School opened timely and we had a full enrollment of 510 students from preschool through eighth grade. Cynthia and I decided that our students would wear uniforms consisting of dark pants or skirt, white shirt, stripped tie, black shoes and socks and a maroon blazer or sweater with Theodore Burns Academy insignia on the breast of the sweater or blazer. To lessen the expense, I purchased the clothing in bulk reducing the charge to our parents by fifty five percent of cost. Our students looked impressive. I could only hope that our teachers made the education impressive.

After the first two weeks of school, Cynthia and I walked through the school and listened to the different teachers. We saw children fixated on their teachers with hands raised and actively participating in the learning process. Our students appeared to be excited about school. We stayed until school was over and talked with some of the students about the school. We heard all very positive remarks and excitement for the next day. One boy said, "Last year I hated school. This school is great. I have learned so much already."

I hugged Cynthia and said, "Once again we did it."

Our best gauge of how the school was doing was our own children in preschool. Amy and Cynthia wouldn't stop talking about preschool and the fun they were having. We noted that they had already been learning colors, shapes, counting and beginning word sounds. They had story time and games. They liked art and playing with clay and colors. Our children looked forward to school every day.

Once the dust settled, and tuition was fully collected, our accountant determined that we would lose close to $300,000 this year.

I smiled and said, "That's not too bad for a startup school. We were generous with the tuition this year. Next year we will tighten up a little more to reduce the shortfall. What is important is that children had an alternative school to attend that would help them excel in life. We took about 470 students from the local school district. The district was quite unhappy with my school and threatened to cancel out Amy's School Kourt.

I replied, "That program has been a tremendous success. I hope you don't retaliate just because I want to provide a different type of education to see how my school compares to schools taught by certified teachers. If my ideas are proven correct, I would hope that the public schools would consider hiring qualified individuals to teach instead of certified teachers that have no real-world experience."

He replied, "I am not canceling the school Kourt program. I am just frustrated because of the funding hit we took when we lost so many students. Our teachers have teaching contracts and get paid whether they teach or not. I have eighteen teachers receiving pay while they sit at home. That is why I am frustrated."

CHAPTER TWENTY-FOUR

We Aren't Done Yet

C ynthia became my day companion. We spent most days together going to parks and getting our children to where they needed to be. Things like swimming lessons and gymnastics took big bites out of our day, three days a week.

I was visiting with Cynthia when I observed an elderly woman open a garbage can at the park and remove some food that a family recently dumped into the can. The woman had to be in her seventies. She carefully picked up the food and wrapped it in her scarf. I watched her visit several other cans before she left the park. I observed an elderly man watching two business men eating their lunches at the picnic table next to him. He was staring at their food and looked hungry and acted like he was waiting on the men to toss part of their lunch for him. He reminded me of the hungry birds waiting for scraps.

I asked Cynthia, "Why are our seniors hunting for food? I need to ask them what is going on."

Cynthia replied, "Please don't embarrass them. Our seniors have their pride, but often not much else once their social security check is spent. Jason tells me all the time that the church is hit up for donations for food and money that seniors need."

I asked, "Doesn't the food bank offer food for seniors?"

Cynthia replied, "It does, but most of their food needs to be cooked and many of the seniors lack the ability to cook and make their own meals. If they don't qualify for Medicaid or other programs, then they are lost to the system."

I did some investigation of the food banks and service industries. We had one mission that provided meals for twenty people nightly. It was a first come-first served basis. That was it. I sat at the park with Cynthia and I asked the woman why she was going through garbage cans.

She replied, "I gotta eat, don't I?"

I asked her why she wasn't going to the food bank for food.

She replied, "I don't have a car and most of their food needs cooking first. I ain't got no cooking stoves no more. I live underneath the overpass in my box. There is no help for people like me so I help myself. Sometimes, like today, I get lucky. Someone threw out most of a sandwich. I can eat this tonight and tomorrow morning."

I asked the man why he wasn't going to the food bank. I mentioned that I saw him watching people eat and commented that he looked hungry. I handed him a sandwich and he explained that the food bank had very little he could use. It was too far to walk and he couldn't carry a full bag of food anyway.

I talked with Rick, Cynthia and Jason that night and asked their opinion on opening up a large senior's center for our neighborhood. Possibly two centers with one on each side of town.

Rick asked, "What do you intend to do with the centers?"

I said, "What else. I want to see that those in need get hot meals and have a place to visit and regain some dignity. I don't care if the seniors come from the highlands or from the streets. I want to make sure that they can get something to eat a couple times a day."

The vote was unanimous. Jason thought the senior center would alleviate some of the pressure put on the church for handouts.

Rick asked me if I intended to become a full-service social agency. I replied, "I intend to do what I believe grandfather would have wanted me to do. He hated seeing people suffer and go hungry. He was the largest contributor to the food banks and you know how he helped me create Amy's Place."

I contacted our architect and explained that I wanted to construct a senior center that would have a full service kitchen and dining room for at least fifty guests; a card and game room; male and female bathrooms and showers; laundromat; television and movie room; a social center for visiting, reading and having coffee and a medical room for visiting physicians.

He asked, "How much do you want to spend?"

I replied, "As much as is needed to provide what I just said."

He drew up the plans and did a detail spec sheet. I contacted my construction superintendent and said, "I have another job for you to do."

Gary replied, "What this time boss?"

I met with Gary and reviewed the plans and specifications. I had located the land and had already obtained the building permits.

He replied, "I can have this built in four months if the weather holds."

I said, "You know what to do. Let's get it done. I want it open, especially with winter coming soon."

I was very proud to announce to the media that the Theodore Burns Senior Center was opening for business on December 4th. I explained that we would be serving free lunch from 11am to 1pm and free dinner daily from 5pm to 7pm. I laid out the amenities and let the seniors know that the center would remain open until 11pm daily and then reopen at 7am. I bought bulk peanuts and bulk candy and we put in a popcorn machine for free popcorn. We had a soda pop dispenser that dispensed free water and pop. We had coffee and tea served in real ceramic mugs. I bought ten dozen donuts for morning coffee. Our center manager mentioned that all of our peanuts and candy disappeared within the first hour of operation. He saw seniors filling pockets with nuts, candy and popcorn, he assumed because of the fear that there would be none the next day. I insisted that we keep filling the bowls and after the first month, seniors began to realize that the bowls would remain full and they didn't need to hoard food. Our donuts didn't seem to last much beyond 8:00 am. Our manager pleaded with guests to eat one donut and leave the rest for someone else. He tried.

Once the center was fully operational, I purchased a food service van that delivered sandwiches to seniors that for whatever reason wouldn't come into the senior center.

Cynthia noticed that seniors were taking showers at the center and then putting on their same dirty clothing. I had Amy's Place deliver pants, shirts, shoes and coats to the senior center for those in need. Over time, we determined the scope of the need for shoes, pants, shirts, socks, underwear, sweaters and coats. I began to see some dignity returning to our forgotten elders and it felt good. They were clean and better dressed. They seemed to enjoy visiting over coffee or tea and telling stories of days gone by. To me, it was perfect. Based upon our food truck assessment, we were reaching most of the seniors in the area and the driver didn't think an additional center was needed at this time. I concurred.

My accountant let me know that the senior center was costing my organization $19,000 per month to operate. I incorporated as a not for profit and began receiving donations to help offset the cost of operation. To me, $19,000 a month to bring dignity to a large group of seniors was an excellent way to use grandfather's money.

When Cynthia and I were at the park, we noticed that there were no seniors lurking around waiting for food to be dropped, etc. We were serving an average of sixty-eight meals at lunch and seventy-seven at dinner. We delivered 250 sandwiches daily to seniors that didn't come into the center. I followed the truck one day and noticed that seniors had identified the truck route and were waiting for their daily sandwich. I thought how perfect and hugged Cynthia for all her support.

I was making my rounds at Amy's Place and I touched base with the two-week emergency tenants that were seeking additional time because of their inability to find work. I authorized a six-month tenancy in one of the furnished apartments to enable more time to find work for this family. Before leaving, the site manager asked me to talk with Jennifer, a single mother that was also looking for work. She explained that she was receiving assistance as a single mother, but the assistance wasn't enough to pay rent and her other expenses. She was on her third two-week emergency placement at Amy's Place. I moved her to a single bedroom furnished unit for six months. I knew that reserving some units would come in handy for such emergencies.

That evening I brainstormed job hunting ideas with Rick, Cynthia and Jason. Unfortunately, none of them had ever looked for work in the traditional way leaving me to my own ideas. I decided that it was best to form a coalition of business leaders to discuss the problem. I was becoming well-known throughout our region and most business owners knew that I inherited grandfather's wealth.

To form the coalition, I called Mr. Knowles and Mr. Poole and invited them to lunch. Both gentlemen had helped me get started with Amy's Kourt by donating $5,000 each. I explained that I needed another donation, not of money, but of job opportunities. I asked them how I can find jobs for people that were truly looking for jobs. I explained about my families, single parents and discharged service men and women presently being serviced in one of our centers.

Mr. Knowles replied, "I am chairman of the Downtown Business Owner's Association. I can arrange to have you as a guest speaker at our next association meeting."

Mr. Poole explained, "I am a director in the Christian Business Owner's Association. I have direct pathways to churches and Christian business owners. I can arrange to have you speak to our membership as well."

I let Mr. Poole know that my husband was Pastor Rick Stevens and Cynthia's husband was Pastor Jason Stevens. They are members of his Association.

Mr. Poole smiled and said, "It doesn't surprise me that you would be married to a man of God. You are truly an angel on earth."

I scheduled talks for both groups. I was surprised that there were so many members in each association. I explained that I wanted to create an employment center and I wanted the business community to place their job announcements with my center. I mentioned that I had accountants, book keepers, secretaries, laborers and military personnel that all were seeking honest employment. I propose to create a profile for each applicant and I would want each business listing to include a detailed profile of the type of applicant you are seeking for your job opening. I have an IT person that will set up a data base for my agency to match profiles of applicants and your job requirements. My agency will do the initial screening and eliminate any applicant that doesn't meet your profile. For example, if you want someone with military experience as an electrician, then we will verify the applicant's MSO and make sure that they were honorably discharged. I am proposing to do your initial leg work. I will only refer qualified applicants in the number that you would like to interview.

Mr. Johnson replied, "I own a large data processing center. I would like prescreened applicants. What do you expect to get out of this relationship? Otherwise, what is the 'quid pro quo'? You can't be offering this service for free."

I explained, "The service will be a free service. The employment agency will be a not for profit service center. If you are pleased with the employees we send to you, then you can consider making donations to keep the doors open. In the interim, I will fund the program with my resources. I think my program will be a win-win if we do our part and each of you does yours."

Mr. Edwards said, "I still don't understand your proposal. What is the profile you mentioned and how will that work?"

I replied, "Consider it like a dating network. You put in your information and the other person puts in their information and the dating service matches up the people based upon the profile information.

Often people lie on their profile. We will be verifying the profile as we match possible employees to your job profile."

He replied, "Now I understand. Thank you."

I asked for their support and received standing ovations at both association meetings. The big question was how soon we could be in operation.

I replied, "I will open up temporarily in Amy's Place while I obtain a facility to house the employment center. We will begin soliciting registrations from job seekers and will develop a profile registry while awaiting your listings."

I turned to Jessica next. She had considerable experience in developing data bases and helped me to create a sixty-point profile for job applicants. On the bottom of the profile application, I listed, "All information provided is subject to verification before being sent on a job interview. Misrepresentations of material fact on your application shall result in your profile being removed from consideration."

I put out an announcement that the Theodore Burns Employment Center was now accepting applicant profiles for employment and job recruitment. Former military are encouraged to apply.

In the first week, we received seventeen inquiries and sent out profiles to the potential applicants. In the second week we received forty-one inquiries and sent out profiles. We were looking for everyone from unskilled laborers to physicians and lawyers.

Cynthia and I kept up with the applications while watching each other's children. I finally reached the point that we needed to hire office staff and a manager for the operations. I was fortunate to find a woman named Victoria that had similar experience with a private placement company in another state. Her job was to find jobs and then match applicants to the jobs.

Victoria commented, "This is so much easier than my last job. You already have over one hundred jobs and the jobs keep rolling in daily."

I explained, "Your job as manager is to make sure that all job specific profile information is verified. For example, don't send an applicant to an interview as a lawyer if they are a paralegal. If an employer wants a journeyman plumber or electrician, make sure that the applicant is actually a journeyman. Ask for verification or this program will fail."

In light of the volume of applicants and job positions, I hired two job placement specialists to help in the recruitment process. I made it a point of visiting the two key business associations monthly to make sure that we were meeting the needs of the employers.

My first quarterly report showed that we received 391 job listings and 485 job applicants. Of the job listings, we provided qualified personnel to fill 348 of the open jobs. The employer's surveys indicated an 88% satisfaction rating. I wanted to know why the approval rating was so low. I learned that the big issue was the lag time from the job posting to the referral of applicants. I replied to the comment by reminding the employers that we were verifying profile information before making referrals. We had a four-step process. First, receive the job announcement; Second, create the job profile; Third, match the job applicant profiles to the job profile and verify profile information to the listed job; and Fourth, make the employment referral. My recommendation was that employers anticipate when they would need staffing and begin the process before the actual need arose.

I instructed the manager of Amy's Place that I wanted job applicant profiles on everyone that requests two-week emergency housing. I did the same for Amy's Place Two. I wanted to make sure that no one fell through the cracks.

The employment center quickly exhausted the space allocated by Amy's Place requiring that I find a new location. I found a former real estate agency office building that had a classroom, six small offices for conferencing, a data processing center and a reception area. The building was perfect for our needs. I bought the building and had minimal conversions. In the classroom, I put tables and chairs for applicants to fill out their profile forms. I used the conference rooms for the applicants to meet with job counselors and review available jobs based upon their profile. Our data center had several computer systems. It was perfect in my opinion. We transitioned over the weekend and didn't miss a day's work in relocating the office. Amy's Place manager thanked me for removing the employment center.

I got home that night and was so excited to see my children. Cynthia was watching them daily as I worked on the employment center project. While our kids played together, Cynthia hugged me and gave me a sisterly kiss and asked, "Are you through saving the world, or what is next in Amy's world?"

I replied, "I think we have it all covered. We provide a neighborhood and school court through Amy's Kourt. That is a tremendous success and Cassandra and Kaylie are wonderful judges. AMY or Arbitration and Mediation Your-way is vastly exceeding expectations. We are booked out three to four months. Amy's Place is meeting the greater needs of the community from food, emergency shelter and clothing to hot meals for anyone in need of food. Amy's Place Two is 96% occupied. The 4% reflect the unused furnished apartments that I keep available for emergency purposes; The Theodore Burns Senior Center and employment center are all doing a wonderful service for the community. The Theodore Burns Academy is full with a waiting list of students. I don't think we have overlooked anyone in need."

Cynthia said, "There are three people that have been getting overlooked lately." Cynthia named Rick and my children Cynthia and Rick, Jr.

I replied, "I know and I feel terrible missing dinner because I am tied up getting the help centers going. I feel so compelled to make grandfather's money work for the betterment of our community. I am grateful that I have met the communities' needs and now I need to meet my families' needs. Tomorrow shall start a new day in our lives."

Cynthia replied, "Amy I hope so. Your family has been missing you." I joking replied, "What were my children's names again? I forget."

Cynthia replied, "Amy, that isn't funny to me. It is time to be a mother again. You and I have done our part for our community. Let's now do for our families."

I replied, "I agree. Let's take a cruise and escape. Do you think that Rick and Jason can find a substitute pastor to relieve them for a three-week cruise?"

Cynthia replied, "I'm sure they can get someone. I will call while you sit and play with the kids." Cynthia returned and said, "It's a go. Let's get the cruise scheduled."

CHAPTER TWENTY-FIVE

Amy's Personal Renewal

The thought of going on a three-week cruise to escape our social programs for a short time was exciting to me. Since I was seven years old, I had been working to improve my neighborhood and later my community. I had my ups and downs, but came out pretty well with a loving husband and two adorable children. Cynthia was four and Rick was two. They were excited to go on a cruise with their cousins.

Our first night onboard the ship was wonderful. We ate too much and sat with our husbands and children and planned out our activities for the next three weeks. We were on a Mediterranean cruise and would have numerous stops to sight see with our families. We laid out where we wanted to leave the ship and become tourists. As we talked, our youngest children began getting agitated and wanted to go to bed. Rick and Jason took the children to bed while Cynthia curled up with me on our Lanai and held me. Cynthia said, "I think we make a pretty good team together. I haven't taken the time to say thank you as often as I should for all you have given to me and my family. Where would I be without you and your generosity?"

I replied, "Where would I be without grandfather's money and your love and help. We are the perfect team."

Cynthia asked, "With all you have been doing, how are your funds holding out?"

I laughed and replied, "The investments I made, coupled with the different businesses breaking even or doing well like the AMY center,

I have only spent down $7,540,000. According to our accountant, I still have $537,000,000 more or less, depending on business valuations. Our community programs are funded from investment earnings and the principal isn't being touched. I asked Cynthia why she wanted to know. Are you worried about your Ten Million?"

Cynthia replied, "Not worried at all. I was more curious than anything."

I said, "I have been rethinking the Ten-Million-dollar gift that I planned for you."

Cynthia interrupted and said, "Amy, you have already given me so much. I don't need your money too."

I replied, "Too bad. As far as I am concerned, your interest is increased to One Hundred Million dollars. However, like before, I have to hold it or I will be taxed more than 55% which I don't want to do. You have access to the money any time you need it. When we get back, I am adding your name as an authorized signor on my accounts."

Cynthia said, "You know, I haven't told Jason anything about my account. You asked me to keep it quiet and I have done that and so has Rick. Do you think that I should tell Jason about my account, or just let it lie for now?"

I replied, "You have been married for almost three years. I think you can tell him if you want to do so. I don't think he will be like Taylor."

Cynthia replied, "I know he is nothing like that. I think I will tell him, if for no other reason than to make him smile. He is such a serious Pastor at times."

Cynthia and I were sitting together with our husbands. Cynthia said, "Jason, there is something that you should know about me. I have been keeping this information away from you, but I need to tell you a little more about me and my finances."

Jason said, "Whew! I thought you were going to say that you had a boyfriend or something. I accept you as my wife regardless of what you are about to tell me. Just know that my love for you is eternal."

Cynthia said, "I would like you to know that I have a trust fund held by Amy in the amount of one hundred million dollars. I have access to the money when needed, but Amy controls the account as my trustee. The money came from our adopted grandfather, Theodore Burns."

Jason replied, "That's really nice. It is helpful to know that we have an emergency fund to fall back onto if needed. However, we are doing very well as a family and I see no reason to change what we are doing because of the money."

Cynthia said, "I knew that would be your response."

Jason replied, "Money can corrupt people. I know that Taylor left you over money issues. I just didn't know what it was all about and Rick never let me know. I take it that Taylor wanted access to your funds and you wouldn't let him. That is what led to him hurting you and your divorce."

Cynthia replied, "You understand the circumstances correctly." Jason replied, "I don't have such desires. The money is yours in trust.

I am not interested except as your husband. I want your love; not your money."

Jason asked, "If you have one hundred million, does Amy have money from your grandfather."

Cynthia looked to me and said, "You can answer Jason if you want to." I told Jason that my grandfather left me approximately $540,000,000.

I set aside $100,000,000 for Cynthia leaving me about $440,000,000 to do community service projects. The service centers I have created are to honor Ted Burns whom I loved and cared for as my adopted grandfather. He entrusted his estate to me to use as I saw fit. I am doing his work in our community and hopefully I will honor him in the process. As far as I am concerned, I am a trustee of grandfather's money."

Jason said, "Wow. I never knew. What a wonderful gift from who appears to have been a wonderful person."

I replied with a tear in my eye that grandfather loved me and took good care of me early on and he has continued to take care of me after his passing. I loved him. He was a great man.

We spent the next three weeks cruising and visiting different historical sites along the way. Cynthia and I were both in a mega-relaxed state of being and enjoying our cruise. Our husbands took care of the kids while

Cynthia and I spent some time together as sisters. We heard comments from other passengers on how cute we were as twins. We decided to have some fun and bought identical bikini swimming suits, towels and cover ups. We also bought identical deck wear and enjoyed looking like twins. We stood in front of a large glass window and noticed that we did truly look like identical twins even though I was Cynthia's senior by seven years. When the cruise ended, Cynthia and I were sitting in the swimming pool room talking as we prepared to swim. Cynthia curled into me again and said, "Big sis, I think I did it again." I asked her, "What did you do?"

Cynthia replied, "I think I might be pregnant. I missed my cycle. Oops!"

I held Cynthia and began laughing and couldn't stop laughing. Cynthia asked me, "What's so funny about maybe being pregnant again?"

I kissed Cynthia on the forehead and said, "Guess what?" Cynthia asked, "Guess what; what?"

I replied, "I missed my cycle too." Cynthia began laughing and then I broke into laughter once again.

Like before, we missed our second cycle and both of us checked in on our OB/GYN. She confirmed once again that we were pregnant and felt our due dates were within three days of each other. The one thing that we did know was that our babies wouldn't be born on June 7th. Our nine-month gestation period would be over in April; not June this time.

I said, "What if we have the same birthdates again. Wouldn't that be fun?"

Cynthia agreed.

We spent much of the next nine months being mothers. We did our walkthroughs of the different programs, but all was running well. I dropped by the employment center and noticed Jerry was completing an application profile. I quietly left the building to avoid a confrontation. Jerry was entitled to seek employment. I learned from the center director that Jerry was placed with a law firm and it was a good placement. I was happy for Jerry, but I didn't want him in my life.

March 9th was Cynthia's targeted due date. My water broke on the 9th at 8:40 pm instead of Cynthia's. She and Jason followed Rick and me to the hospital. I had been lying in the delivery center for hours without a delivery. The day changed to the 10th and I had contractions, but no delivery. At 11:40 am, Cynthia's water broke and she was in contractions immediately. She delivered at 3:05 pm. I delivered at 9:42 pm the same day. We laughed like two little girls playing dolls. I had another boy and Cynthia had a little girl. She named her daughter Elizabeth after our mother. I named my son, Brian Theodore after my father and Grandfather. Cynthia and I decided that three children were enough for both of us.

CHAPTER TWENTY-SIX

The Road Well-Traveled

I took the time to visit each of our social and business centers and I was pleased with what Cynthia and I created with grandfather's money. We were meeting the needs of the hungry; the working poor; our valued senior citizens; those individuals in need of emergency food, clothing and housing; and those wanting to improve their lot by finding jobs.

I thought back on my life from a little seven-year-old that started my own judicial system that expanded from neighborhood disputes to school disputes to full arbitration and mediation services across the state. I thought back to the young girl that sold drugs to feed her little sister and the sisters that just wanted shoes without holes in the bottom. I was proud of Cynthia's and my work bringing dignity to those in need and the opportunity to help others while helping themselves. Amy's Place was a wonderful gift to our community.

I thought about those needing affordable housing and we met that need on an emergency basis and for a much longer term through Amy's Place Two.

I thought about the senior citizens going through garbage cans for food and how they now had clean clothing and two hot meals a day.

I looked forward to my next step in life. Cynthia and Amy were nearly five years old while Jason and Rick were three and our youngest were one year old. Our children would be attending school at the Theodore Burns Academy. Since it's opening, its scholastic achievements outshined the public school with our students routinely testing outside the margins of the test parameters for each grade. Using teachers that worked in the field before teaching improved how students learned. What was clear to me was that holding a certified teacher certificate didn't mean that someone could effectively teach. I wanted students to learn and exceed beyond grade levels and that was what happened in our school. Our students learned by applying the subject matter; not just reading and testing for the basic knowledge.

I was twenty-eight years old, but felt so much wiser than my years. I learned so much from those people around me. From grandfather and Cynthia, I learned to care and share. That is who I am and I am proud to say my name is AMY. I started out wanting to be a judge. I became so much more through the love of my family and especially my loving sister Cynthia that I adore. I would suspect that we will live out our lives together, at least next door to each other. We both love to swim and our homes are connected by an indoor swimming pool.

My children will be raised working with our service agencies. No silver spoons in my family. I want my children to love life and care for others like they care for each other. Cynthia is committed to the same philosophy. The last thing either of us wants is our children referring to themselves as "Trust fund" children. There are no free rides in life. Our husbands keep all of us grounded in God and in spiritual awareness of our surroundings. Like grandfather, I hope I don't need a mediator between God and Satan when it comes time to take my soul.

My name was placed in a ballot box for woman of the year. I learned of the nomination and quietly placed Cynthia's name in the same box. Our community decided to name us both as Women of the year and outlined all we had done for our community. I held Cynthia and said, "Please never let go of me."

She held me tightly and said, "I will never let go. Please never let go of me either."

We held tightly to one another and raised our families and continued to fulfill the needs of our community. What we established worked without our continued involvement and would survive our passing in the future.

I thank God and especially thank grandfather for all the help given to me and later Cynthia on our road through life. I pray that we continue in the fight for dignity and hope others of means take some time to help out someone else with less means. That is my lesson of life.

James A. Gauthier, J.D.

CPSIA information can be obtained
at www.ICGtesting.com
Printed in the USA
LVHW041753311019
635978LV00001B/124/P

9 781951 306496